JAZZ AND DIE

JAZZ AND DIE

STELLA WHITELAW

ROBERT HALE · LONDON

Robert Hale Limited
Clerkenwell House
Clerkenwell Green
London EC1R 0HT

www.halebooks.com

2   4   6   8   10   9   7   5   3

Printed in the UK by Berforts Information Press Ltd

To

Jackie Harvey, good friend and writer,
and her wonderful wasp

ACKNOWLEDGEMENTS

Many thanks to Fred Lindop, organiser of the famous Swanage Jazz Festival, and all his stewards. So much kindness and help as well as gorgeous music.

And thanks to Swanage library staff, Worthing library staff and Oxted library staff. What would I do without you?

Also thanks to Dr David Thomas for his invaluable medical details.

Lastly, thanks to several retired police officers who put me right.

Any mistakes are entirely mine but writing this book has been an absolute joy.

ONE

To tell the truth, I'd never given it a thought. I'd never been anywhere really high before. But now I stood on the open walkway, terrified, the key trembling in my hand. Perspiration broke out on my brow, knees shaking. I felt sick.

'What have I done?' I asked myself. 'I've made a terrible mistake. This is vertigo. It's awful.'

A nightmare lay ahead if I was going to get vertigo every time I tried to go along the open walkway to my new flat, in either direction. It was four floors up over a two-storey supermarket and restaurant. The drop was down onto a tarmac car park. One of those parking spaces was mine but I didn't have a car yet to replace the burnt-out ladybird. Herring gulls swept by, showing off, squawking, indifferent to my predicament. Vertigo never bothered them.

My reflection in the smeary kitchen window was pale-faced and terrified. Even my wind-blown tawny hair had lost some of its fiery colour.

I clung to the door handle. It was cold and slippery. There was nothing else to hang on to. A north-easterly wind was blowing off the South Downs and it went straight through my jeans and sweater. I would freeze to death if I did not get my feet moving soon.

'It's all in the mind,' I told myself. But it felt as if it was all in my stomach. I'd been staying in a Travelodge since I was turned out of my two bedsits. The adjoining bedsits had been my home and refuge for half a dozen years. I loved them but the miserly landlord had decided he'd get more money if he let them as offices, so it was goodbye to Jordan Lacey's unusual home. I'm still a private investigator and still owner of First Class Junk, my remarkable antique shop at the far end of Latching.

My few pieces of good furniture were in storage. Other belongings were about to be shunted from shop to new home in cardboard boxes and carrier bags. At least, that had been my initial plan.

It had been a big mistake, viewing the flat on a wet and stormy day. The estate agent had kindly walked on my left-hand side, to protect his damp client from the rain. I did not even get a glimpse of the drop. It wasn't there in the mist.

But the view from the sitting-room window had banished any uncertain thoughts. The fourth-floor flat faced the sea and I stood quite still, mesmerized by the diagonally crashing waves, the pounding surf, the cascading spray against the end of the pier. It was as if the whole world was being unrolled before me, a carpet of shimmering water. Not blue as on a calm summer's day, but the coffee-brown froth of turbulent churned sand and debris.

I fell for the tempestuous view. I barely looked at the tiny bedroom and closets, also facing the sea, the miniscule kitchen and bathroom both at the back. The balcony seduced me with visions of long summer evenings ahead, sitting there with a glass of wine and a book, being civilized, watching the world go by. Living the F. Scott Fitzgerald life.

'I'll take it,' I said, without a second thought.

'Excellent,' said the estate agent, smiling. 'I'm sure you'll be very happy here. I can see that you like the view.'

'I love the sea.'

'If you'd like to come back to the office and sign the agreement, give us your bank details. As it's empty, you can move in straightaway.'

That decided me. I could move in straightaway. No more shunting between shop and Travelodge. I could hang up my few clothes in the built-in closet, make my own coffee in the proper kitchen. The kitchen even had work surfaces, the kind you could wipe clean. Those bedsit kitchens didn't have work surfaces. I had to chop salad on the draining board. This was going to be, oh, so like a normal person.

The estate agent politely escorted me along the walkway, again shielding me from the rain, to the lift at the far end. The lift took us down to street level, near the supermarket entrance.

'Let's hope the lift never breaks down,' he joked. 'It's quite a climb.'

So I produced proof of identity, signed a six-month agreement, paid a deposit and the first month's rent. It was a lot more than I had paid for the two bedsits but look what I was getting for the money. A proper kitchen with granite work surfaces and a wide window view of the South Downs, a bathroom on the same floor and a magnificent expanse of ocean. I would have paid that much just for being able to look at the sea any time of day or night.

I eventually managed to get the key in the lock. It turned stiffly. Salt got everywhere. I pushed open the door, which was almost blocked by a pile of post. I went into the narrow hallway and shut the door, standing firmly on the floor, ankle deep in offers of takeaway pizzas and broadband. My head cleared. The vertigo receded.

It was like a miracle. Everything was all right inside the flat. My balance was normal. I took off my wet trainers and padded through to the sitting room. The view was still there. It hadn't gone away. No mirage. I hadn't imagined it. The tide was going out but the acres of wet sand were calm, the raging sea far out on the horizon.

Pigeons and seagulls flew backwards and forwards, weaving and darting. They thought this high block of flats was a cliff. They were cliff pigeons.

'This is not a cliff!' I shouted at them but they ignored me.

I had brought a few essentials from the shop. Electric kettle, coffee, tea bags, cheese, yogurt, a sleeping bag and mobile phone. But no mug or plate.

I leaned against the door to the balcony, keying in DCI James's mobile phone number, chewing on a lump of cheese.

'DCI James,' he said, sounding distant. He was a long way away. He'd recently been promoted and moved further along the south coast from Latching.

'I've moved in,' I said.

'Good for you. What am I supposed to do? Cheer?'

'I get vertigo on the walkway. It's four flights up over a double-storey supermarket and restaurant.'

'Surely you knew that?'

'I didn't notice.'

'You'll get used to it.' DI James was busy on a cold case murder. He sounded really vague. 'This is what you have to do to overcome vertigo. Go outside and count to ten, then go back indoors. Next, go out again and count to twenty and then go back inside. You can cure yourself, but it takes time. Don't look down till you are steady enough to walk.'

'I'll give it a try, otherwise I'll have to stay inside the flat for ever.'

There was a chuckle. The chuckle that I missed so much. I missed the man too.

'I'll post you a sandwich.' Then he rang off.

The kitchen window was dirty. I took out a damp J-cloth, no old newspaper. I would do ten seconds' worth of cleaning a corner of the window and then go back inside. It worked, after a fashion, if I breathed slowly and deeply. I phoned the storage company and asked them to deliver my furniture the next morning. It looked as if I was going to sleep on the floor that night, not for the first time in my life. I'd slept in some funny places: up a tree, even a priest's hole.

Outside again, cleaning the kitchen window for twenty seconds more. I did not look down or at the distant green South Downs. I could manage twenty seconds without passing out. It seemed like a milestone of sorts.

But when it came to actually walking along the open walkway

to the lift, past the front doors of three other flats, I was immediately sweating and gasping for air. I had to go to work at the shop: it was my bread and peanut butter. No way was I going to be marooned in a flat with a view for six months, especially without a mug. No vertigo in the lift taking me down.

The seafront seemed like heaven. I could have kissed the pavement like that nice old Pope with white hair. I went into the supermarket and bought milk, lettuce and rolls.

'Have a nice day,' said the girl, mouthing the mindless platitude.

'Is that a promise?' I said, putting the purchases into my bag-for-life. The store charged five pence for a new carrier bag.

Every step along the pedestrian area to First Class Junk felt as if I had stumbled into happiness. Now I needed some cases to solve. I have a tidy portfolio of cases solved or abandoned, as well as my years of experience as a policewoman.

We don't talk about why I left the police force. Let's say that I normally tell the truth in order to catch a criminal and this senior police officer thought otherwise. The rapist went free. I reported the officer. End of my career in the police.

My shop was floundering a bit. The numerous charity shops were in hot competition. They were getting more and more upmarket, some actually selling antiques. First Class Junk sold low-grade, flotsam antiques. If I spotted something really classy, then I passed it onto a top dealer and took a percentage. I occasionally found a gem. I discovered a Moorcroft sugar caster in a box of junk. It paid the rent for a few months.

A young man was waiting outside First Class Junk. It was a corner shop with small optician-size windows on either side and a splayed flight of steps up to the front door. Over the front door was an elegant wood carving from some demolished portal. It was all painted a dark maroon.

'Sorry, I'm late,' I said, unlocking the door. 'A case of unexpected vertigo.'

'Valium, that's the answer. Take one before climbing,' said the young man. 'My mum used to get it. Right as rain now. She can climb any lighthouse.'

'Isn't Valium on prescription?'

'I could get you a couple. Internet.'

I bustled in, turning on lights, wondering if he was a client or a customer. I stood behind the small counter expectantly. If he was a client, I would take him into my office at the back, seat him on the Victorian button-back chair, make him a coffee.

'Those maritime compasses in the window,' he said. 'Could I look at them?'

He was a customer. He paid six pounds for one. He chose the best. Everything in the shop was priced six pounds. It saved on making out new price tickets. I wondered if it was time to put the price up. Everything else was going up.

It was a fairly busy day. A stream of customers, buying or not buying. No cases, not even a lost tortoise or a wandering husband. Wandering husbands had less money these days to spend on other women. I missed DCI James now that he had been promoted from Latching and moved to Hampshire or Dorset on a temporary replacement post. We occasionally spoke on the phone but James was always preoccupied. It was a serious case.

I needed a car. Arriving at a crime scene or interview on a bicycle was hardly promoting the right image. My ladybird car, bright red with black spots, had been ideal. Everyone knew it, even the villains. And a villain had set fire to it, burnt it to a smouldering wreck. It had been a moment of anguish. That the target had been me was no consolation.

I wandered round the used car sales spots, uninterested in the family saloons and 4x4s on sale. I wanted something different, a vehicle with style.

There was time for a long walk along the seafront before it got dark. My legs needed stretching. The council kept changing the seafront. The palm trees were perfect. Sometimes their fronds were netted for the winter, some years not. There was now a wood seascape on the pebbles. Bits of gnarled wood sticking up for no particular purpose. Something vaguely artistic; cost a lot of ratepayers' money.

Two elegant white-walled houses along the far end had been demolished. Flats were going to be built on the site. It was sacrilege but I supposed people had to have somewhere to live and flats brought in money, council tax to the council, parking fines to the traffic department.

It was yellow, a sort of sunburst yellow. It could not have been brighter. I could only see the roof because it was a low-slung two-seater, parked on the road below the seafront promenade. Something about the fact that it was parked on the sea road, late at night, made me stop and peer down. There were hastily posted sheets of paper plastered on the windscreen.

FOR SALE
MAZDA MX5
One careful owner
MUST GO

I wrote down the phone number in my notebook. I loved the yellow car instantly. It might not be discreet enough for a private investigator but then neither was the red and black ladybird. Its name could be wasp. It had black stripes on the luggage rack. I was into insects. I should have been a biologist.

I dialled the number on my mobile, leaning against the sea wall, listening to the sound of the waves crashing on the shore. The waves hissed: Buy It. Buy It.

'Your yellow peril car,' I said. 'Is it still for sale?'

'Absolutely,' said a male voice, almost jumping out of the phone. 'I have to sell it immediately. I've been posted to Doha, Qatar, for two years. I'm flying out tomorrow morning. If I leave it on the street, the vandals will demolish it in days. Do you want to buy it?'

'Yes, I think so. I have a secure parking space.'

I visualized the vertiginous parking space below the flats.

'I'm coming down with the insurance documents and the keys,' said the young man. 'A secure parking place? That's a bonus. Of course, we have to agree on a price. But I should be happy with a down payment, and monthly instalments.'

'That would suit me,' I agreed faintly. My bank balance was shrinking. It was teetering on the edge of insolvency.

Half an hour later I was the new owner of a Mazda MX5 California, a burst of sunshine on wheels. I had agreed that if Mike Reed, who was selling the car, wanted to buy it back at the end of his two years in Doha, he would have first option. By then, he might be loaded with dollars and looking at a Porsche or a Lamborghini. It was worth the chance.

The car was a dream. A different sort of dream to the ladybird. The ladybird had been square and solid and not sporty-looking. This two-seater looked fast and ready to take off. I had to unfold my legs and duck my head to get into it. The steering wheel was yellow and black.

'You realize that it's retro, don't you?' Mike said, peering in.

'What does that mean?' I asked, thinking no oil or something.

'No electric windows, no clock, no air bags.'

'I can wind down a window. No air bags? I'll bring a cushion.'

I drove the sunburst car slowly along the seafront, getting the feel of it. The engine sounded powerful. I managed to work the unused card-entry system to the reserved car-parking space. The barrier arm rose and allowed me to drive into the car-parking area. I found the space, the number painted white on the tarmac, and parked with a sense of achievement. The leather upholstery was cream and soft, the dashboard more like aircraft controls than a car.

So far, so good. No funny feelings in the lift. But when I got out on the fourth floor, the vertigo swept back. It seemed even worse now that it was dark, faint neon lights along the walkway, one outside each front door. Yet I couldn't see how far down there was to fall. My body had programmed itself to having vertigo.

I crept along, like a crab, facing the kitchen windows of the other three flats, trailing my hands along the brickwork, seeking something to hold onto. These flat owners would be alarmed at seeing a pale-faced stranger peering in. Not a good relations exercise for making friends with new neighbours.

My phone rang. I'd changed the ringtone to Vivaldi's Four Seasons. It sounded good, invigorating. Now it sounded loud.

'Hello,' I croaked.

'How's the window washing?'

It was DCI James, the man of my long-time unfulfilled dreams. The elusive detective who seemed to like me and then ignored me for weeks. But now he was phoning. I chalked up a bonus point.

'I did t-ten seconds and then t-twenty seconds' window washing.'

'There you go. Where are you now?'

'Marooned on the walkway. Two flats away from my front door. It's dark. I can't move. My legs have disappeared and I feel sick.'

There was a pause and I faintly heard the tapping of a keyboard and far-off voices. James was still in the CID office, working late. It must be a serious case, a major investigation.

'I can't come and rescue you,' said James.

'So? I shall have to stay here till they find me frozen stiff in the morning.'

'Don't exaggerate, Jordan. No one freezes to death in July.'

'Dehydration, then.'

My breathing slowed down a fraction. Talking to James had taken my mind off the vertigo for a few moments. He seemed to know what had happened.

'Shall I talk you home?' he said as if it was the most normal thing in the world. 'Is there a rail? Put your hand on the rail.'

'It's wet. It's wood.'

'Is the rail firm, not wobbling or anything? No, so don't look down. Look straight ahead towards your own door. Tell me what you have been doing. Start moving, one foot at a time. Left foot, now right foot.'

'I've bought a car.'

'Yesterday you rent a flat, today you buy a car. This is mega investment time, Jordan. Have you won the lottery?'

'It was necessary. I've needed a car since the ladybird was incinerated.'

'Is this another ladybird?'

'No, this is a wasp. She's beautiful.'

'A wasp?' She heard his deep chuckle. 'Does she sting?'

'She's sunburst yellow with hooded headlamps like eyes.'

'And the petrol consumption? Keep moving.'

'I don't know. I didn't ask.'

'I bet you've bought a gas guzzler. She sounds an expensive lady. Where are you now?'

I found with amazement that I was almost outside my own front door. I fished in my bag for the key. I had not looked down once onto the darkened car park.

'I'm right outside my own front door.'

'Put in your key and open the door.'

It took some willpower to let go of the handrail and launch myself towards the door. But I made it. The key turned and the door opened to the hallway. I stumbled inside and leaned against a wall.

'I'm in.'

'There you are, Jordan, home and dry. Have you got your breath back? Are you listening? I've got a case for you.'

A case? James had a case for me? I must be dreaming. What was the opposite to insomnia? Whatever it was, I must have it.

TWO

But I wanted to hear more. I needed a case. I needed some income after the marathon spending of the last few days.

'So,' I said, putting down my bag, 'a case for me? That's something new. When did you ever think I might be starving, living off crumbs that a seagull wouldn't even consider?'

James ignored the tirade. 'You like jazz, don't you? Starting tomorrow, there's a three-day jazz festival down here. They are busy putting up the marquees now on a field facing the sea. If I mention names, you'll know them. All famous musicians. This is a top-class jazz festival.'

My interest was stirring. I had never been to a top-class jazz festival but it was something which excited the music in my blood. 'So?'

'One of the top musicians has brought his teenage daughter along with him. She turns the pages or cleans the instruments. But he came to the station this morning because he's been getting threatening letters. Someone is threatening to abduct his daughter during the festival. He wanted me to put twenty-four-hour observation on his daughter.'

I was beginning to see the light. Not the song.

'This is not something I can do,' James went on. 'I don't have the resources and the evidence is flimsy. Besides, I have a murder investigation going on. But I thought of you.'

'Is the father willing to pay for this twenty-four-hour bodyguard?'

'Yes, though when I tell you who he is, you'll probably do it for nothing, just for a seat at his concerts.'

'Who is it?'

'Chuck Peters. And his daughter is fourteen-year-old Maddy Peters. He's willing to pay.'

Chuck Peters. I would have given my right hand for a seat at one of his jazz concerts. He was a multi-reed player, played everything – trumpet, sax, trombone – with spine-chilling skill. He was a world-class musician. He could reach a top F. He'd played in the Albert Hall, on the Jools Holland show, New Orleans, all over the world.

'Have you mentioned me?' I could hardly get the words out.

'I have recommended you. I told him you were the best. How about that cruise that you went on as a bodyguard? A great success.'

It could hardly be called a great success, since I had been set up, but I was not going to argue with James.

'Can you get down here by tomorrow afternoon? The jazz festival starts Friday afternoon with a cruise on a steamer to Poole Harbour. Maddy is going on it.'

'I don't know the way,' I faltered.

'Can't you read a map?' He sounded exasperated. 'Take the coast road. Point your yellow wasp towards Littlehampton, Southampton, Bournemouth, then take the ferry across to Studland Bay and straight down to Swanage. I'll meet you at the bus station.'

'I thought you said you were in Hampshire.'

'Dorset. Swanage is in Dorset. You'll love it. The Jurassic Coast is awesome. Dinosaur bones and fossils all over the beach. Call me when you arrive.'

He rang off. It was all happening too fast. My furniture was being delivered tomorrow morning. I had to unpack and then pack again. I needed some sleep. Driving the wasp all that way would be getting to know her. I hope she liked me at the wheel.

I surfaced from a tumbled sleep in a sleeping bag on the floor.

Sleeping on a floor was nothing new. Locked in a windmill, in a cave, on the floor of an empty hotel, in my car. This was almost luxury because there was a normal flushing bathroom along the hallway, not a hole in the ground.

I was out early since I had to get clothes and essentials from the shop. The walkway did not seem so bad this morning, and anyway I was in such a rush there was no time to think about vertigo. In an hour, I was back, laden with stuff from my bedsits. A few clothes, mugs, food, toiletries. I had a mania for washing my hair.

The postman was on the walkway, clad in his red and yellow jacket. 'Hi, there,' he said. 'You moving in?'

'Yeah,' I said. 'Not used to the height yet.'

'I've been on a lot worse,' he said. But he walked along with me, stopping to put mail through letterboxes. 'Sorry, only junk today.'

I was at my door and I had not noticed so company helped. 'Nice to meet you.'

'Take care,' he said, going onto the one flat further from me. I had not met any of my neighbours yet. I'd had no neighbours at all next to my late bedsits. This was a plus, if I ever saw them.

Now I could make coffee, in a mug. Muesli in a bowl. Sort out what I was taking with me to Swanage. I did not have much in the way of clothes, mostly jeans and shirts and sweaters. I had one dress, given to me years ago, but it was way out of fashion now. If Chuck Peters threw a party, I would have to go shopping.

The wasp had a reasonable-sized boot behind the two front seats. No seats at the back. It would take a couple of travel bags. I put my anorak on top. It was bound to rain. I realized that DCI James had said nothing about accommodation. I'd worry about that when I got there.

My furniture arrived at 9 a.m. on the dot. It didn't take long for the two men to haul the lot inside. A four-foot pine bed and mattress, a white chest of drawers, a three-seater pale green tapestry sofa which they had to haul up the stairs as it wouldn't fit into the lift. Two bookcases, CD player and a desk and chair. I had acquired quite a few new pieces since the cruise. Several heavy boxes of books.

I had to give them a decent tip because of the sofa. And they reassembled the pine bed without being asked. I suppose I looked tired or helpless.

By ten I was out again, packing the wasp with bodyguarding necessities. I'd need torches, batteries, my personal alarm, camera, phone charged. I couldn't believe that I was actually going to meet Chuck Peters. He was one of the best. I had some of his CDs.

In the euphoria, I'd almost forgotten that I would also be seeing DCI James, if he had the time or inclination. Perhaps the Swanage sea air would generate more romantic feelings than windy Latching. He seemed to like it there.

I drove the wasp out of the car park as if I had lived there for years. The barrier arm rose perfectly. It was a steep and winding slope through the multi-storey car park down to street level. The multi-storey was already filling up. I was glad I did not have to use it. The ramps were always full of dark muffled sounds and echoing shadows. Creepy.

The wasp trusted my slightly erratic driving with patience. The gear box looked different. I stopped at a Little Chef for coffee and to fill up with petrol. The coffee was good, the petrol expensive. She was a thirsty lady.

The coast road was straight and easy at first. I took the A27 to Littlehampton, bypassed Bognor Regis and onto Portsmouth. Then it was motorway, the M27 to Southampton, where I knew I would get lost and I did. Finding a signpost for the A31 to Bournemouth was a relief. I began to relax.

It took some time, though, wandering around Bournemouth's residential streets, to find the ferry terminal. So many lovely old houses had been knocked down for retirement flats and nursing homes. Eventually I joined a long, steep, downhill queue and jolted up the ramp and drove onto the ferry. I was amazed to see it was pulled by chains from either shore, no machinery or anything.

'Where do I pay?' I asked.

'When you get off, miss.'

The ferry was packed tight, crowds of holidaymakers, lorries, an open-top bus. The schools had already broken up. Several kids clustered round the wasp, admiring her. She was quite an eyeful.

'What kind of car is this, miss?'

'Is it a James Bond car? Has it been in a film?'

'Can it do stunts, like shoot out guns or flames?'

It was only a ten-minute ride on the water and I didn't have time to make up the entire history of the wasp, although I was getting quite a few ideas. Mike hadn't told me much about her past, so there was no harm in elaborating.

I only got back into the driving seat in time before I was beckoned off. Lots of kids waved to me. I handed over cash at the pay-desk. There were different rates for the size of vehicle. But I had probably saved that much in petrol, instead of taking the long land route via Wareham to Swanage.

Sandbanks was a vast expanse of sand with scattered holiday-makers in caravans and tents. Sand dunes and grasses waving in the breeze, windswept trees giving shade. A great holiday spot.

The Dorset scenery was lovely. Rolling hills and endless glimpses of the sea. Corfe Castle was a gaunt ruin atop a steep hill, lots of history but not much castle left. Perhaps I'd get to see it one day. I liked ruined castles especially when the stones talked to me.

The winding tree-lined road was going steeply down towards Swanage which was surrounded by more hills and headlands. So unlike Latching, which was miles of flat, flat, flat.

I drove slowly along the seafront. It had a promenade, but it was a narrow pavement unlike the wide expanse of Latching. There were beach huts on the sand and more beach huts on part of the road which was blocked off for cars. I had to drive back into the town, passing several white marquees already erected on a field above the seafront. It began to look exciting. Marquees mean music.

The jazz festival was getting ready to start. I hoped I was in time for the jazz cruise. I could see that there was a sketchy sort of pier, maybe Victorian, at the far side of the harbour. Nothing like our Latching pier which had a theatre pavilion and an amusement arcade. This pier was a plain structure purely for pleasure boats and steamers.

I found the bus station and a car park, slid the wasp into a vacant spot. 'Thank you,' I said, switching off. The engine died away. It always paid to be polite to a car.

A tall figure emerged from an unmarked car. I had not seen him for weeks but a rush of emotion threatened my throat. That dark crew-cut, tinged with grey. His weather-beaten face, strong jaw, blue eyes like the ocean depths. He walked over, didn't smile, opened the driver's door.

'You took your time,' said DCI James, his eyes roving over the interior.

'How did you know I was here?'

'We've been tracking you. A bright yellow car is hard to miss. Radar picked you up at the ferry. You've certainly acquired a beauty but hardly the right car for a private investigator. Nothing anonymous about yellow.'

I was not going to be drawn into an argument. The wasp and I were mates. We were going everywhere together. I didn't need anonymous.

'Am I too late for the jazz cruise?'

'They are waiting for you.' He took a blue laminated badge out of his pocket. It was on a silver chain. He hung it round my neck. 'You're an official jazz steward. It will take you anywhere. You can get in anywhere that Maddy goes.'

'Does she know I'm guarding her?'

'No. She's a normal fourteen-year-old and would be pretty stroppy about it. It's up to you to make friends with her. Get in my car and I'll take you down to the harbour. You'll need a fleece. It can be pretty blowy out at sea.'

'What about my wasp?' I hesitated.

'Give me the keys. I'll get one of my constables to drive it away. Don't worry, he does know how to drive.'

'Where am I staying?'

'At the Whyte Cliffside Hotel. I've booked you a room with a view of the sea. Many of the musicians are staying there, including Chuck Peters and Maddy. It's within walking distance of the marquees and the pubs.'

'It's not high up, is it?'

James relaxed for an instant, a glimmer of warmth in his eyes. 'No vertigo, Jordan. I promise. But the hotel gardens do go down to the cliff edge so keep away from them. You'll hear the sound of bees in the honeysuckle and crickets at night. Nothing to be alarmed about. You'll like it.'

It was a long time since I had sat in a car beside James. I could smell his aftershave and the cleanliness of his skin. Even his clothes seemed familiar although I had not seen them before. He knew his way around the town. There were several complex one-way streets. Quite confusing.

'What's this major investigation you are here for?' I asked. I could see the pier gates ahead and at the far end was a white-painted steamer, tied up. 'Is it important?'

'You don't want to know, Jordan. It's not nice. You stick to the jazz festival and guarding young Maddy. Leave me to worry about my case.'

He stopped at the gates and I got out, the steward's badge swinging against my sweater. I didn't have a clue what a steward did. I hoped someone would tell me. But I wasn't the last person to board the steamer. There were several women hurrying along the walkway, waving their tickets.

'Don't worry, ladies,' I said, flicking my steward's badge at them. 'I'll make sure you get aboard.'

'Thank you, thank you.' They were all overweight, short of breath. 'We didn't realize it was such a long walk to the pier.'

There were two other stewards waiting at the steamer gangplank, checking tickets, marking off the numbers. One of them, a thick-set gentleman in a navy waterproof coat, glared at me.

'You're late,' he said.

'Traffic,' I said sweetly. 'All those confusing one-way streets.'

'We couldn't set sail till you arrived. We have to have the right number of stewards on board for the number of passengers.'

'Health and safety,' explained the other steward, a pleasant woman with crisp-cut white hair. 'In case there's an emergency.'

'Everything by the book,' I said. 'You are absolutely right.' I flashed around several of my high-voltage smiles. I always went to a good dentist.

I could hear the sound of music already. It was traditional jazz from New Orleans, not quite my scene, but pulsing music just the same. I was instantly at home, my feet tapping, my body swaying to the rhythm. This was going to be a job after my own heart. Now I had to find Maddy and make friends with her so that she would get used to me being around.

The steamer was easing off the pier, backwards, its engines thrashing. Some of the passengers had gone down into the salon where the four-piece band had set up its instruments and amplification. There was also a bar and a coffee counter. But a lot of the passengers preferred to sit on the stern deck outside so that they could see the famous Jurassic cliffs and the soaring coastal scenery.

It was awesome. Latching didn't have cliffs. These sheer white cliffs had been there before the beginning of time. It was not hard to spot the caves and gullies of the rock quarries, where men and women had worked, blasting out marble for the pavements of London. The gulls were screeching overhead. They hoped we were going fishing. Cormorants perched on crops of rock, doing their own fishing.

I found Maddy easily because she was the only fourteen-year-old among a crowd of middle-aged and elderly music-loving passengers. She had blonde hair tied back in two ponytails. She was chewing gum. She did not look happy. I could see trouble ahead.

THREE

Maddy was wearing current teenager gear. Cropped bl
denim shorts that could not have been any shorter. A brig
red, sleeveless T-shirt, falling off one shoulder. Black ribbed tight
and sloppy Ugg boots, in the middle of July. I ask you.

Her make-up was to the nines. She was even wearing sparkly
false eyelashes in the afternoon. I was not surprised that Chuck
thought his daughter needed a bodyguard. Her eyes were glued
to the drummer. He was a lean young man with a mop of dark
hair, all brushed forward so that the fringe hid his eyes. He kept
his eyes down. Perhaps this was his way of hiding from the bev
of beauties who no doubt followed him around wherever he w
playing.

He was drumming the rhythm with careless inattention.
music was good but I don't think Maddy was listening. She
propped against the half-open door that led to the bows of
boat. There was a stiff wind blowing away the mugginess
salon.

I went back upstairs onto the stern deck, pulling on my
The skipper was giving a running commentary from the b

'Soon we shall be passing the Old Harry Rocks, a mag
150 feet tall white stack standing out to sea off Ballard He
the rocks are 65 million years old, the Cretaceous worl
and me, folks. The smaller rock is called Old Harry's W
had been an earlier spouse but that rock disappeare
trace.'

You could tell he was reading from a script by his monotonous tone.

'A marital dispute,' said a passenger. Everyone laughed.

'Old Harry is another name for the devil so it was not surprising. Now we are coming along to Studland Bay and you may be able to spot a few nudies.'

There was suddenly a rush of keen photographers. We passed Sandbanks, where millionaires build big houses facing the sea, and then Brownsea Island which is a nature reserve for animals who build their own more discreet habitats. Red squirrels, silka deer and lots of birds: I remembered learning about them in a BBC documentary.

'We shall soon be boarding a pilot to take us through the narrow channel to Poole Harbour. It's very shallow in parts and we don't want to get stuck in the sand.'

Poole Harbour looked an interesting place with a jumble of buildings along the seafront. The boat did a tight turn at the far end of the harbour for the trip back. Poole Harbour deserved another visit, if I ever had time.

It had been a glorious afternoon, sailing with a background of jazz. Maddy had hardly moved, yet someone had given her a can of Diet Coke and she was drinking from it. I kept an eye on her red shirt. There was hardly a cloud in the sky and even the water seemed bathed in a golden light.

It was magic.

The magic was abruptly shattered. There was no premonition.

There was a loud grating, grinding noise, a crash and a jolt. I staggered back. The whole boat shuddered. The engines stopped. There was a stunned silence. Even the band stopped playing. Surely they should keep on playing? They obviously hadn't seen *Titanic*. The band always played on.

A few passengers knew what had happened. They peered over the sides of the boat. We had gone aground near the Old Harry Rocks. The devil's work? Was he still around? Was this his day off and he was bored?

There were several more jolts and crashes and grinding noises

as the skipper tried to manoeuvre the boat off the rocks with bursts of the engine. It didn't move. I could see the jagged rocks below the choppy green waves.

Passengers began talking nervously. Some peered at the rocks. Maddy was talking to the drummer who had stood up to look outside. She was animated. Her day was made with a few minutes of his time.

The portly steward came bustling over to me. He had a clipboard in his hand.

'Have you checked the lifejackets?' he asked.

'No.'

'You were supposed to check the lifejackets. That's your job, to check all the safety equipment.'

'No one told me. But there are plenty of lifejackets. Look, they are stowed away under the seats on the deck. Dozens of them.'

'Then you could start checking names,' he said, thrusting the clipboard at me. He was panicking. 'Check that everyone is here.'

'No one has fallen overboard,' I said calmly. 'I would have seen it happen. Or someone else would have seen and shouted out.'

Several scenarios flashed through my mind. Mayday. The skipper would radio ashore for lifeboats to come to our rescue. Was it my duty to see safe transfers into the lifeboats? Children first, so that would be Maddy. There were a lot of heavy ladies and elderly gentlemen to transfer. Would this include the double bass?

If the boat holed, water would start coming into the lower salon first. I would keep calm, helping passengers into life jackets. Maddy would help elderly ladies with the buckles. The crew would launch the orange rafts from the stern decks. Was it my duty to transfer again? I began to feel hollow with dread. A cold sweat swept over me.

I knew I could swim the distance ashore but over all those rocks, so sharp and visible under the waves? I didn't know if Maddy could swim. She'd probably refuse to jump in on the grounds of losing her eyelashes in the sea.

There were a lot of scared faces now. They were facing watery danger. A couple of hours ago they'd been ashore, having a pub lunch or fish and chips. Now an unknown hazard threatened their lives.

It was several years since I'd been a policewoman but the first thing we learned was crowd control. 'Keep calm, please,' I said, moving among them. 'The skipper has everything under control. He'll soon have us off the rocks. Nothing to worry about. Stay calm, everyone.'

I moved forward to the front of the salon. Maddy was shivering in her little red top. I took off my fleece and hung it round her shoulders. She pushed her arms into the sleeves. They were still warm.

'Thanks,' she said. The drummer had left her to talk to his band mates. She looked forlorn and desolate.

'Soon be back to the pier,' I said. 'Not long now. I'll look after you.'

'My dad will be worried. I'll have to phone him.'

I didn't want her phoning her dad and alarming him. He'd think that she had been taken hostage by pirates. He'd have half the police force out.

'Don't phone him yet,' I said. 'We'll only be a little late.'

A crackle came over the loudspeaker. It was the skipper at last with an announcement. 'Would all passengers please go to the front of the boat, please. The front end is the pointed end, folks, the bows.'

He wanted us all to move forward. A shimmer of white-faced panic spread among our jazz enthusiasts. A woman started crying.

'Like the *Titanic*,' said a helpful joker.

There was a reluctance to move. Those on deck did not want to go down into the salon. They wanted to stay on deck. Many were elderly and the stairs were too much for them. I began to help them down the stairs. Maddy, to my surprise, began to guide a frail woman.

A woman in the salon was sobbing into her husband's thigh. She was rigid with fear. I took her hand.

'Everything is going to be all right,' I said, full of confidence.

'The skipper knows what he is doing. He's shifting the weight of everyone aboard so that the boat will tilt forward and the stern will lift off the rocks.'

She didn't like the phrase *tilt forward*. Nor did the other passengers. They imagined the bows dipping under the water with the extra weight, tipping the boat and waves rushing in through the salon.

I gave a running commentary as efficiently as possible as if it was an everyday occurrence and I'd done it many times before. The woman crushed the bones in my hand. It was crippling.

There was a sharp burst from the engine. 'Now the skipper is doing a quarter turn forward,' I said, not really having a clue. People seemed reassured. Then I felt a different movement. There was a buoyancy. The boat lifted.

'Now he's gone into reverse and we are backing out towards the sea,' I said hopefully.

'Thank goodness. God bless the skipper.' It was a chorus.

I looked out of the nearest steamed-up window. We were backing out to sea. Old Harry, the devil, was further away. I didn't want to see him again. The crew were inspecting the box that housed the propeller shaft. We were still not clear of the woods, or of the waves, as you might say.

As the boat moved clear of the rocks, there was spontaneous clapping from the passengers. The relief was tangible. Couples were hugging and kissing, laughing. Maddy was grinning. Many couples held hands for the slow two and a half miles back to Swanage landing pier. The skipper was not risking an engine breakdown. Perhaps the danger had healed rifts, reaffirmed lost affection.

I was used to danger, but this unexpected danger, the uncertainty of being pitched into a watery disaster, had sharpened my awareness of life and our fragile hold. None of us know what will happen next.

'It was the skegs you heard,' the skipper told me when I climbed up to the bridge to get his viewpoint. 'They're steel blades, reinforcing the after end of the keel and the rudderpost.'

There was another cheer when the coastline of Swanage came into view and the spindly legs of the pier were growing closer. Passengers started to gather up their belongings. The band were also packing up. The drummer had the biggest load of equipment to carry off. He was zipping his drums into bags. Maddy was trying to help, putting his sticks into a zipped pouch.

As we docked, another cheer went up for the skipper and more clapping. There was not exactly a stampede to get off but it was obvious that solid mother earth was a magnet.

'Sign here,' said the chief steward, still glaring. He held out his clipboard. I wrote a barely legible signature. Not a word of thanks.

'You did very well, my dear,' said the other woman steward. 'Kept everyone calm. Don't worry about old Felix here. He's a grumpy old soul till he's got a few whiskies down him.'

I saw Maddy fly into the arms of a figure I knew well. It was Chuck Peters. He had come to meet his daughter. A short man, but full of vigour and life. A man who could make music from any instrument.

'So you got back safely,' said a voice I knew. A bolt of happiness shot through me. James had come to meet me. He stood back from the crowd, not rushing.

'There were a few scary moments,' I said.

'We heard it all. The skipper radioed us to stand by with ambulances. But apparently, Florence Nightingale kept everyone calm and there were no casualties.'

'She has a way of reappearing, even centuries later. But I didn't have a single candle. Why are you here?'

'You don't know how to get to the Whyte Cliffside Hotel. There is a way along the beach and then up a steep path to the cliff top. Not your regular way, even without vertigo. The entrance is a couple of roads back and hard to find. I'll take you but don't expect this every day.'

'What do I have to do this evening, being a steward?'

'You keep close to Maddy. You are not there to act as a steward.'

'Felix thought I was.'

'No one knows.'

Great. I was there, wearing a steward's badge, but I didn't have to do any stewarding type things. I was there to be with Maddy. I was juggling several balls.

'Chuck Peters wants to meet you this evening before the gigs start. His room is 520. Maddy won't be there. She would hate the idea, apparently. But Chuck wants to meet you.'

'He wants to meet me?' I could have fainted. James started driving his car away from the pier entrance. It was his usual soulless black Saab. I sat back in the passenger seat, vowing to never go on another jazz cruise. Dry land for me from now on.

'Six-thirty in his room. Look efficient. Wear your badge.'

'I know why you are here,' I said as he drove along the sea road towards the other side of the bay. Hills rose on all sides above the sea. 'They were talking about it on the cruise. A girl's body has been found at Corfe Castle. A girl who has been missing for three years. A cold case.'

There was a long pause as James negotiated an open-top bus coming the other way. It was a narrow road when cars were parked along the seafront.

'Since you know that much, it was Corfe Castle. She was found buried in the grounds of the castle. At first we thought very old bones – centuries old – but then forensic dated her clothes fragments to Primark. That's when I was brought in.'

'How old was she?'

'About fifteen, they think.'

'Scary.'

'That's why you are here. There may be a connection.'

James took a steep left turn and drove uphill, then another right into a cul-de-sac. The front of the Whyte Cliffside Hotel was all that one could wish for in a five-star hotel. Automatic doors, manicured shrubs and plants, plenty of lighting, a foyer made of glass. My wardrobe seemed more and more inadequate.

'What sort of connection?' I asked, hoping the wasp was parked here safely with my luggage.

'We think she had something to do with the jazz festival. She was wearing a silver bracelet of linked key notes.'

FOUR

A group of musicians apparently had a permanent booking for the whole of the top floor. They worked late, partied late and never got up for breakfast, so other guests staying at the hotel were not disturbed. The guests who were regular jazz enthusiasts and had a stroller ticket for the three days felt it was a bonus: they often caught sight of their favourite sax player or drummer.

I was in room 410, the floor below the musicians. Unless the hotel had well-insulated walls, I would hear their late arrivals. But maybe I would be with them, my eyes on Maddy, making sure she was safe.

'I've never stayed in a big hotel before, apart from a Travelodge, and you know what they're like.'

'This has five stars,' said James, getting into the lift.

My room earned every one of those five stars. The bathroom was a joy in itself, gleaming white shower, big bath, free toiletries, four different-sized fluffy towels. I wandered round, touching everything. And instant hot water, not like the bathroom that went with my previous bedsits. Luke-warm had been its middle name.

The double bed was covered in a cream and blue stitched quilt with matching cushions. Cushions on a bed, for decoration, I ask you. I had more hanging space and storage drawers than I had clothes. There was a comfy armchair and a desk at the window. There was a hospitality tray on the desk, not just regular tea and coffee, but hot chocolate, a bottle of still water, biscuits, even herbal teas. And it was all mine. Perhaps I should move in.

'Don't forget you are here to work,' said James, following me, carrying my two travel bags. He'd seen me eyeing the hospitality tray.

'I'm seeing Chuck Peters at 6.30 p.m.,' I repeated. I put my alarm clock by the bed, ignoring the digital timepiece already in place. I would never be able to work out all the buttons and instructions.

James put down my bags. 'I may drop in at one of the gigs tonight,' he said. 'It all depends.'

He turned and left me before I could thank him for carrying my bags up. At least that meant that the wasp was safely in the hotel car park. I felt I ought to go and check but I was drawn to the window. I was high up because the hotel was on a cliff, but my feet were anchored to the carpet and there was no trace of vertigo. Was I becoming cured?

There were chairs and tables scattered on the lawn below that stretched to the cliff edge. I might not feel so safe down there. Guests were sitting, reading, drinking, dozing in the late afternoon light.

It was so different from Latching. Swanage Bay was full of yachts and surfers and motorboats – a busy, busy scene – whereas the English Channel had a few trawlers and liners so far in the distance binoculars were needed. Across the bay loomed more rolling hills, green and verdant, very walkable. I wondered if Maddy liked walking. Probably only if the drummer came along too.

The phone on the desk rang.

'Miss Lacey?' I knew the voice instantly. I'd been to his concerts at the Pier Pavilion. His vocal cords were raspy from years of blowing, sometimes singing his lyrics, a bit like Rod Stewart.

'Hello, Mr Peters,' I said. I had to control my voice.

'As it's such a pleasant evening, I wondered if you'd like a drink on the lawn? The weather changes a lot at Swanage. Could be torrential rain tomorrow. We'll find a private table somewhere

where we can talk.'

'I'd like that,' I said, swallowing. I was going to have a drink with the famous Chuck Peters. I was about to enter a period of good fortune.

'What shall I order for you?'

I had no idea. I would have drunk mud happily in his company. 'A white wine, please, if it's not too early.'

He laughed, a raspy laugh. 'It's never too early.'

He put the phone down.

I had to test the shower. It was perfect, standing in a waterfall of warming dew. I washed my hair in free shampoo. The biggest towel wrapped right round me. There was a hairdryer, firmly attached to the wall so guests could not take it home as a souvenir. As if I would.

At 6.25 p.m. on the dot, I went downstairs and found the way out through the veranda doors from the glassed-in lounge. I spotted Chuck Peters immediately, sitting at a far table. He was a short, burly man, with dark hair cut into disobedient tufts. He wore gold-rimmed glasses, which often fell off when he was playing. He already had a glass of cold beer.

I hurried across the velvety grass, not looking at the cliff edge. He got up when he saw me. He had a big grin on his face. His front teeth were distorted in level and shape from blowing horn for so many years.

'Miss Lacey?' he said, holding out his hand. It was long and slim with musician's fingers. 'Come and sit down. Your wine is coming now. I didn't want it to warm up.'

'Hello, Mr Peters. I am not going to embarrass you by saying that I am a great fan, even though I am.'

'It's on your face, lady. No need to say it. Just enjoy the music. Any requests, tell me. It would be a pleasure. Ah, here's your wine.'

A waiter came over with a bottle of wine in an ice bucket and two glasses, a bowl of nuts and a dish of carrot sticks. He was in his thirties, dark-haired, Spanish-looking.

'Thank you,' I said. He nodded and smiled.

'The service is the tops. That's why I always stay here. That and a decent bed.' He was pouring out a glass of wine for me and pushed it towards me. 'Those hills over there are a world heritage site. Dancing Ledge is fabulous. I ought to write a piece called Dancing Ledge.'

'Thank you.' I didn't seem to know any other words. 'Dancing Ledge would be a great title.'

Chuck reached into an inner pocket and pulled out a wedge of paper. It was time to talk business. 'I've been getting this stuff for the last six months. I'm at my wits' end. Maddy is the love of my life. I've shown them to the police but, of course, show-business people get a lot of strange mail. It might be a weirdo. Have a look at them, Miss Lacey.'

'Jordan, please.' At least I could remember my own name. I sipped the wine, which was heavenly, and leafed through the papers. They were not exactly letters. They were blunt threats to harm Maddy in different ways, with a specific countdown. Someone was counting time, marking off days. I could see the threats were perilously nearing zero.

'Zero is this weekend, the Swanage jazz festival,' said Chuck, the words snagged in his throat. 'You've got to do something, Jordan. Catch the bugger before he hurts my Maddy.'

'I'll never leave her side, I promise,' I said. 'I'll be like a stick of glue.'

'She's a bit rebellious, y'know,' he said. 'Typical teenager. No mother to take care of her. Been doing what she liked for years.'

I didn't ask about Maddy's mother. This wasn't a good time. I'd find out later. Meanwhile I was going to have my work cut out, sticking to a rebellious teenager who would rather be with a certain mop-haired drummer.

'Does she come to all your gigs?'

'She never misses. Always has, ever since she was a toddler.'

I smiled at Chuck Peters, remembering. 'I saw her come up on stage once in her pyjamas, to say good night to you, while you were playing. She must have been about five or six. You never even stopping playing, but ruffled her hair, gave her a pat and she went off into the wings.'

'She doesn't do that now. Happy days. You've a steward's badge so you can go in and out of all the shows. No problem. We have a suite upstairs with adjoining bedrooms. But I can't keep a check on her all the time.'

'Nothing will happen to Maddy while she is in my care,' I said. 'And I've good friends in the police who will come the instant I call.'

'DCI James? He told me you were once in the police force but prefer being a private investigator. So you've a good solid background of detective work.'

I wouldn't say a good solid background but there have been successes. And occasionally reward money. Most of which I had now spent on a flat I couldn't reach without vertigo and a classy car that was a fuel alcoholic.

'Your fee,' he went on. 'I'll pay whatever you say. The accommodation is naturally in the package, so don't worry about that.'

'A few of your CDs would be nice,' I said modestly.

'Negotiable.' He grinned. He reached down onto the lawn. 'This is your fleece, I think? Maddy said it belonged to a red-haired steward. She thought you did good on the jazz cruise. Keeping everyone calm. So she likes you already.'

'It might not last. I can be strict if I think she's doing something foolish.' Like going off at midnight with the drummer.

'You can be as strict as necessary. A firm hand wouldn't hurt her. I'm feeling more confident about this now that I have met you. Like the gear. Wish Maddy would wear more clothes.'

I had to laugh. I was in my best indigo jeans, a pale blue long-sleeved denim shirt that was fringed, cowboy boots. My almost dry hair was tied back with a ribbon. Too wet to plait.

Chuck stood up. I didn't get up as I was taller than him. 'Gotta go. Got to go through my pad, decide what we are going to play. The first night is always important. Keep the wine. Take it back to your room. They won't mind.'

'Thank you,' I said again.

I sat back in the chair, drinking in the last of the sun, swallowing gulps of ozone fresh air and white wine, nibbling a few carrot sticks. No lunch.

I had become so bewitched with Latching, I had forgotten that there were other wonderful places along the UK coast. And this was one of them. The Purbeck Way. The Jurassic cliffs. Chuck should write a song about the Dancing Ledge. Maybe I'd think up some lyrics.

I sat till the sun chilled my skin and I had to shrug on the fleece. Time to find Maddy and work out how I was going to follow her. I had not asked Chuck if she knew about the threats. Probably not.

The first evening programme of the festival was so complicated, I wondered how I was ever going to keep Maddy in sight. Five different venues. Some needing stroller tickets, some free. The pub ones were free. Buy a drink instead.

The drummer was the magnet. If I worked out where he was playing, then it would be easier to follow Maddy. She might think I was competition. Hard cheese. I was ten years older than him. I searched through the programme. The drummer on the cruise quartet was Ross Knighton. He was also in Chuck Peters' band. Now there's a surprise. And tonight was a tribute to Louis Armstrong. I could not believe my luck. If DCI James was also there, then I would have stumbled into happiness.

I would take the wine back to my room. No one would be bothered. Perhaps rules were lax while the jazz festival was on. Jazz is different. Jazz is a release of the soul. Not many people know that.

Perhaps Chuck Peters ran up a big bill.

I ran into Maddy outside the lounge, still clutching the bottle of wine. She looked at me, her eyes flashing.

'Has my dad paid you to follow me?' she asked suspiciously.

'Sort of,' I said. I said nothing about the threats. 'He's worried about you.'

'I know what I'm doing,' she said.

'That's great. Good for you. But he doesn't know what you are doing. I know what it's like, being young and infatuated by a musician. It happens all the time. I've been there, got the T-shirt.'

For a second, she relaxed and grinned. It was a breakthrough. She obviously realized that I was not going to stop her doing what she wanted to do.

'My remit is to make sure you get back to the hotel safely,' I went on. 'Is that unreasonable? You can spend as much time as you like watching Ross banging the life out of his drum kit. I shall maintain a certain distance as I have concerns about damage to my hearing.'

'And you won't interfere?' she asked suspiciously.

'I promise.'

'That's all right then.' It was a grudging acceptance.

'I'll give you my mobile phone number. So if you feel you need my help in any way whatever, you can call me.'

I wrote the number on a plain card, not one of my business cards. Maddy would not welcome the news that I was a private investigator. She thought I was one of the volunteer stewards.

I needed to check out her room but I could hardly follow her upstairs. A drip of icy water on my T-shirt came like an answer. The ice was melting in the wine bucket.

'Fancy finishing this in your room?' I suggested. 'Nowhere in public as you are underage for alcohol.'

'I'm fourteen.'

'That's still underage. If you've any lemonade or soda water, we could make spritzers.' The French did it, didn't they? Diluted wine for their children.

'OK.' She was tempted. 'Sounds cool. Come on up.'

The top floor showed signs of occupation by a different race. Doors were not closed, people stood chatting in the corridors, instruments lay around. There was strumming on a guitar. It was alive, thriving. None of the stillness and propriety of the other floors.

Maddy's room was furnished a lot like mine but it had a

connecting door to the sitting area and her father's bedroom next door. Her room was also incredibly untidy. Clothes, towels, magazines, cosmetics tossed around, on the bed, on the armchair, on the floor. She'd brought enough clothes for a month's stay. She went into the bathroom and came out with two glasses.

'Will these do?'

'Perfect.'

The diluted white wine loosened Maddy's tongue. She chatted about hating school, needing new clothes and a lot about the amazing Ross Knighton. He was wonderful. He was a great drummer. The greatest new star on the jazz scene. He was so good-looking. All I had to do was nod and agree.

'He's terrific. Wait till you hear him play,' she went on, her eyes glowing.

Eventually I tore myself away from the eulogy of praise and left with the empty bottle and bucket. I needed some real food. A few carrot sticks were not exactly sustaining. It was going to be a long evening.

As I closed the door behind me, a piece of A4 paper fluttered to the floor. It had been stuck to the door with a lump of Blu-Tack. I picked it up. The writing was in a thick black felt tip. It read:

Only three days to Zero and baby Maddy will be shredded meat.

FIVE

It was a sheet of lined paper torn from a school notebook, with a ragged serrated side edge. The writing was well formed, not illiterate. It seemed to be the same writing as on those earlier threats which Chuck had given me to read – but I would need to check.

I scrabbled in my shoulder bag for a specimen bag. The kind of thing a modern girl always carries about. Using a tissue, I picked up the tiniest corner and eased the sheet of paper into the plastic bag and sealed the top. DCI James might be interested. He might find some prints or DNA. DNA was so quick these days. No more waiting for six weeks for a result. They could do it in hours.

There was no point in telling Chuck. He was concerned enough. And he had his first big concert tonight. It would be jazz to blow your mind. What worried me was access to this top floor. It was too easy for anyone to get up here. There was a medley of musicians wandering about into each other's rooms, staff of the hotel delivering room service, other guests finding themselves on the wrong floor, accidentally or on purpose, autograph books in hand.

I sent DCI James a text, saying I had some evidence he might want to see. I was not adept at texting but my style was improving. I didn't do little sideways faces at the end or LOL. He'd know that a *JL* signature was not Jennifer Lopez.

The stalker could be in any of those hotel categories. I didn't think there was a noun for a threatener. But there it was. I looked it up on my laptop. Threatener did exist but no one ever uses the word these days. It was classified as archaic.

One of the signs of a jazz enthusiast was to wear a beard or a hat. I couldn't manage a beard so I wore a real cowboy hat borrowed from my Latching shop. I could have sold it several times to Latching cowboys. If you were in a jazz parade then most women carried a highly decorated umbrella. You wouldn't catch me spending time decorating an umbrella.

A crowd were already queuing to go into Marquee One for that night's gig. Another steward spotted my badge and grabbed me. He looked frazzled, nice round face, brown haired, a bit on the heavy side. It looked like too many quick burger and chips lunches, washed down with a lager.

'Thank goodness you're here. Can you man this front entrance, please? Check everyone. Red wristband for tonight's stroller or a single ticket purchased at the box office. Don't let anyone in on any excuse. They will say anything.'

'OK,' I said dubiously. I was keeping an eye on Maddy. She was already in the tent, helping to set up the stage, manfully carrying in some of the percussion gear. Ross was playing with her dad's band tonight. He must be good. The sound engineers were testing everything on site. Rows of uncomfortable grey plastic chairs sat in a semi-circle round the stage. Chuck didn't like regimented rows so the layout was always changed for him. Lots of regular old-timers brought cushions to sit on.

I stood at the entrance, looking official. The evening was already cooling and the sky darkening. Street lights were coming on in the town below. The field was high above the shore line. No vertigo but I could see a couple of steep paths which might be tricky in the dark.

'Wristbands or tickets, please.'

'My husband has got mine and he's already inside.'

An unlikely story, madam. I smiled at her. She had a set-hard face. 'Then he will probably come looking for you, won't he? Please wait outside.'

'I've left my wristband at the hotel.'

'Lucky you. You've got time to go back and get it.'

She agreed, reluctantly.

'I've brought the wrong colour. I've got on a blue wristband.'

I checked with the chief steward, the heavyweight who was in charge. He said blue was tomorrow's colour so her story sounded true. She had bought a weekend stroller. I let her in. She looked relieved and flashed me a big smile.

'I'll buy you a drink in the interval,' she said.

Things were looking up.

It was a long time since I had heard any really good, authentic jazz. My trumpeter friend of old, who occasionally played at Latching, had vanished from the circuit. Please play 'Here Comes That Rainy Day', I thought. 'Rainy Day' is the lament they play for musicians who have died. It's quite beautiful and always makes me cry even if I don't know the musician. They could play it for me, one day.

Tonight's big band concert was full of unexpected delights. They played 'You Do Something To Me' and 'When Can I See You?', both full of rhythmic energy. 'Moonlight In Vermont' is one of my favourites with its gentle, insistent swing. 'Shake, Rattle And Roll' had the tent flaps vibrating. 'Watermelon Man' finished the first half.

Jazz was changing. It was a marvellous confusion of complexity, genre-mingling. It was every kind of jazz that there had ever been, all mixed up. Harmonies, grooves and anti-grooves, funk, fusion and free-jazz. It was a ground-breaking sound; made my head spin.

Maddy wandered over towards the bar. She was probably getting something for Ross. Musicians get thirsty. I remembered seeing the great Maynard Ferguson drinking champagne throughout a whole concert at Wigan. It was a wonder he remembered what he was playing or could still stand.

I didn't get that promised interval drink but I bought myself a cool lager. The marquee was hot, pulsing with heat under the canvas.

'Hiya, Jordan. Are you enjoying it?' Maddy asked, strolling

over. Tonight she was wearing purple tights, black shorts and a vivid skimpy sequinned top. Quite a dazzling outfit. It was a wonder Ross could keep his mind on the score.

'Fabulous,' I said, even though I had to stand. I was keeping an eye open for an empty seat. Stroller tickets could move onto one of the other venues. But no one ever left a Chuck Peters gig. So never a vacant seat.

'Now you know that Ross can really play the drums. My dad thinks a lot of him. Did you hear those brush strokes? And his suspended time fills and cymbal patterns?' Her eyes were glowing, brighter than the diamanté lashes.

She was talking a foreign language. But I nodded. 'Great sense of timing,' I added. 'Spot on.'

Maddy seemed pleased. 'He always plays inside a song.'

Inside a song? I had a lot to learn.

I was glad they didn't play any Glenn Miller. Although he was a great musician, his compositions had been done to death. Not exactly the right phrase since he disappeared on a night flight during World War II and was never seen again. But there were some of his numbers I never wanted to hear again. (Do not mention a certain pearl necklace.) It was not fair to a great band leader, of course. But he did arrange masses of other music which no one ever seemed to play these days.

Mandy came back with a diet coke for herself, a lager for Ross and a can of orange juice for me. 'OK for you, Jordan?'

'You're a star,' I said, taking the juice. 'Thanks.'

It was a step forward. We were going to get on.

Apparently I had other duties when the concert ended. Rubbish to collect in black bin bags. Straighten chairs. Collect lost property. Fogged by the music, people left everything behind, walking away in a cloud of sound. Coats, bags, drink were left under chairs. Excuse me, I am here to watch Maddy, but it was not difficult to do both. Ross's gear took the longest to cart back to his van. No mistaking his van. It had *DRUMS* stencilled on each side, the *U* in the shape of a kettle drum. I bet sometimes he wished he'd learned to play the flute.

Chuck was, of course, surrounded by admirers. He sold and signed a pile of CDs. They had to make money somehow. He spotted me and waved me over.

'Coming to the party? It's at the Bull and Horn tonight.'

'What about Maddy?'

'She's coming. She likes you, so thumbs up.'

It was going to be a long night. I felt tired already and the comfy bed at the Whyte Cliff beckoned. Last night I had slept on the floor of my new flat in a sleeping bag. Strangely, I already missed my new flat. It was so right for me and an unexpected dream after my two bedsits.

He was standing behind me. I knew without even looking. Did my shoulders have a sixth sense or was it because my hair knew that he had once touched it? Perhaps my hair remembered that moment, had stored the memory in its roots. It was DCI James, in a waterproof jacket that was glistening with rain. He waited until I had finished a bin bag collection.

'I'll take that outside for you,' he said. 'It's started to rain.'

'Thank you,' I said. 'But I've got to follow Maddy.'

'To the Bull and Horn. It's a party. I'll take you. A party sounds good. Then you can tell me about this riveting new evidence that has me leaving my real work.'

'It's another threat. Untouched, except by the writer. I found it pinned to Maddy's bedroom door with Blu-Tack. There might be something on it.'

'Did you get the Blu-Tack as well?'

'Of course.'

'Blu-Tack sometimes absorbs sweat. Useful.'

The chief steward came lumbering over. I liked him. He'd had a stressful evening with far too many people trying to get into the marquee but he had never lost his temper. The entrance couldn't be closed because of people leaving to go onto a venue elsewhere. But he had made the overflow form an orderly queue. They didn't mind. They could still hear the music outside, standing in the rain.

'Well done, lass,' he said, wiping his face with a handkerchief. 'Don't know what I would have done without you. The other steward on the rota didn't turn up. They do that, you know, say they'll do a duty and then go and listen to something else they fancy at another venue.'

'Don't worry, I'll always help you out. It's been a pleasure,' I said. 'Great jazz. Music for the soul.'

'Tom Lucas,' he said, introducing himself. 'Are you coming to The Bull? I'll buy you a drink.'

Tom Lucas was at least twenty years older than me and twice my weight, but he was tall with it and moved easily. And he had an open, generous face with pleasant grey eyes. His brown hair was heavily flecked with grey. No oil painting but looks weren't everything, as the magazine agony aunts are always telling lonely females.

'I'll see you there,' I said, zipping up my fleece. I wasn't going to miss out on a lift with James. Besides, I had to give him the threatening note.

Tom Lucas wasn't leaving yet. The marquee had to be secured for the night. Alcohol securely locked away. A couple of youths had brought sleeping bags and were spending the night in the tent. Nothing was safe these days but the boys thought it was a great lark. They'd listen to music half the night.

It was a fine steady drizzle. I hoped James's car was not too far away or I would be drenched. Thank goodness for my boots on the wet grass. I'd seen lots of women in open sandals. The cowboy hat was like a miniature umbrella, keeping some of my hair dry. But rain dripped off the brim like Aussie corks.

'I don't suppose you know where the Bull and Horn is?' James asked.

'I don't know where any of the pubs are. You're the police. Surely it's the first thing you learn anywhere. The trouble spots.'

'Just testing.'

He was teasing me. It made a change. He was usually so serious and remote that I wondered if he had any normal social feelings at all. Perhaps he was glad to see me. He could hardly relax with his new colleagues when he had this castle murder to solve.

I closed the car door, glad to be out of the rain. It was persistent stuff. Maybe Dorset rain had a relentless quality left over from its Jurassic days. Latching rain seemed softer unless it was blowing a force seven gale.

I opened my shoulder bag and gave James the specimen bag. He read the threatening words through the plastic.

'So it's more of the same. Did Chuck show you the others?'

'Very similar, although the countdown has changed. If that is a countdown.'

'Don't take any notice of that. He probably got it off a television show. I've seen other examples of a countdown time factor being used to increase the tension.'

'It's effective. It works.'

He asked me a few other things about Maddy: what she was like, what was her relationship with the drummer. He drove carefully through the rain. The street lights were awash with haze, gutters splashing with rain running off the steep streets.

'Adoration from a distance, I think,' I said. 'I don't believe he's interested in her. She's useful to have around as a besotted little slave, carrying stuff.'

'Watch him as well.'

'Sure, I've got eyes in the back of my head. Hadn't you noticed?'

He drew up outside the pub. It had only been a few minutes but still I liked being with him in close dark confines. I turned to him, imaging the clear profile, the firm jutting chin, the bold nose and curving mouth. 'Aren't you coming in?'

'I think one admirer is enough for you to cope with tonight,' he said, meaning Tom Lucas. 'You go in and enjoy yourself. But remember you've a long day ahead tomorrow. Jazz starts with the ten o'clock parade from the bus station, then it is relentless non-stop jazz till the last gig at midnight.'

And I was tired already.

I said good night to James and got out of the car, stepping

straight into a puddle. Water splashed up my legs. The pub was all lights but it looked solid and workmanlike, loads of red brick and beer signs. Rows of wet benches sat outside on the pavement but they were empty of their normal clientele.

I went inside, shaking the rain off my cowboy hat. The bar was packed. I couldn't see a face I knew. No sign of Maddy. They did say all the pubs were in walking distance but that could be wishful thinking.

'Hey ho, here comes a new face,' said a voice close beside me. 'It makes a change to have a new steward, instead of all the old faithfuls. So where do you hail from, little lady? Texas?'

'South of West Sussex,' I drawled.

'Did you come on your horse?'

I'd been lassoed by the joker from this afternoon's steamer trip. I recognized the voice and the tireless joviality. There was nothing wrong with a jolly soul but I was too tired to respond or be receptive.

'Yeah, he's tied upside outside,' I drawled. 'I've come in to buy him a bundle of hay.'

He laughed heartily and I managed to side-step his approach. I was not going to be saddled with him half the night. Maddy had appeared, wet and wistful, standing on her own at the edge of a crowd. The drummer was surrounded by admirers and he was drinking. Perhaps he was dehydrated, sweated a lot.

I went over to Maddy. Her make-up was a mess. Smeared lipstick and smudged mascara. Tears and kisses.

'How about we both go to the ladies and tidy up? That rain can be the devil. I feel like I've been wrung out and hung up to dry.'

Maddy smiled wanly. 'OK,' she said. She was carrying a straw bag the size of a picnic hamper. We went into the ladies. It was pretty full. Women didn't like the portable cabin loos at the marquees unless they were desperate.

Maddy found a space at a mirror and began to repair her face. It was a major make-over. I had to admire her dexterity. I rarely got beyond a quick application of mascara and lip gloss. She could teach me a thing or two.

She was out in ten minutes, face flawless. I had washed my hands three times. She went straight for the group round the drummer. He had his sticks flying. He was playing a beat on anything, the chairs, the windows, the walls. The other musicians, who had brought along a trumpet or a saxophone, began to join in.

We were in for a long night.

The impromptu was dazzling. I hardly recognized anything. Maybe 'Sugar Foot Stomp'. Maybe 'Poor Butterfly'. They improvised whatever came into their head. I was mesmerized.

'You're new, aren't you?' It was big Tom Lucas. He was holding a pint of lager and offered me a glass of red wine. 'Is this all right for you?'

'Perfect,' I said. 'Thank you. I needed that. It's been a busy evening.'

'It'll be even busier tomorrow, or is it already today?' He looked at his watch. 'Ye gods, look at the time, my wife will be chewing her nails.'

'She doesn't come to the gigs?'

'No, she dislikes jazz. Fortunately she allows me my once-a-year indulgence at the festival. As long as I am home at a reasonable time.'

Oh dear, Tom Lucas, nice man as he was, was yoked to a jazz-hating female who wanted him home on time. Still, there was no harm in making his once-a-year indulgence as happy as possible.

'So you must enjoy every moment,' I said. 'I'm around all weekend, so let me know when you want to skive off to listen to some other group. I can cope.'

Total exaggeration. I had no idea how I would cope and look after Maddy at the same time. Tom Lucas was obviously tied to a long marriage and jazz was his only escape. He had probably been good-looking when he was younger and he had a certain gentle charm about him. Something sweet that still clung to him.

'That would be great, thanks. Where are you staying?' he asked.

'The Whyte Cliffside.'

'Very posh,' he said. 'Do you like it?'

'Great hotel. I'm lucky. Chuck Peters booked it for me.' I was saying too much. It was the wine on an empty stomach. Tom looked interested.

'You know him that well?'

'I only met him today. It's a long story.'

I had no idea what story I would tell him. I would have to think up something plausible if he probed me again. Maddy saved the day. The improvised gig had petered out. Everyone was tired. She was leaving, clinging to Ross's arm. More smeared make-up? I had to follow them.

I gulped down my wine.

'I'll give you a lift,' said Tom quickly. 'It's on my way home. Whyte Cliffside is quite a trek up the hill in the dark and some of the street lights go out at midnight. Cuts, you know.'

I saw Ross's van leaving from outside the pub as I got into Tom's car. It was heading towards the hotel. Tom's car was a Honda, comfortable and clean. I hoped I wasn't going to have to fight him off.

No, he was the perfect gentleman, trained and muzzled by the jazz-hating wife. He dropped me off at the end of the hotel drive and made a swift turn-round, one eye on his watch.

I checked that Maddy was safely in her room. I could hear her weeping. Her dad could sort that out in the morning.

My room, 410, beckoned with its warmth and comfort. I stood under a lukewarm shower for a few minutes, then sat on the bed stark naked, eating oatmeal biscuits. It was therapeutic.

I checked my phone for messages before I turned out the light. There was one from DCI James. It was blunt and to the point.

'The DNA matches,' it said. What did that mean? DNA of what? And what did it match?

SIX

The breakfast room was almost empty. No Chuck Peters, no Maddy, not a single bleary-eyed musician. I was the only jazz steward, apart from their normal guests. I had survived the night and emerged in one piece in the morning.

I had slept like a log. The bed was a tumble of dreams but all so fleeting that I could remember none of them. Morning light crept in, hanging on ropes. That first cup of tea, sipped in bed, was hot sweet nectar. I had obviously died and gone straight to heaven. Was an angel serving me? A jazz angel?

Another shower. I was living in the shower, a warm bath of memory. It was becoming my second home. I might turn into a mermaid. I ought to check for a tail.

In the dining room, I was shown to a window table by yesterday afternoon's waiter and invited to help myself from a long buffet table. It was laden with goodies. My survival instinct prompted me to pocket cheese, biscuits and an apple in case of imminent worldwide disaster and starvation. Fortunately I had enough propriety to stop myself.

I took cranberry juice and a bowl of muesli and fruit back to my table. Same waiter hovered with a silver coffee pot. He had a thick head of dark hair, smoothly combed back. It was all so civilized.

'If madam would like a cooked breakfast?' He flourished a long menu. I was not a full English breakfast person. All that fried grease and meat. I went for a simple cheese omelette. This would last me all day and it was going to be a busy one.

The omelette was perfect. It oozed golden grated cheese.

'That looks lovely, thank you,' I said.

It was not easy following Maddy around. I wondered if Ross would be joining the jazz parade at ten? Drums are not usually walked around the town down to the seafront. A few kettle-drums maybe to help everyone keep in step.

After his cryptic text message the previous night, I expected DCI James to contact me again that morning. I wanted to know what he meant. If the maniac threatening Maddy had a connection to the castle murder, then he was seriously dangerous.

I checked upstairs. Chuck Peters came to the door, bleary-eyed, unshaven, in a paisley silk dressing gown.

'Maddy's slipped out, gone to the umbrella parade,' he groaned. 'Sorry, Jordan, got to go back to bed. Catch a few more hours.'

'Can I get you anything?'

'A new head.'

I had on my trainers so I could run along the seafront. It had stopped raining. The speckled shore was all fresh and pristine sand, beach huts and paddle boats to hire with enticing names: Desiree, Ruby, Estelle. It was altogether different to Latching, which was an endlessly flat vista, always so clean and distant.

This was a small bay, with honeyed bands of sailing boats, swimmers already splashing around in the sea, the crescent shape of hills and high cliffs either side like enveloping arms. It was if a giant had scooped out some of the land with a shell and flung it into the sea.

The cordoned streets drew me towards the bus station where the parade would be assembling. The police had already stopped the traffic. People were lining the pavements, eager for a good view. I tussled through crowds, trying to find Maddy.

Maddy was with the umbrella brigade. She didn't have a deco-rated umbrella but was standing close to Ross. He had brought along two cymbals. He was going to clash them with the New Orleans band, who were ready to lead the march. It was also a fund-raising march, and volunteers roamed the pavements rattling their cans, in aid of the street children of Cambodia. The children who begged, ate and slept nights on the streets.

I'd seen a documentary film about these orphan children but did nothing about it. Another cause ignored. Now I put a fiver, one of the blue ones, in a can. Not a lot. I was ashamed of myself. I could have afforded a lot more. Instead I had spent the money on a high-rise flat and a yellow car.

The sky was a clear blue, not a cloud in sight. The sea was whispering to the waves. No rain today, surely?

The march started off, led by the grand marshal, resplendent in braid, silver-knobbed cane and top hat. Then came the New Orleans jazz band, followed by the umbrella mob, twirling their brightly decorated umbrellas. What did the band play? All the old stomping favourites. There was a drummer but he had a big bass drum slung round his neck, beating the tempo of the march.

'Putting On The Ritz.' 'Sugar Foot Stomp.' Maddy was safe enough, alongside Ross, who clanged his cymbals whenever there was a pause in the music. He was clear-eyed; no sign of a late party.

There was a big police presence. Streets closed to traffic, crowds to control, whatever else was threatened. Maybe a protest of some sort.

DCI James was suddenly at my side. I saw him put a tenner, one of the brown ones, in a can. He sidled up to me, grave-faced.

'You got my text? The DNA matched. Don't let Maddy out of your sight. She is in danger if it's the same homicidal maniac.'

'But you didn't tell me anything.'

'The DNA matches items found at Corfe Castle. You don't need to know any more.'

'You've no idea how difficult it is. I can't keep track of her. She is besotted by this young drummer.'

'Then follow the drummer and you'll be following Maddy. Where's your umbrella? Join in the march.'

I don't know what made him do it. Perhaps it was the joyful New Orleans music, throbbing the air. But James put his arm round my waist and drew me close. I could hardly speak, hard against him, breathing in the scent of his skin.

'But spare some time for me, Jordan Lacey, private investigator. It's pretty lonely down here in the wilds of Dorset. Too many ghosts in the castles.'

Then he had gone. What did he mean? Ghosts in the castles? He'd vanished into the crowds like another dark shadow. Work always came first for James And my work must also come first, guarding this wayward lass.

The drummer, Ross Knighton, looked almost presentable in daylight. It was all that floppy hair and shadow of an unshaven chin. But his jeans and T-shirt were clean. That's always a big plus. He took little notice of Maddy, prancing at his side. She was fourteen. He was in his early twenties. She was a baby in his eyes, even with the false lashes and provocative clothes.

I sidled up to him. He might like older women. But my job was not to put Maddy's pert nose out of joint. He might be intrigued by the idea of a threesome, in a platonic way. If we were both protecting Maddy, it could make life easier. I felt sure he was not the writer of the threatening letters. He probably couldn't even write straight. He grinned at me, wondering where he'd seen me before.

'Hi, Ross,' I said, in a break in the music. We had reached the harbour where the New Orleans band were going to play a free concert for forty minutes or so. The musicians were milling about, arranging themselves for the gig. A flotilla of small boats were tied up, advertising trips to the Jurassic cliffs or to go fishing.

'Hi,' he said, his eyes sweeping over me. 'Like the hat.'

I was in my cowboy outfit again, plus fringed suede waistcoat against any chilled air. Maybe when I was sixteen or seventeen, I would have gone for the Ross type. But I don't remember being sixteen or seventeen. Had I skipped those years?

'I'm a steward,' I said, pointing to my blue badge. 'And a friend of Maddy Peters. Perhaps we could be useful to each other.'

I was not quite sure what I meant, but it was a start. Ross raised a dark eyebrow, wondering. I suppose I looked ancient to him. Nodding thirty might be ancient in his eyes.

'If you could keep her out of my hair for five minutes. There are other birds I fancy at this festival,' he said, combing his fringe back with his fingers.

It was not exactly the answer I expected, but I knew what he meant. Maddy had drifted off to buy ice-cream cones from a stall. She sure was trying hard to capture his affection. She was wearing tight washed-out and torn jeans this morning and a festival T-shirt. She looked almost normal.

'This could be a mutual arrangement,' I said hurriedly. 'If you keep an eye on Maddy when I don't know where she is, then I will keep her occupied other times so that you have the freedom to chase . . . other jazz enthusiasts.'

'Sounds good,' he said, unwrapping a slice of gum. 'So what's in it for you?'

'A set of Chuck Peters CDs.'

Apparently that was the right answer. Chuck was his hero. He would do anything for Chuck as long as he could play in his band. Ross was not ready to start out on his own. One day he would be a top percussion star, but not yet. Maybe even play at the Albert Hall at a promenade concert. It was his dream.

'OK,' he said. 'So this is just for the festival? You keep an eye on Maddy some of the time and keep her out of my way. And I'll do the same for you if you've lost track of her? Sounds fair, even when I can't prise her off me. She's like a dying lobster, clinging with all claws. I've got scratch marks. Sometimes she smells as bad.'

'She wears a lot of cloying perfume.'

'It stinks.'

'Here comes your ice cream.'

'I hate ice cream. You have it. Buy me a beer.'

But he did take the stick of chocolate off the top before handing the cone to me. It was synthetic white stuff swirled up to a stiff point. Tasted like cold shaving cream. Perhaps it could be used for both.

A crowd was gathering, sitting on the harbour wall or buying coffees at the cafe where they also got a seat for the price. A bit early for lunch from the seafood bistro. It was licensed so I got Ross a can of beer. It was the best I could do to consolidate the arrangement.

'It's probably revolting,' I said, handing it over. Maddy shot me a jealous look. 'Don't recognize the brand. Maybe it's a local brew.'

'It'll do,' he said carelessly, flicking it open.

I sat at a distance from the band, making sure I could watch Maddy. The good humour had returned to her young face now that I had backed off. The harbour seafront had railway lines set in the cobble stones. Once the quarry men had hauled their carts of rough stone along these lines to the waiting ships. They were historic, preserved. People walked on them now, not noticing that they walked on history.

New Orleans jazz is not my favourite. I can only take so much. I prefer big band jazz with all its changes of mood and tempo. The umbrella brigade were still twirling their decorated umbrellas. Their arms must be aching. They'd walked a long way to the harbour in unsuitable shoes. Other parts of their anatomy must be aching too. They were tough ladies.

My ears suddenly registered a difference. There were no clashing cymbals. I ran towards the crowd, jostling through people, but both Ross and Maddy had gone. The gap in the band had closed in. The brass were playing ear-piercingly loudly. It blew through my head.

'Have you seen Maddy?' I asked some of the players. They shook their heads, their eyes glued to sheets of music clipped to their instruments. 'Have you seen Ross anywhere?'

But one of the umbrella ladies had eyes in her head. 'They went off up the headland,' she said, nodding towards the rising sweep of hill westwards past the bandstand.

'Thanks,' I said. 'Smashing umbrella,' I added. It was black and white stripes decorated with red and gold tassels. Her dress and hat matched. It was quite an eye-catching outfit. 'You look great.'

I raced towards the headland, past the tall Greek columns that had been scavenged from the streets of ancient London, and brought to Swanage as ballast in the quarry boats. It was a steep climb up the grass sward. The pair of them could be anywhere. There were dozens of worn paths going off in different directions, half hidden by shrubs and wild brambles. The band might have been a hundred miles away but still the brass sound carried. I could almost make out a tune but couldn't put a name to it.

A bulky figure in a windcheater was walking towards me, two light tan Labradors romping around his feet, enjoying the freedom of the grassland, the wind blowing through their silky coats. I recognized him. It was Tom Lucas, the number one steward from last night's concert.

'Hi there, Jordan, enjoying these lovely views?' he called out. 'All free gigs this morning. Our work starts at one o'clock prompt. Where did the rota say you should be?'

Time had been kind to him. He had such a sweet smile, strong teeth and pleasant voice. No wonder Mrs Lucas stamped her ownership, accepted the jazz.

The dogs came rushing over to me, scenting a friend. 'Hello, boys,' I said, giving them my hand to sniff before I ventured to stroke them. I'm always scared of dogs. I've seen too many injuries from bites in my WPC days.

'They're friendly,' said Tom. 'They won't hurt you.'

'I'm always careful. In case I'm not welcomed.'

'You're welcomed. They like you. They're called Ant and Dec.'

The dogs were a little overweight like their master. They didn't get enough walks. I wondered if Tom had a job with long hours that kept him within four walls or perhaps Mrs Lucas overfed them. Too many doggy treats.

'I'm looking for Maddy,' I said. 'Chuck Peters' daughter. I think she was with Ross, the drummer.'

'Are they up here?'

'Someone saw them coming this way.'

'Oh, I know the chap. Wild and windy hair. No, I haven't seen them. They haven't come this way. Be careful, Jordan, the path veers very close to the cliff edge up here. The council ought to put up a fence.'

Very close to the cliff edge? Fear rose in my throat. Supposing there had been an accident and Maddy had gone over and Ross was scrambling down to rescue her? I would have to look.

Vertigo. It all came rushing back, my acute vertigo outside my new flat. The dizziness, the sickness, the trembling legs. What could I do? I could hardly ask Tom to look when he had two lively dogs, Ant and Dec, to look after. I could hardly ask him to hold onto my belt while I peered cautiously over the cliff edge, white faced and sweating.

I wished I was up here to enjoy the view of the bay for it was a glorious sight, fresh and windy. The air was sweet, tinged with wild flowers, sea-thrift and clover, and salt blown up from the turbulent sea below was blowing through my head. I could hear it thrashing on the rocks. No sand or sailing boats here, only cliff falls.

'You're looking very worried,' said Tom.

'I am worried.'

'I'm sure that young lady can look after herself. Ross wouldn't dare try anything on and lose his spot in Chuck Peters' band. It's his big chance in the jazz world. He'll go far.'

'The cliff edge?'

Tom chuckled. 'They've probably headed for the bushes.'

I didn't say that Maddy was the one who wouldn't care if Ross lost his place in the band. His career didn't mean anything if she could get what she wanted. She was a determined young woman. She would get her claws into him, whatever the cost. He'd have a job fighting her off.

As if to back up my thoughts, I caught sight of Ross running downhill further inland, half sliding on the grass, his shirt flapping off his back. He was glancing back over his shoulder as he ran, panting, trying to keep his balance on the steep slope.

'There he is!'

'And there's young Maddy.'

Maddy had emerged from a scrub of bushes, brushing leaves

from her clothes, trying to fix her hair. She started waving her fist at him, her face contorted.

'I'll make you pay for this, you bastard,' she shouted, her words carrying on the wind. 'Wait till my dad hears about this. You won't last five seconds in his band if I tell him about this. And don't you deny it. I'll tell him.'

Tom looked at me and said one word: 'Trouble.'

I sighed. 'Double trouble.'

Maddy was a handful, no doubt about that.

SEVEN

Maddy didn't notice Tom and I standing some way higher on the headland, two dogs leaping around. She rushed down the slope, slipping and sliding, but then her bulging straw bag flew open and a cascade tumbled around. She stopped to scrabble among the grass to collect her belongings.

It gave Ross the breathing space he needed. He fled down to the harbour seafront, hurrying through the stragglers, losing himself in the crowds.

The New Orleans bandsmen were packing up, making their way to the nearest pubs. Jazz is always thirsty work. The umbrella ladies were taking it easy, putting up their feet with cappuccinos at the harbour cafe.

'Did you say you were keeping an eye on that young woman?' Tom asked.

'Sort of. She's too young to be on her own all the time.'

'You'll need more than one eye.'

It was tempting to confide in Tom but not exactly a sensible move. DCI James might object if I took on board a civilian. Besides, the situation could become dangerous and I didn't want to deprive Ant and Dec of their cliff walks.

'I'll see you around,' I said, giving the dogs a farewell stroke. I couldn't let Maddy out of my sight. She was on her knees, searching in the long grass.

'It'll be a pleasure,' said Tom, nodding.

Perhaps Mrs Lucas wasn't around much to cook and that's

why he lived on burgers.

I sauntered over as if I had appeared by accident. 'Hi, Maddy,' I said, letting the wind comb through my hair.

'I've lost my best lipstick,' she moaned. 'It was brand new. Cost a bomb. Passionate Peach it's called. I just love it and now I can't find it. Hell's bells. This isn't my day. Ross and I have quarrelled and I'll never speak to him again. He's a mean, rotten so-and-so bastard. I hate him, hate him.'

She went on, mumbling incoherently, a waterfall of words.

I didn't want to know what they quarrelled about nor did I correct her language. But I had a vague idea of the circumstances. Ross had been the one escaping down the slope, not young Maddy.

I did a bit of kicking around with the toe of my boot. The gods were on my side. Perhaps one of them suffered from vertigo on his cloud. I caught a glint of gilt and bent down. It was a fat, shiny lipstick case.

'Is this your Passionate Peach?'

I was nearly knocked off my feet. Maddy hugged me ferociously.

'Thank you, thank you, darling Jordan! You're my best friend forever. It's the most fabulous colour. Look, look.'

She unwound the gilt cover and showed me the barely touched lipstick. It was a sort of pink or sort of peach, whichever light it was held in.

'Wow,' I said, who only owned one lipstick, shade of a forget-table rose. 'Fab colour.'

'Isn't it? I'm so pleased. Let's go and have a coffee to celebrate. I feel like celebrating.'

I guess I felt like celebrating too and never said no to a coffee. Breakfast now seemed a long time ago.

'Good idea.'

'My treat.'

We strolled into town. Swanage was a pleasant seaside town, lots of souvenir, bucket and spade shops, the usual quota of charity shops, cafes and fish restaurants. The two chain supermarkets were sited further back in the town with a couple of banks and travel agents on the way. I remembered I might need some sort of glam top if I got asked to a party. It wouldn't hurt to have a glam top in my meagre wardrobe.

The town was packed with holidaymakers and jazz enthusiasts. They crowded the pavements and spilled onto the road. *No Vacancy* signs hung in every window of the guest houses.

Fresh fish was the top dish of most restaurant menus, it seemed. Local fishermen downloaded their catches in the early morning. The menu boards were enticing. DCI James would be in seventh heaven. He loved fish and chips with a big dollop of tomato sauce. It was always his first choice.

We sat on the front at a cafe near the new cinema, bathed in sunshine. I had a straightforward latte, no extras. Maddy had something more complicated and a cheese bagel. She had skipped breakfast.

'Would you like to take a look round the charity shops?' I suggested. 'We've got time before the first gig or are you giving them a miss after this morning?'

'No, I'm going to my dad's. One o'clock in Marquee Two. But we've got time for a quickie shop crawl. I love shopping.'

The first charity shop was useless. It was a muddle. Too old, too dated, dusty, creased and overpriced. And the assistant was snooty which, as a seasoned shop owner myself, always puts me off.

'Are you looking for anything special?' she asked, looking down her nose.

'Have you got anything special?' I asked.

Maddy giggled. She was already halfway out of the door. She didn't like it either.

The next charity shop was a delight. Clothes were hung in sizes, colours and occasion. I went straight to the black rail. Black was right for any party. Maddy started combing the most recent summer gear. I bought a silky black tunic top with simple plaited straps instead of sleeves. Maddy bought two T-shirts, one a bright blue with a polar bear on an ice floe and the other a kaleidoscope of razzle-dazzle sequins. No missing her on a dark night.

'Come on. Marquee Two. We'll just make it,' I said before Maddy started on the rail of swimwear. 'We ought to hurry.'

'We must come shopping again,' said Maddy happily. 'I'm sick of all my clothes. They stink. I'm going to dump them.'

I wasn't sick of any of my clothes. I didn't have enough to feel that any of them deserved such a fate. But I loved the new silky top. I now wanted an occasion to wear it, to show off my tanned shoulders, preferably with James around. The Latching sun had been kind to my skin. Even with my tawny hair, I never got burnt. I didn't stay out long enough, half dressed, in the sun.

A few clouds had gathered in the sky, like uncertain mourners wondering if they were at the right funeral. They hovered over the bay, casting shadows where before had been sunlight. I shivered, glad of the waistcoat.

Maddy darted into the marquee. She had a musician's pass despite not playing a single note. No one could deny Chuck Peters' daughter free admission. No one could deny her anything. The public were already filing in, showing the correct colour wristband, armed with cushions and sandwiches. There were plenty of stewards around so there was nothing much for me to do.

I tried to look inconspicuous, picked up a programme to read, cruising around. Names were beginning to be familiar.

Maddy was already in her usual place at the side of the stage. She had not offered to help Ross carry in his drum kit. She was giving him the cold shoulder this afternoon.

'Do you know how to draw a pint?'

A steward I had never seen before, short, dark and wiry, rather harassed, had appeared from nowhere. He was flapping a list.

'I don't know,' I said, helpfully.

'The barman hasn't arrived. We need another hand at the bar. There's a queue and the customers are getting ratty. These are the prices.'

'I can do prices,' I said, leaning heavily on my shop experience.

'Then you are the perfect person,' he said, beaming. Did all jazz stewards have wonderful smiles? It must be the music infecting the soul. 'Someone will show you how to draw a pint.'

I eased round to the bar at the back of the marquee. I could still see Maddy, sitting cross-legged at the side of the stage. It was a makeshift sort of bar with three barrels at the back and a cool cabinet with bottles of white wine, soft drinks and water. The red wine was already out on the counter. There were different sized plastic glasses for every kind of drink. Not exactly rocket science.

The three barrels of beer were different local makes. Beer drinkers are connoisseurs. They don't drink any old beer. Someone showed me how to work the pump to draw a pint up to a certain line on the glass. It was a skilled art, believe me. All that froth suddenly appearing. You had to stop before the foaming top became Niagara Falls. This was something new I could put on my CV: bar experience.

It would help, if I had to get a job.

I thought I was good at maths but when a punter ordered two pints, a red and a white wine, three cokes and a bag of crisps, my mental arithmetic was thrown. I got out my PI notebook and dedicated the back page to adding up mechanics.

Every ten seconds I glanced at Maddy. They were playing 'Lullaby Of Broadway'. Music to dance to. 'My Blue Heaven.' Any time, any day. 'Poor Butterfly' always made me want to cry. The saddest piece of music ever written.

'Half a pint, miss. Local brew,' said a deep-toned voice in my ear. 'Don't rush the draw. I don't want a wet glass.'

'What are you doing here?' I hissed at him. The front of my shirt was damp and I was harassed.

'What are you doing here? You are supposed to be guarding Maddy.'

'I am guarding her. I can see her. I know where she is. She won't move till Ross moves.'

His half-pint was drawn with extra care. I didn't want another sarcastic comment.

'The DNA and prints on the note are confirmed. They match DNA and prints from my castle victim. The girl we found was also fifteen, a lot like Maddy: pretty, very modern, skimpy clothes. But she came from a decent family, was taking her GCSEs, an above-average student but not a tearabout. She was always home by a certain set time, except this once. Her family are still devastated. I want closure on this case.'

DCI James leaned on the bar counter, sipping his half-pint. I pushed a bag of crisps in his direction. This was probably his lunch.

'We don't want Maddy to be the next victim.'

I shivered, a chill running down my spine, like that moment on the headland this morning. I took another ten second glance at her. Maddy was leaning forward, her chin in cupped hands, mesmerized by the rocking percussion.

'She's in her usual trance,' I said.

'She could be knifed in a trance,' said James.

'She's got a scream that would stop traffic,' I said, remembering her shouted abuse at Ross.

'I'm sure it would, if it was plunged into her ribs.'

James leaned over towards me, his ocean blue eyes hard and glinting. 'This is not like you, Jordan. A bodyguard guards a body. It doesn't draw pints. Hang up your tea-towel and take Maddy a diet coke. Put it on my bill.'

'Yes, sir,' I said. 'Right away, sir. And I'll have a red wine.'

It was an unidentifiable bottom of the house red but I needed the raw alcohol after that reprimand. Bright red liquid in a small plastic beaker hardly soothed my ruffled feelings. I abandoned the bar. No one seemed to notice. There was no queue now. I took the drinks down to the front and handed the can over to Maddy.

'This is your lunch,' I said.

She nodded, hardly noticing it was me, her new best friend. She opened the can and began to drink fast as if dehydrated by the music.

There was a spare chair at the end of the front row, next to the marquee flap. No one was sitting there because it was draughty. I could feel a chill wind round my legs as I sat down. It was lethal and uncomfortable. No wonder everyone had given it the cold shoulder, or cold bum. I drank some of the red stuff. It didn't help;

wet and weak, tasteless.

The vocalist was singing Ella Fitzgerald's 'Goodnight My Love' when I heard the first pattering on the tent roof. At first I thought it was brush strokes, then I realised it was raining. After such a glorious morning, some sort of cold front had swept across the bay.

A middle-aged woman leaned towards me, tapped me on the shoulder, smiling. 'You're the steward who saved us all yesterday when the boat crashed onto the rocks, aren't you?'

'Well, it wasn't exactly me on my own,' I said modestly. 'The skipper had a lot to do with it.'

'Still, you kept us all from panicking. You were the only one with any sense. Silly lot.' She nodded in agreement with herself and settled back to listen to the jazz. I remembered her. She had been the one crying.

The band were tiring. I could feel that the energy had gone. Chuck Peters meandered among his musicians, indicating a change in programme.

'We are going to end our session this afternoon with the perennial favourite "Sing, Sing, Sing" featuring our talented drummer, Ross Knighton.'

Maddy's face was bathed in adoration.

I wondered if Ross could cope with this number. Long ago I'd heard the world-famous swing and jazz percussionist, Eric Delaney, play this number and he'd been ancient even then. He'd played everything on stage: the walls, the chairs, the lights, the microphones. It had been a performance to remember. As well as his drum kit, he'd had on stage a xylophone, glockenspiel, timpani, military side drums, tubular bells, Chinese gongs and tam tams.

Ross handled it well. He was not yet a virtuoso performer but his technique and artistry was way above the normal bash and bang drummer. Maddy was entranced, as usual, never taking her eyes off him as he leaped around the set.

The applause was deafening. Chuck went through the customary naming of each of his musicians so that they got their share of the applause.

'That's all, folks. See you again this evening, eight o'clock in Marquee One. Got your brollies? I think it's raining.'

That was an understatement. It was pouring, a steady relentless rain. The sky was dark with rain clouds. Stewards hurried out with lanterns to hang on the poles along the entrance so that no one slipped on the path. The wet grass could be treacherous.

Ross was zipping up his kit into their waterproof bags. It was costly equipment and he never left it lying about. Maddy had apparently forgiven him and was helping stow away the sticks.

Chuck was wiping and packing up his instruments to take along with him. He was due to play at another venue at four o'clock but first he wanted a quick liquid lunch and a steak sandwich. He said something to his daughter but she shook her head and flounced off.

He looked around the marquee; spotted me. He grinned and waved.

He hurried over, putting a folded twenty note in my hand. 'Make sure Maddy gets some proper food inside her, will you? She won't survive tonight's partying on a packet of crisps.'

'Sure,' I said. My cheese omelette was already a distant memory. 'There's a great fish and chip restaurant right on the front, highly recommended.'

'I know the place, the one on the corner? It serves round the clock. And get a taxi. You'll be soaked in this downpour.'

Maddy was valiantly helping Ross to carry his gear out to his van. I saw her disappear through the tent flap with some of the drum stands. Next I heard a scream. It was indeed a scream that could stop traffic.

I ran outside, half blinded by the rain. Maddy was standing in the middle of the field, her arms outstretched in terror. She had dropped the stands. Huddled at her feet was a heap of black and white material and a seeping puddle of red.

It took me a few seconds to recognize that it was a woman. It was the black and white umbrella woman on the street parade this morning. But now the sharp ferrule of the decorated umbrella had been planted into her chest. The seeping red was blood.

EIGHT

I rushed over to the woman and knelt down onto the grass. I felt for a pulse in her neck. It was faint but it was there. I didn't touch the umbrella.

'Where's your phone?' I said to Maddy. I'd left my bag under the bar. But she was still screaming hysterically, unable to do anything except open her mouth. I pulled her back into the marquee, grabbed my phone out of my bag and dialled 999.

'Ambulance and police,' I said. 'The top field near the seafront where the jazz festival is being held. Swanage. A woman has been stabbed. She's still breathing but only just. Hurry.'

I didn't wait to give them my name and address. I wanted something to cover the woman to keep in her body heat. My new silky top was hardly suitable; neither were Maddy's T-shirts. There was a sleeping bag rolled up behind the bar, stored from the previous night's vigil. I hauled it out and hurried outside to the woman. A crowd had gathered, undeterred by the rain.

'Don't touch anything!' I shouted. A man was on his knees, trying to remove the umbrella. 'Don't touch it!' I shouted again. 'You could do more damage than good. Leave it alone.'

'But shouldn't we try to get it out?'

'No,' I said. 'Let the medics do it.' Didn't he ever watch those helicopter rescue shows on television? Latching police had always been glued to them. I unrolled the sleeping bag, carefully easing her into the recovery position, covered her so that at least there was some warmth. It was sleeting now, the wind flinging the rain into horizontal shafts. I was soaked through although I didn't notice until later.

'Close the gates,' I said to today's chief steward, the short harassed one. He was even more harassed now. He was white-faced and sweating. 'No one should leave. There might be a witness. The police will want to question everyone.'

'The police?' he mumbled. 'What about the festival? Will they close it?' He had already forgotten all the emergency and first aid training given to the stewarding group. I'd read the rule book and hand-out given to every steward.

Patience, Jordan, I said to myself. Keep calm. 'The police and ambulance are on their way. I suggest you ask everyone to return to the marquee and sit down and wait. No point in everyone getting drenched.'

Maddy. I'd forgotten all about her.

'That's Elsie Dunlop,' said someone. 'She's a regular on the parade with her umbrella.'

'Will you stay with her for a moment?' I asked the same onlooker. He looked steady and reliable. 'I'll be back in a moment.'

'Certainly, miss.' He put up a striped golf-size umbrella to keep some of the rain off Elsie Dunlop and himself. 'Anything you say.'

I went back through the flap, dreading what I might find. Another stabbing? But Maddy was sitting on the stage, being consoled by Ross. He was patting her hand, if you could call that consoling. She was sniffing and sobbing, mascara on the run again.

I hurried over to him. 'Thank goodness. Keep her warm, keep her calm, give her something to drink and don't let her out of your sight.'

'It's my turn to babysit, is it?' he said. 'Is the woman outside going to be all right? Looked pretty lethal.'

'We don't know yet. Hardly all right with an umbrella in her chest. Must go. I can hear the sirens coming up the hill. They were pretty quick.'

The field was suddenly a mass of lights, police and paramedics arriving at the same time. The Scenes of Crime Officer was already unrolling his tape. No music in the marquee tonight. They would dust every blade of grass for prints.

A female detective inspector had arrived in the first police car. She was slim and short with raven black hair cut smoothly to frame her face. She was wearing a navy waterproof with a high collar. She flashed her ID card at me but I couldn't catch her name. She was high-octane efficiency.

'Did you find the victim?' she asked me curtly.

'No, it was Maddy Peters. She's inside the marquee, very upset. I made the 999 call.'

'You're supposed to give your name and address. It could have been a hoax.' She was quite abrupt, standing feet astride.

'I thought it was more important to take care of the stabbed woman. There was no time to waste on details. You can have my name and address now.'

'Where's this Paddy Peters?'

'Maddy Peters. She's in the marquee. She's only fourteen.'

'Then I need an adult present before I can speak to her.'

'There is an adult with her now. His name is Ross Knighton. He's a drummer with the festival.'

Her expression said that anyone who was a drummer could hardly be an adult too. Did DCI James have to work with this woman? I began to feel a certain amount of sympathy.

'He's taking care of her.'

The paramedics, as efficient as always, were working on Elsie Dunlop, fixing an oxygen mask on her face, putting her on a saline drip. They were wrapping her in foil, the umbrella still in place, wondering how to get her into the ambulance with the attachment. It was a big umbrella.

'We could saw off the handle,' one suggested.

'Too much friction,' said the other.

'You need a cradle for it,' said the same sensible onlooker who had recognized Elsie Dunlop. 'I'll make one in a jiffy.' He went back into the marquee and returned with several empty crates and a roll of duct tape. 'Will these make a cradle? A bit on the makeshift but the best I can do.'

There was hardly any room in the back of the ambulance once they got Elsie on a stretcher, the umbrella cradled in crates and the medic beside her. I was glad when the doors closed. The sleeping bag was left on the grass. It was still only afternoon. It felt much longer.

Her name was apparently DI Ruth Macclesfield. She and her officers were marshalling everyone, efficiently but without making many friends. She wanted every name and address.

'But when can we go? I've got a stroller ticket. Another gig to go to.'

'No one is leaving yet.'

'You also need to ask where they are staying in Swanage,' I said to her in passing. 'They have come from far and wide for this festival. It's famous. You might want to speak to some of them again before they go home.'

She glared at me and said something to a nearby constable.

'And who are you?' she asked. 'Fast lady to the phone, but reluctant to identify yourself. Name and address, please.'

'My name is Jordan Lacey. I'm staying at the Whyte Cliffside Hotel.' My new flat's address in Latching was barely imprinted on my memory. I couldn't remember the exact postcode. I could only remember the vertigo.

'Home address?'

'Currently moving,' I said. Now that sounded really suspicious. I rummaged through my shoulder bag to see if I had written anything down anywhere. There was no letter or card and nothing attached to the front door key, except a blue plastic dog tag with eyes that swivelled. I could hardly say that I had forgotten the exact address, having bought the flat in a hurry, but that it was on the fourth floor, facing the sea, above a well-known supermarket and restaurant.

'I can vouch for this young woman,' said DCI James, not betraying by the flicker of an eyelash that he had once kissed me quite passionately in a fishing boat. That had been a happy day.

'Her name is Jordan Lacey. I have known her for three or four years from my previous deployment in West Sussex. She was a police officer, now retired from the force.'

'If you say so, sir,' said DI Macclesfield dubiously.

'Carry on, Ruth. You're doing a good job.'

He turned to me. 'What can you tell me, Jordan? Is Maddy all right? Where is she?' He led me to an almost empty row of chairs. I sat down with relief. My legs were beginning to feel the strain and I was very wet. My jeans clung to my legs. Thank goodness my hat wasn't soaked, too. Cowboy hats had a certain resistance to the weather.

I told James all that I knew, which wasn't very much. I hadn't noticed Elsie Dunlop sitting anywhere at the gig although I had been pretty busy at the bar. Nor had I heard her scream. I'd only heard Maddy screaming.

'Is there any possible way that the attacker could have mistaken Miss Dunlop for Maddy?' James asked.

I shook my head. 'They don't look alike at all. They weren't dressed alike. No way. Maddy was on the field, carrying gear out to Ross's van,' I said. 'Our Maddy isn't similar to Miss Dunlop in any respect: different age, height, clothes.'

'I'll have a word with Ross.' James returned moments later. 'Apparently Miss Dunlop had spoken to Ross afterwards, but only briefly, saying how much she enjoyed his "Sing, Sing, Sing". So she was in the marquee for the show?'

'Her last words,' I said forlornly. 'If only she hadn't spoken to him. Maybe somehow the attacker confused the two of them.'

'Or deliberately confused them. Maybe it was another warning to Chuck Peters. Pay up or this is what will happen to your daughter.'

'Pay up? Has there been another demand?'

'Did he tell you?'

'No, nothing about another demand. And another weird thing. It was pouring with rain but her umbrella wasn't up. It was unfurled.'

'Perhaps Miss Dunlop didn't want it to get wet. All those

elaborate decorations. Not for normal usage.'

I couldn't imagine it. Her hair, her hat, her smart dress. Surely her first thought would have been to protect them from the rain?

'I think someone stole or borrowed her umbrella,' I said. 'Find that person and you may have her attacker.'

DCI James sighed. 'You make life so much fun, Jordan,' he sighed. 'I love your priorities. Now I'm looking for a lost umbrella. I shall be at Poole Hospital all evening, in case Miss Dunlop regains consciousness. If she could give us a description, we'd have something to work on.'

He went over to talk to DI Ruth Macclesfield. 'Are you sure?' I thought I heard him say. Maddy was calming down now. Ross was agitated, checking the air for me. He waved me over.

'Hi, Jordan. I have to play at the con club in fifteen minutes with the Wilson Boys Trio. It takes me that long to unpack and set up my kit. I have to go. They are my mates. I can't let them down.'

The marquee was almost empty. It looked forlorn.

'Of course not, Ross. You go off and do your stuff.' I nearly commented on his brilliant 'Sing, Sing, Sing' but thought it might be tempting fate. Last words and all that. 'Break a leg.'

'I need the loo,' Maddy whimpered. I knew she would refuse point blank to use the portable loos lined up at the end of the field. I didn't blame her. They were always damp. And it was still raining.

'I don't have a magic wand,' I said. 'I can't produce a sole-use en suite for you in the middle of a field. You'll have to wait.' It was all those diet cokes she drank.

'Think of something,' she said. 'Fast.'

'My hat?'

This brought a glimmer of a smile to her wan face and took her mind off her bladder. She should have strong muscles at her age. DCI James came strolling back, looking grave. His short hair was silvered with raindrops.

'No one seems to remember Miss Dunlop even being at this afternoon's session,' he said. 'That's puzzling. She's a striking-looking woman. No one sat next to her or behind her. Do you remember seeing her?'

'I was chained to the bar, remember?' I said. 'Perhaps she was waiting outside. There was a queue.'

'Oh yes, you were the new serving wench.'

'What's a wench?' Maddy asked.

'Archaic word for servant,' I said. 'My customary role.'

'I could give you both a lift back to the hotel so you can get into some dry clothes but DI Macclesfield wants you to go to the station first and make a statement, Maddy,' said DCI James, refastening his waterproof.

'I need to go to the loo,' said Maddy anxiously.

'I believe they have several at the police station. All mod cons.'

It was not a pleasant drive to the police station in the patrol car. The shiny inside smelt of fear and vomit and disinfectant. Maddy huddled into a corner on the back seat, not looking at anything. The driver hardly spoke, but he did offer back a tube of Fruit Gums.

'I only like the red ones,' she said petulantly.

'I'll have the green one,' I said, always ready to oblige. 'The next one looks like red. Thank you.'

I'd seen so many police stations in my life. This one looked no different. Austere concrete and brick surroundings, grey plastic chairs, awful green paint and a tiled floor. But it was equipped with the latest in technology, computers, scanners and printers on desks and coded locked doors.

Maddy followed me reluctantly.

'Could you direct us to the nearest cloakrooms?' I said to the desk sergeant before Maddy could get her demands in. 'It's rather urgent.'

'Through the swing doors, first on your left. I can't spare a female escort.'

'We don't need an escort,' I said, steering Maddy through the swing doors. 'I'll look after Maddy.'

The loos were as bleak as always. Chipped white tiles and scratchy paper towels. Four cubicles. We both used them. Maddy changed into her new polar bear T-shirt and busied herself repairing her face. The Passionate Peach came out again. I could hardly put on my black silk so I stayed damp.

The statement didn't take long. What could Maddy say? I sat beside Maddy, being the required adult present. She gave her name, address and age.

'Tell me in your own words,' said DI Macclesfield, her eyes like peanuts. Perhaps she had missed her lunch.

'I came out of the marquee with the sticks pad to take to Ross's van. I'd been helping Ross. I'm his assistant. It was raining and I could hardly see where I was going and then I nearly fell over this woman. She was right in my way,' Maddy added truculently. 'There was blood everywhere. It was h-horrible.'

She began to cry again but not much because the mascara was fresh. Cosmetic firms must make a fortune out of her, I thought.

'Did you see anyone running away?' asked DI Macclesfield, leaning forward. I could see a tan make-up smudge on the neck of her white shirt. It was the wrong shade for her skin. Very unprofessional. I had always kept a spare white shirt in my desk and spare underwear. You never knew when you might need a quick change.

'No.'

'Did you see anyone acting suspicious at all?'

'I don't know what you mean.'

'Anyone who looked different.'

'You mean anyone with vampire teeth or a neck covered in blood?' Maddy was recovering her wits quickly.

Ruth Macclesfield was not amused. She had a seriously injured woman in Poole Hospital and a vicious attacker at large. I had a fellow feeling for her but said nothing. She didn't generate sympathy.

'You must remember something.'

'All I remember is masses of blood.'

'That's all for now but if you think of anything, please let me know. I'll get your statement printed out and when you have signed it, you can go. I take it you can read and write?'

Ouch. Below the belt, DI Macclesfield. And hardly necessary.

'Miss Peters took her mock GCSE exams this year,' I said. 'We will forget you said that. Discriminatory remark.'

DI Macclesfield made no comment but left the room with the laptop.

'What did I say?' Maddy was bewildered.

'Nothing. Don't worry. She's stressed out. She's got an attempted murder on her hands and no clues. '

I phoned for a taxi. We didn't want to arrive at the hotel in a police car. The sooner we got back to some sort of normality, the better. As I suspected, Maddy had no intention of missing the evening gig in her new self-appointed role as assistant to Ross.

Whyte Cliffside Hotel appeared out of the rain, a haven of peace and civilization. The manager met us in the foyer; word had spread fast. He appeared quite concerned.

'Please ask for anything that you want,' he said. 'Perhaps you would like room service in your room, some privacy. People can be so intrusive.'

'Thank you, that's very kind,' I said. 'We'll order a late tea or early supper or whatever is on the menu.'

'I have to go to Dad's evening gig in Marquee One,' said Maddy. She was recovering fast from her fright.

'First, a hot shower, a change of clothes and something to eat,' I said firmly. 'And lock your door. Only open it to me. I will bring your room service order.'

She looked as if she was about to object but then saw the sense of it. 'OK, Jordan, if you say so. I'll only open the door to you. But I still want to go out this evening.'

I pushed her towards the lift. 'First things first,' I said firmly. I was the one who was desperate for a hot shower and some dry clothes. I was damp and clammy and harrowed by events. That comfy bed beckoned me. Half an hour with my feet up and I would be as right as rain.

Wrong word. It was raining hard. But the jazz enthusiasts would still turn up in hoodies and waterproofs, no doubt about that.

Maddy ordered a cheeseburger, diet coke and a banana split. I took the tray in to her. She opened the door carefully, wrapped in a big towelling robe. She'd washed her hair as well. It was rolled up in big rollers.

'Don't leave without me,' I said. 'We'll go together. We'll go in my car.'

'I didn't know you'd got a car.'

'Wait till you see it, Maddy. You're in for a surprise.'

'As long as I don't have to push it,' she said, with a surprising touch of humour. She closed her door and I heard her locking it.

The hot shower was a dream. I stood under it, mesmerized. My supper tray arrived. I had ordered a crab salad, roll and butter and a fruit yogurt. There was also a miniature of three-star brandy on the tray which obviously the manager thought I might need. He was right. A few sips warmed me up immediately.

I sat on the comfy armchair re-reading the rules and hand-out which Tom Lucas had given me. It was all there: what to do in an emergency. But nothing actually covered someone being stabbed with an umbrella.

My supper was delicious. I ate the lot. I could have nodded off so I made some black coffee to keep myself awake. My phone rang. It was probably Maddy demanding to be taken somewhere.

But it was James. His voice went straight to my heart. The man held my happiness in his voice, in his eyes, in his smile. But he didn't know it.

'I'm calling from Poole Hospital. Are you both all right?' he asked.

'Yes, the dragon didn't eat us. Plenty of spitting fire. A bit scorched round the edges.'

He absorbed this information, then he chuckled. The sound I loved. 'I get bitten every day.'

'Why don't you take her out for a drink? Get her drunk. She might mellow.' But I didn't mean it. I didn't want James to have anything to do with his soulless detective inspector.

'I think it's been tried,' he said with resignation. 'She has a concrete-lined stomach.'

'That explains the frozen face.'

'Jordan, I have something to tell you which I think you ought to know. It is relevant to the unfortunate attack on the field this afternoon.'

'Oh no, poor soul, has Elsie Dunlop died?' The words caught in my throat.

There was a pause. 'It's not that she has died. But she's not Elsie Dunlop. She is a *he*.'

'What? I don't understand. What do you mean?'

'Elsie Dunlop is a man.'

That explained all the make-up.

NINE

Maddy was impressed by my wasp. She walked round the car as if the yellow beauty was something beamed down from outer space.

'This is actually your car? You own it?' She ran her hand over the wet and gleaming yellow bodywork. 'It's fabulous. I wish Dad would get something like this. He drives a stupid, middle-class black Saab.'

I won't hear a word against Saabs. James drives a Saab. It suits him; solid and reliable but with a hint of speed when necessary. It could ram a tank.

Maddy was done up to the ears in a red parka with fur-trimmed hood. She looked like a little animal peeking out from under the fur. It was still raining. Where had the glorious morning gone? It was a different country, sodden with water, an empty beach with pock-marked sand, boats moored, but the restaurants, cafes, theatre and jazz venues were packed. Dark clouds swarmed over the sky as if in combat for the grimmest face. I heard a distant rumble of thunder, saw a far crack of lightning. The sky had got indigestion.

I unlocked the car and climbed in before my newly washed hair got a second rinse. Maddy was fast after me, sliding in, not finding the slow-slung roof any problem. She shook off the rain once inside. I hoped the wasp would start after its lonely wait in the headland hotel car park.

The car responded immediately, sweet thing, with a low throb.

Obviously longing for something to do, somewhere to go. She needed taking out every day. Tomorrow I would give her body-work a loving polish. Shopping: buy best polish, soft cloths.

'Let's go,' said Maddy merrily. 'Shame we can't put the roof down. That would be fab.'

I had never put the roof down yet. It was not automatic. You had to unfasten clips, do some folding thing with the windows and unzip something else. Mike Reed had explained but I had only been half listening, dazzled by the prospect of imminent ownership.

I reversed slowly out of the car park, hardly able to see in the rain-splashed mirror. It was not a long way down the hill, then along the coast road and take a right up towards the jazz fields. Five minutes at the most. It would take longer to find a parking space.

'Let's go for a spin,' said Maddy excitedly. 'We're quite early. Ross can set up his own stuff for once. I'm not his slave, his wench.'

'OK,' I said. I didn't argue with her. James had given me a map of the area. I would have to drive carefully because of the recent miniature brandy. I didn't want to collect any points. 'We'll go up to the top of the headland, towards the golf course and Langton Matravers. There's a special quarry site called Dancing Ledge that looks like a long cliff walk from the road. Another time, perhaps. And there is the Great Globe at Durlston Country Park. All worth a visit.'

'I'm not into history much,' said Maddy, pulling down her hood. Her newly washed hair was still in big rollers.

It was a steep climb; the road seemed almost vertical. I had to go into the lowest gear. The wasp responded with a rasping growl, her wheels gripping the wet road with confidence. The road was lined with guest houses and small hotels. Thank goodness we weren't staying here. The walk uphill would have killed me.

'Wow, what a hill,' I said. 'Maybe one in four?'

On the top of the headland the air was clearer; it was still raining but the wind was blowing it inland. We could see misty miles of rolling white-topped waves, each crested and tumbling towards the cliffs. Even Maddy seemed mesmerized by the surging power of the sea, thrashing against the rocks.

'Nature's open book, this is called,' I said. 'There have been a lot of shipwrecks along this coast. I saw a whole history of ship-wrecks in the library.'

'Not much of an open book today. Can hardly see a thing.'

'I think we ought to go back soon,' I said. 'We don't want your dad to get worried about you.'

'He worries about everything,' said Maddy. 'He thinks I'm five years old, still playing with plasticine in kindergarten.'

I asked what I had been wanting to know but had been unable to find out. 'Is your mother still around?' It had to be carefully worded. She might have died from one of the dreaded female illnesses.

'You bet she's still around but not around for Dad or me.' Maddy almost snorted. 'She went off with some jazz musician, not even a famous one. They are always broke, live in a caravan half the time, play at one-night gigs in pubs. I once saw him playing his sax in the street with a hat on the pavement. There was about fifty pence in it. I nearly died of embarrassment.' She paused, then added: 'But he did play well. Good clear notes, good control.'

'Did he know you?'

'No. I've never met him, thank goodness. I might spit in his face.'

I was sorry I'd brought up the past. I turned the car carefully in a lay-by and headed back toward the town. 'Is Ross playing tonight?' I said, changing the subject. Maddy's thoughts switched immediately.

'You bet. Ross'll be there. Acid jazz tonight. Acid jazz digs the new breed, you know. Wait till you hear it.'

Acid jazz was not part of my scene. I liked mainly swing and blues and big band jazz. I wasn't even sure what acid jazz was.

The wasp climbed the shorter hill to the jazz field and I

let Maddy out after she had removed her rollers and brushed through the big waves. Marquee Two was still cordoned off with SOC tape, definitely not in use. Only Marquee One was functioning tonight. Stewards had laid coarse matting across the grass to the entrance to prevent mud being stamped inside.

The field was already a swamp. The rain wasn't draining away down to the sea as it ought to. The field must be sitting on rock. Maybe Jurassic rock. Maybe the dinosaur bones were getting a shake-up with the jazz rocking.

The wasp was small enough to fit in a tiny parking space that had been overlooked by bigger cars. She backed in easily and the engine died with a sound that almost asked me not to leave her too long.

'Won't be long,' I promised. Now I was talking to a car.

Tom Lucas caught sight of me from the booking office. 'Thank goodness you're here. We have twice as many people coming because of the cancellation next door. We're going to put in some extra rows of seats. No leg room for anyone tonight. Can you help?'

'Sure,' I said. 'Let's get it done.'

Nobody wanted to move once they had got a seat. It took all my persuasion and wacky charm to get the extra rows in. 'There's a special prize tonight,' I improvised. 'It's hidden under one of these extra chairs. It's a voucher for Chuck Peters' latest CD.'

It got people moving. There was an immediate shift.

Tom was amused and grateful. 'I'll pay for it,' he offered. 'No need for you to fork out. Do you know how Miss Dunlop is?'

I shook my head. I didn't want to say too much. DCI James had told me in confidence. 'Still unconscious, I think. She's under guard at Poole Hospital.'

'Oh dear, poor woman. I wonder what caused such an awful attack.'

'We might never know.'

I had my own theory. She/he had recognized someone. Someone who did not want to be recognized. Someone from her/his previous life. That might be the answer. Clear as soggy mud.

'We'll know when she regains consciousness. She may be able to give a good description of her attacker.'

'It hasn't stopped the crowds coming in. I thought there might be a drop in numbers but all the venues are reporting a big turnout. Thank goodness. We have to cover costs. The festival gets more expensive every year and we don't want to put ticket prices up.'

I agreed. 'People can't keep paying more and more. There is a limit to their pockets, especially these days.'

The marquee was swarming with people, body heat, wet clothes, muddy feet. It would soon be steaming. It was like being in a sauna.

I asked around about acid jazz. I got a variety of answers. It was infectiously catchy early hits. It came to life on the dance floor. It had party energy. It united style tribes. I was beginning to like the sound of it, whatever it meant. I was no wiser.

'We're packed. Healthy and safety,' said Tom, sweating.

We had to close the entrance, only allowing people to leave. But no one wanted to leave once the Chuck Peters band began playing. He started with the lively but haunting 'Night And Day'. There was a patient line outside, waiting under dripping umbrellas, ready to leap inside if anyone left. They could still hear the jazz but it was damply uncomfortable.

Maddy was sitting on the edge of the stage, near a tangle of electric cables. Hardly safe, I thought, but if I moved her, where else could she go? I leaned against a bin in a far corner. It was killing my back but this was what I was being paid to do. That reminded me that my fee had not been finalized. Would it be enough to get my new flat redecorated? Nothing had been written down. So much for efficiency.

My thoughts drifted to James and his new responsibilities since he had been promoted. This poor girl whose body had been found in the grounds of Corfe Castle was also only fifteen, almost the same age as Maddy. Her parents would be distraught, even though it was three years ago. The pain would never really go. I wondered if his investigations were progressing.

James would have no time now for a glass of wine with me. Or a fish and chip supper at a local restaurant down on the front. The Gorgon would have her sights fixed on him, day and night.

Chuck was echoing the tune of 'Fascinating Rhythm' (Gershwin, 1924) with his tenor saxophone, taking it to new heights. It was magical music. If only James could be here to share it with me. It would take his mind off the disasters of the world, the realities of police work.

We were supposed to have our phones switched off but occasionally one began ringing, much to the owner's embarrassment. Sometimes the phone belonged to a musician on the stage but they were never fazed. They answered the phone with one hand and went on playing at the same time, as if nothing had happened.

When my phone went off, I dived out of the marquee as if I'd been stung. There was a scurry of amusement, also some annoyance. I took no notice. I held the phone under my anorak. I could hardly test its weatherproof properties.

'I can't hear you,' I said.

'I can't hear you at all.' It was James.

'I'm standing in the pouring rain, outside the marquee.'

'Can't you find . . . somewhere quieter?' he shouted.

There was a big oak tree in a corner of the field. I squelched across the mud to the shelter of its sturdy branches and canopy of leaves. Although I was almost out of the rain, the tree provided a different cascade of big drops falling from the laden leaves. It was darkly green, luminescent, Jurassic.

'Is Maddy all right?' he asked.

'She's pretty resilient, recovering well. Nothing deters her from Chuck's gigs and Ross's company. Maybe she'll have nightmares tonight.'

He didn't ask if I was all right. I'd seen enough unpleasantness since I'd been a private detective. That nun on a meat hook had been pretty nasty. 'Is Miss Dunlop stable?' I asked. I didn't know what else to call her. 'Has she said anything yet?'

'Unfortunately no. And she is not going to be able to tell us anything. Elsie Dunlop died an hour ago. The ferrule had pierced a lung. There was copious bleeding. The surgeons couldn't do anything to save her.'

The drops falling from the leaves were cold and invasive. They went down my neck, trickling onto my warm skin with icy fingers. I froze onto the ground. I did not want to feel dead.

Death had come to a happy place. Jazz was always happy. Death had no right to disturb the happiness.

'That's so sad. I'm sorry. Have you anyone you can contact?'

'There's no one apparently. No family. But I need to interview some of the other umbrella ladies. Can you get me a list of names?'

So I was working for him now, was I?

'Maybe. I'll try. If I can take my eyes off Maddy for ten seconds.'

Would there be a pauper's funeral? I had never been to a pauper's funeral. Mozart had one, didn't he? Before they dug him up and put him somewhere else.

'If anyone asks, what shall I say?' I asked.

'You can tell them the sad news. There's no harm. I'll be in touch later. By the way, find out what school Maddy goes to. Just a thought.'

I went back to the marquee, wet and soberly. So Elsie Dunlop had died. End of story. It would be pretty difficult to track down her killer now. No clues. No forensic evidence. The umbrella had been washed clean by the rain. But it was not my problem. Maddy was my problem.

She was half asleep, sprawled on the stage, looking almost like the five-year-old who used waddle up on the stage in her pyjamas to say good night to her father, still playing his brass. She was curled up, head on her arms.

The music was talking to my soul. Jazz does that. It moves some of us but does nothing for others. Some people don't like jazz but I'm beyond understanding why. Perhaps they don't have souls. They have a lump of stone, or maybe a sponge.

I was keeping an eye on Maddy. What else could I do? Chain

myself to the belt of her jeans?

They were playing 'Swanee' (Gershwin, 1919). Where did they get these great arrangements?

'So Miss Dunlop has died, has she?' It was big Tom, at my side. He looked bulky and reliable. How did he know? I'd said nothing.

'Yes, so sad. She never came round,' I said. 'How do you know?'

'Grapevine,' he said. 'Some of the police lads get a few free tickets. It's nothing special. They check on the parking.'

'No one is supposed to know yet.'

'You can't keep anything secret these days. You look cold and starved. Have you had any supper?'

'I don't exactly remember. Yes, I had a crab salad but it was ages ago.'

'We're all going for a pizza after the show. Do you want to come along? Nothing special. Just a gang of us.'

'I'll let you know,' I said. 'It depends on Maddy.'

Tom grinned as if he understood. 'Maddy. I guess she'll come along if Ross is coming.'

'Do you know any of the other umbrella ladies?' I threw in.

'Quite a few. They are regulars. They spend all year decorating their umbrellas. Different design every year. There's one of them over there – the woman with the big white straw hat.'

He was so easy to get along with. Where was the custodial Mrs Lucas while he was jazzing around ? I had no way of finding out. And he was almost a different generation. At least twenty years older than me, but did that matter these days? He was young at heart. This music made it so. Jazz rejuvenates the soul.

I eased away. I wanted to ambush the white straw hat before she moved to another venue. But she was glued to the music. I kept half an eye on her. I had to leave room for the unexpected.

I sidled up to Maddy. 'Going for a pizza with the boys afterwards?'

'You bet. But my dad'll be mad at me if you don't come too. You can drive.'

So I was her chauffeur now as well.

The jazz was coming to an end. They played an encore, then another. 'Foggy Day In London Town', then 'Misty'. The audience wouldn't let them go. Their hands must be sore from clapping.

The white straw hat was moving. I scribbled my phone number down on a page from my notebook and managed to put it in her startled hand. Her eyelashes were as black as soot, rimmed with eye-liner. She had frizzled white-gold hair.

'It's about umbrellas,' I said quickly. 'Please ring me.'

She nodded, bemused, and hurried out. Obviously going to catch one of the later venues down town. There was no stopping her.

So that was decided. I went along with Maddy as specified. She was revitalized. She jived, she danced, she sang, her curled hair bobbing about. The pub served huge pizzas, piled high with pepperoni, peppers and three kinds of cheese. I took a slice, big enough to last me a week. It was delicious, filling. Tom put a glass of house red on the table.

'Not sure what you would like, Jordan. Is this all right? I can change it.' He was certainly out of practice. Hadn't he said the same thing last night?

It was a fun party. The musicians were playing again. Did they ever stop? It was improvised jazz, soaring round the crowded room. Where did they get the energy? I was dead tired. I wanted to sleep. Any minute now my ears would shut down. Maybe I would hibernate.

I found myself a corner seat, almost cushioned. Nothing on which to rest my aching body. I didn't want to talk to Tom, however nice, or Maddy or Ross or the incredible Chuck Peters. My head was already giddy with sleep.

'So, sleepy-head, is this how you spend your working time?'

I could barely open my eyes but I knew that deep voice.

'You're supposed to be the one working,' I croaked. 'Not me.'

'I am working. Maddy is my chief witness. My only witness.'

'So? Go get another statement.'

'You're still wet. Didn't you dry off at the hotel? You'll get pneumonia.'

'Maybe a severe illness will rate a substantial bonus.'

DCI James had half of lager in front of him. He was still on duty. He was looking at me with a strangely wistful expression. 'Did you let it be known around that Miss Dunlop had died in hospital?'

'Not me. Quite a few people seemed to know already. Why?'

He shifted along the seat towards me. His waterproof jacket was hardly wet. He slid his arm along the back of the bench, almost brushing my hair. It was like electricity touching moisture, setting off high voltage. I could catch the whole of my life in his arms.

'Because, Miss Sleepy Private Investigator, between you and me, happily it isn't strictly true. It was a tactic. She is still unconscious and under guard. But if the attacker thinks she's died, he'll feel safe now and might come out into the open.'

'So none of us are safe? And I'll have to take extra care of Maddy. He's on the loose, still here at the jazz festival. It could be anyone.'

James nodded gravely. 'It could be anyone. Even your new admirer.'

'I don't want an admirer. I'm done with men.'

'All of them?'

TEN

I could see the sense of this. If the attacker thought Elsie Dunlop had died then she could not give the police a description, a clue, a motive, an account. He would consider himself off the hook, untraceable.

'My new admirer, as you call him, has a name. He is Tom Lucas and he was working in the box office when Elsie Dunlop was attacked.'

'How can you be sure? You say you have eyes in the back of your head. You are supposed to be watching Maddy.'

'My head swivels.'

James looked amused. 'It certainly does. One of your main attractions.'

He finished his lager and got up, stretching his legs. It had been a long day. I didn't know where he was staying or if he had accommodation. Perhaps the Gorgon was giving him bat-proof roof-room in her house. Once she had shaken the snakes out of her hair.

'You're leaving,' I said.

'That's what it looks like.'

'I found one umbrella parade woman with a white straw hat. She's phoning me.' I mentally added, 'I hope.'

'Good on you.'

Where had he got that from? Had he been to Australia in the few weeks I hadn't seen him? His life was a mystery to me. I knew, of course, about the tragedy of his ex-wife and the children.

He had eventually told me, when he could put the distress into words. He knew all about grieving.

'Nothing concrete yet.'

'Phone me when you have some names. Don't stay on late here. Tomorrow will be another full day. And don't drink any more and drive or I'll have to book you. You'll lose points.'

'Is that a promise? My licence is clean.'

I went over to Maddy. She was drinking juice. At least it looked like juice. You can add vodka to anything. It was the perfect disguise. 'Time for bed,' I said.

'Don't be a spoilsport. The night is young.'

'It's not night. It's already the morning.'

'I could have danced all night,' she warbled, out of tune.

'You won't be looking your best for tomorrow. Ross has his special gig. Are you planning to miss it?'

She did a re-take. She had forgotten about his solo spot. It was unusual for a percussionist to take the stage. There might be some other musicians, whoever cared to turn up and add a few notes. He had a lot of friends.

'OK. You can drive me. I don't want to go with Ross.'

'Good on you,' I said. Where had I got that from? 'Let him simmer on a slow burner.'

She grinned and nodded. 'You bet. I like that.'

'He'll think you've gone home with another young man. There are a few others around. Have you noticed?'

It was still raining. But the wasp was watertight and moved like a dream. Maybe she knew I needed careful handling and responded with similar restraint. The same parking space was still vacant at the hotel. The wasp slid in, almost gratefully, as if she was the rightful owner.

'Back tomorrow,' I promised her as I got out into the rain.

'Are you talking to your car, Jordan? You're mad.'

I made sure Maddy reached her room safely, checked it over, heard her lock the door behind me. The rest of the floor was quiet. Very few of the musicians had returned yet. They had stamina.

My own room, a floor below, was again a haven. I fell into it, threw off my clothes, tumbled into bed, wrapped myself in the duvet. All I wanted to do was sleep; catch a dream or two.

'Sunny Swanage' was how the Tourist Office advertised it. And yet it was still raining the next morning. The marquee would be flooded by now. I looked out of the window, rags of last night's mist swirling over the bay. A few dog owners were being taken for a compulsory walk along the sand.

The organizers of the jazz festival must be biting their nails. They relied a lot on the day-tripper, the casual ticket sales. The weekend stroller tickets were a reliable source of income but they needed a few hundred more punters with ready money. The musicians still had to be paid current rates.

The jazzmen didn't mind. They got paid whether they played to a dozen punters or 200. They enjoyed playing jazz. It was their life. They would have played for nothing, only don't tell anyone. It was their life blood, the notes coursing through their veins.

My jeans had dried off and I had a long-sleeved black T-shirt to wear under the suede waistcoat. A skinny coating of warmth. The same waiter served my breakfast coffee.

'Would you like an omelette this morning?' he asked.

'Yes, please.'

'Cheese, mushroom or 'erb?'

'Mushroom, please.' I could do 'erbs myself, any day. I thought of my new kitchen awaiting my culinary skills. That was the second best thing about this flat. A proper kitchen with worktops and cupboards with shelves and doors that opened and closed. The first best thing was always the glorious view. I wondered if the sea at Latching was churning with this wind and rain. It seemed a million miles away along the coast, on another far planet.

I saw a smack of blue appearing in the sky. Was the rain being chased away to another county?

'Is it going to rain all day?' I asked the waiter, making small talk.

'Oh yes, all day. You stay in hotel and drink wine, I promise.'

'Are you Spanish?' I asked. 'You have a Spanish look.'

'My mother was Spanish. But she met a handsome Englishman who was on a Thomson holiday. No more late-night Sangria.'

I had to laugh. This waiter was amusing. A bit like Manuel *in Fawlty Towers*, only younger, taller and with better English.

My phone rang. It was a woman. I didn't recognize her voice or her name. Her voice was suspicious.

'It's Betsy Nicholls. Betsy Nicholls. You asked me to phone you. Last night, remember?'

'Ah, the umbrella parade? You have a wonderful umbrella. Fantastic decorations. It must have taken hours.'

I could hear her thaw over the phone. 'Yes, it did take hours, my own design, and nearly got ruined in the rain. What's this all about? Why do you want to speak to me? Is it about Elsie?'

'Yes, I'm afraid it is. I'm so sorry if she was a friend of yours.'

'Elsie was not exactly a friend. More of a long-time rival. She's won the prize for the best umbrella three years running. It's about time someone else got a look-in. Though, of course, not this way.'

Could this be a motive? Surely not? But sometimes feelings do run high.

'I need some of the names of the other ladies in the umbrella parade. Can you help me? I'd be very grateful.'

'What for? Are you police?'

'No. It's to eliminate people from their enquiries. A few names, please, and where they are staying, if you know.'

'Most of us are staying at the Elysium Bed and Breakfast, two roads back from the front. We always gather there. We book it every year.' She began reeling off a list of names. I scribbled them down in my notebook. It sounded as if they booked a lot of twin doubles or perhaps they shared family rooms, being friends. It saved money to share a room.

'Thank you very much, Miss Nicholls. You've been most helpful. Let's hope we have a drier day today.'

'My umbrella's ruined. It'll have to be completely renovated.'

'You may get a brilliant new idea.'

'I've got several already. I need the time.'

My omelette arrived. I took a few mouthfuls before phoning DCI James. Omelettes get cold so quickly. It was creamy and delicious. The chef was a genius.

'Unpaid slave reporting,' I said when he answered his phone. He was probably already at his desk with a mug of lukewarm brown coffee and a couple of doughnuts. His eating habits were dreadful. He would die young. That's what the scaremongers said.

I reeled off the names while I could still read my writing.

'Thanks, Jordan. You're a treasure. The Elysium B&B? Sounds like a heavenly guest house.'

I refused to laugh. My melting mushroom omelette was more important.

'Did you find out where Maddy goes to school?' he went on.

'Completely slipped my mind,' I said.

'Well, slip it back in,' he said and rang off.

Maddy appeared in the doorway of the dining room. She was wearing the sequinned T-shirt she had bought yesterday, totally unsuitable for the weather. She searched, as if for a friendly face, and caught sight of me. She came over to my table, swinging her straw bag. She never moved an inch without it.

'Hi, can I join you?' She sat down without waiting for an answer.

'I thought you were going to have room service?'

'Sick of room service. I want to see some life.'

The half-empty dining room was hardly life but she was looking at the buffet table with normal teenage greed. Buffets always have that appeal. Help yourself to as much as you can carry. It was universal.

'Help yourself,' I said.

She sauntered over to the buffet and poked around the selection. No crisps, popcorn or cereal bars. She helped herself to a strawberry smoothie, two warm croissants from the hot tray and a chocolate spread. It was a start.

'Where are we going this morning?' she asked.

'There's a local youth big band playing at ten o'clock.'

'They're school kids.' She dismissed them. 'No big deal.'

'We could look in and see if they are any good.'

'If you like. I don't care. Then we could go shopping.'

I supposed a lot of shops would be open, even though it was a Sunday. They needed the holiday trade these days.

'Great idea,' I said, thinking of the wasp. 'I need some polish.'

She looked at her sparkly mauve nails. 'Yeah, I need some polish too.'

We decided to walk down the hill into town while there was a break in the rain. The fresh air would sharpen our senses. It had rained heavily in the night and the uneven road and pavement was a waddle of puddles. More rain ran down the gutters, drains overflowing with swirling debris, echoing ye olde London and Dickensian streets.

'This is going to ruin my boots,' Maddy complained. Her Ugg boots were having a rough time. She'd probably buy a new pair this morning. I took a bet on it.

The youth big band was tuning up in the only useable marquee. The grass inside squelched underfoot. Stewards were putting down more rough matting, straightening chairs, checking wristbands.

'Need any help?' I asked.

'All under control, thank you.'

The youth big band were hardly kids, they were mostly fifteen or sixteen years old. Maddy looked fractionally more interested in the taller boys. They all wore navy blazers, white shirts and red ties, even the girls. It was a smart outfit.

'We'll listen to a couple of numbers and then we'll go,' said Maddy, slumping into a chair. She opened a can of Pepsi and a packet of crisps.

The band leader began with a long introduction about how they had been formed from several schools in the county, where and when they rehearsed, etc. I could sense Maddy shutting off. Then they began to play, several well-known standards, nothing difficult. Some of the brass was too loud, not quite on the note. They were nervous, couldn't take their eyes from the sheet music.

'I can't stand this, Jordan,' said Maddy, fidgeting. 'Time to go.'

I could hear the rain starting to patter on the marquee like tiny feet. The thought of getting wet again was abysmal. 'One more number,' I said.

The band leader was making an announcement. 'Unfortunately we are without our vocalist this morning. She has a sore throat and doesn't want to strain it.'

Maddy snorted. 'Sore throat. They always say that. Cold feet, more likely.'

'But as we have rehearsed the number, we will now play it. That old favourite, "As Time Goes By", ladies and gentleman.'

The old favourite was slower and more melodic so the band was making a better job of it. Though playing slow is not always easy. It takes a lot more control.

Maddy got up. I thought she was leaving. But instead of going to the exit, she was going up onto the stage. She spoke to the band leader, who was busy conducting, and took a mike from him. I froze with apprehension.

'A kiss is just a kiss,' Maddy began to sing. She was in tune. Her voice had a faintly husky quality, quite unique for a fourteen-year-old. She had all the confidence in the world, singing as if she sang every day of her life with a big band. Had her mother been a singer? Did Chuck Peters know his wayward daughter could sing?

There was thunderous clapping at the end of the song. Some of the band members were clapping too. Maddy looked around, flushed with pride. The conductor spoke to her, giving her some loose sheets of music.

'I know all of these,' I heard her say. I sat back with relief. It didn't look as if we were leaving yet. It was still raining.

The disconsolate look had gone from her face. She didn't always want to be Chuck Peters' daughter, in the wings, listening to her father play or waiting hand and foot on Ross. She wanted to be up there, singing, being herself.

She sang the classic 'Moonlight In Vermont' and then the up-tempo 'You Do Something To Me'. A little bit of nerves beginning to show but it was to be expected. I wondered if she had sung in front of an audience before. 'I've Got A Crush On You', which I knew was Gershwin 1928, finished her debut.

She came back and sat beside me. She was trembling, licking her lips. I could sympathize. 'You're very good,' I whispered. 'Well done.'

'Thanks.'

'Do you want to go now?'

'No. They've asked me to stay and get to know some of the band afterwards. They seem pretty cool. They're serving lemonade and cakes.'

Who could resist lemonade and cakes?

At some point, I had to prise Maddy away. She had almost signed up her life to the youth band. She had agreed to sing with them tonight at the farewell concert.

'I need more clothes,' she said. 'For tonight's farewell.'

I thought she had enough clothes for a six-month safari of the Sahara Desert.

'Where do you go to school?' I asked in an empty moment.

'Cowdry Private. It's a very posh boarding school, fees cost thousands. Dad thinks it'll turn me into a lady. Fat chance.'

I had to agree with her. Fat chance.

We went on to another gig, then another, different venues, tramping around, getting wet. My head was spinning with jazz. I like jazz, always have, but sometimes non-stop is more than any human can cope with. It was blowing through my head, occasionally with crescent-shaped pain.

The same charity shop was open. Maddy made a dive for the cocktail rail and came up with a couple of tops, one in gold lamé, the other a slinky blue folded satin. I tried not to look at anything.

'How do you know if they'll fit? They look very small.'

'They'll fit,' she said dismissively. They both had miniscule straps. Maddy would be cold when the sun went down.

'What about a cardigan?' I suggested.

Maddy looked at me as if the word was obscene. 'My gran wears a cardigan,' she said.

We took refuge in a tea shop which advertised Cornish cream teas, – a bit odd for the county of Dorset. It was packed with holidaymakers in steaming raincoats. The girls were rushed off their feet, hardly giving anyone time to read the long menu. This was going to be our lunch.

'Coffee and a toasted cheese sandwich,' I ordered, not even looking at the list.

'Strawberry ice cream and a can of coke,' said Maddy. Her diet was certainly a weird one. 'And two packets of crisps.'

I spotted a familiar white straw hat. Betsy Nicholls was sitting with a coven of animated cronies. I recognized a few faces even without their umbrellas. They were putting the world to rights, including Elsie Dunlop's world. Or what had once been her world. They did not know that she still had some world of her own, even if it was motionless and dark.

'Ross's gig is the next big show,' said Maddy, stirring the ice cream into pink mud. I wondered if it had ever seen a strawberry. 'We mustn't be late. I promised I'd help him get set up.'

My phone rang. I took it out of my bag. 'Hello.'

'I thought you'd like to know that Elsie Dunlop is showing signs. Moving a bit, eyelids fluttering. So that's progress.'

'That's good news. I'm very glad,' I said.

'Is that your dishy detective?' said Maddy, her eyes bright, sucking on the spoon. 'The one you are sweet on?'

'It is not and I am not,' I hissed.

'You've gone all soppy-faced.'

'Will you leave me alone?' That's one thing I could pride myself on. My face never gave away my feelings. Maddy only said it to rile me.

'Who are you talking to?' James asked.

'We're in a tea shop, having coffee. It's our lunch break,' I said. 'I'm with Maddy. She keeps interrupting. She's a typical nosy teenager.'

Maddy started giggling. The impromptu singing had done her good. She was almost her normal age group.

'So, did you find out what I wanted to know?'

My mind went blank. 'What?'

'I asked about Maddy's school. You know, algebra and verbs and all that educational stuff.'

Turning my head away so Maddy couldn't hear, I said, 'Cowdry Park. It's a private boarding school. Very expensive apparently.'

There was a silence at the other end of the phone, although I could still hear the faint bustle of the police station, numerous phones ringing, doors slamming, loud voices.

James sounded grim, almost threatening. I heard a sharp intake of breath and a rustle of paper.

'The fifteen-year-old girl, the body found in Corfe Castle. She went to the same school, Cowdry Park. Don't let Maddy out of your sight.'

'I won't,' I said, ringing off.

'Why was he asking about my school?' asked Maddy, dipping crisps into ice cream.

'It was probably a recommendation for one of his friends.'

The casual words could not disguise my fear. The same school. It was too much of a coincidence.

ELEVEN

The nightmare suddenly got darker. If both girls went to the same boarding school, maybe there was a connection. It didn't sound good. The girl who died had been fifteen and that was three years ago, so Maddy would have been around eleven when she disappeared. They probably didn't even know each other. It could be an unfortunate coincidence.

Maddy was scraping out the last of her ice cream. She discovered a film of pink foam on her lips. She got up, scraping back the chair, reaching for her straw bag on the floor. She didn't need to tell me where she was going.

I could talk now. I rang back DCI James. 'Is there any significance to that?' I asked. 'It being the same school?'

'It doesn't seem much, but it's something. One girl murdered. Another threatened. Same school. There has to be a link. The jazz festival?'

'Maddy is in danger.'

'I think so. There must be another link, apart from the silver key-note bracelet. I don't think Corfe Castle itself holds the answer. Although the murder was about the same time as the jazz festival, three years ago.'

'Maybe the girl liked jazz or her parents did. Perhaps they came here. Did you ask them?' There was a pause. I let him off the hook. 'Can I have the girl's name, please? I hate referring to her as the body in Corfe Castle. She deserves a name.'

'Sarah Patel. She had an Indian grandfather but English-born parents. He came over from Bombay, made a lot of money with a family hot curry recipe. Sarah was knifed with some sharp instrument then buried in the grounds of the castle. She was found because the torrential rain this summer had washed away the topsoil. An American tourist found her. They don't get many visitors because it's such a steep climb to the castle ruins.'

'Not much of a souvenir,' I said, immediately regretting the flippant remark.

'On the contrary. Sarah had been missing for three years. At least her parents know where she is now. They can begin some sort of grieving. They are still doing forensic tests. Every detail helps. Very Patricia Cornwell.'

'Maddy's coming back now. Fresh lipstick. Passionate Peach.'

'See if you can find out anything about Sarah Patel. But don't alarm Maddy. We don't want her running away.'

'How's Elsie Dunlop?'

'Still unconscious but vital signs all improving. We live in hope.'

'One bit of good news.'

He rang off. I tucked my phone into my shoulder bag. It would need recharging. A Post-it note on forehead would be necessary.

'Ross is starting soon,' Maddy reminded me. She was used to getting her own way. But this time I didn't mind. A watery sun was peering out from behind a cumulus cloud as if uncertain of its welcome. A haze was rising from the sea. The marquee would not have dried out yet. The ground would take weeks even if the canvas dried.

'Sure. We've got to get a good seat for this.'

'Won't you be stewarding?' Maddy asked.

'Maybe. It all depends on the rota.'

Enigmatic. It all depends on what rota? Nothing, actually. My life felt as if it was being washed on a wave, drawn this way and that by the moon. I did not seem to have any control over it. If I was the next one to get an umbrella in the chest, would anyone care?

There was already a queue waiting for the Ross Knighton

Ensemble, as he called himself this afternoon, but what exactly did he ensemble? Maddy wouldn't wait in any queue. She ducked under a flap round the back and marched up to the stage. Ross already had his set in place and was testing the sound and acoustics.

'You didn't wait for me,' she said.

'You didn't say you were coming.'

Usual teenage stuff.

'I've made a list of requests,' she said, bringing out a scrappy bit of hotel paper from her straw bag. 'Will you play them?'

'The programme is already arranged, babe. I don't do requests until the end of the gig.'

It was a good start to the afternoon. I made a swift retreat. I could see that they were getting along swimmingly, even if it was deep water. It took me twice as long to get out under the flap. My long legs are not made for such manoeuvres. And the grass was wet. This was going to be a loud session. I wished I had brought some ear plugs. Drums I can stand, and even like, but not the excessive amplification.

Tom Lucas was in charge of this one. He waved to me. I picked my way over to the muddy canvas pathway, grateful for some adult conversation.

'You're not down on my list for this afternoon,' he said.

'I'm a stand-in, in case someone doesn't turn up.'

'Great. That's what I like to hear. Glad to have you on board again. At least you know what you're doing. Some of the stewards are less than conscientious. I guess they only volunteer for some free jazz.'

'Jazz lovers will do anything for free jazz.'

Ross was warming up, getting his wrists loose.

I suddenly realized what I had said and retreated before Tom took that as an invitation to hear his CD collection while Mrs Lucas played Beethoven in the kitchen.

But he hadn't noticed.

'I haven't had any lunch,' he went on. 'Can you take over the box office for ten minutes while I catch a sandwich from the bar on the front? I won't be long. I'll show you the ropes. Ticket prices, strollers and single gigs here. We don't take cards. Nothing half price until 8 p.m. this evening.'

'I can do that,' I said. 'I used to run a shop.' Used to run? When had I given up First Class Junk and sold the stock off? Never. It was all waiting at Latching for me. I couldn't wait to get back, open up and take down the CLOSED FOR RENOVATIONS sign. I'd flick around a few splodges of paint, blow off the dust. And I would need some new stock. The charity shops here might give up some treasures. Not so easy these days. Everyone was more alert to spotting scrimhaw or a Troika. Don't mention Moorcroft.

'Then you're perfect.'

'Enjoy your lunch, Tom. Give the pickled onions a miss.'

Now I was the Almighty Custodian of Money and Tickets. I got a proper chair and a table and a window in the marquee where people could stand and argue about prices. There was a lot of arguing about prices. It was a sign of the times. Everyone was hard up. As if the musicians played for half price on the last day.

'But there's only half a day left.'

'And there are still eight different venues you can go to. The jazz goes on till midnight.'

'I've got to catch the last ferry back. It leaves at 11 p.m.'

'It's a pity they don't run a late ferry for the jazz festival. Someone ought to suggest it.'

Travelling around Swanage was a problem if you didn't have wheels. The railway line had been closed by Dr Beeching and now steam trains only ran from Swanage to Corfe Castle and back, a round trip of ten miles.

This customer didn't buy a ticket but stomped down into the town to find the free venues. I gave him a programme to cheer him up. There was a whole unsold box full of programmes. We were downhill. They'd be recycled tomorrow in some landfill.

The marquee was filling up, wristbands being checked. Maddy's sequinned top was barely visible from where I was sitting. Tom's sandwich had turned into more than a sandwich and a lager or two. But I sold quite a few tickets to day visitors who turned up because of the improving weather. I was worth my weight in gold.

My stomach told me that the mushroom omelette had not tided me over a toasted lunch. I was not exactly growling with hunger but some small animal was prowling round inside. I found some soft mints in my bag. They would have to do.

'Are you in charge now?' Maddy asked suspiciously, strolling over.

'That's right. I'm in charge. Do you want to buy a ticket?'

'I thought you were supposed to be looking after me.'

'I am looking after you. I can see your sequins from any point on the planet. If you suddenly disappear, the tracking device I attached to your bag will alert me.'

She looked startled. 'You're kidding me? A tracking device?'

'Go check,' I said nonchalantly. 'I bet you a packet of crisps that you can't find it.'

'I don't believe you.'

'Suit yourself. Have you got a good seat?'

'Front row. Ross won't let me sit on the stage.'

'He wants it all to himself. It's not surprising. After all, it's his show. You might break into song.'

She grinned, remembering her morning's triumph, sat on the edge of the table, swinging her legs. 'I was good, wasn't I?'

'You were good,' I agreed. 'Great voice.'

'Ross has never heard me sing.'

'He has a treat in store.'

'I'm going to sing at the farewell bash tonight.'

'Then you will surprise everyone, including your dad.'

I could see it was going to be some party. I could wear my black silk top. It would go great with my best jeans and boots. Time to look with it, whatever with it meant these weird fashion days. Girls wore any mixture of clothes and called it fashion.

The marquee was crowded, especially as the weather was improving by the minute. No more waterproofs and Wellingtons. A few summer tops arrived, straps, halter necks, bare shoulders.

I was not into bare shoulders. Perhaps that's where I had gone wrong with DCI James. Maybe he liked a bit of skin showing.

Ross could play. He had talent. He was going places, way out of Maddy's reach. He would be playing in the Albert Hall when Maddy was still at school.

I felt sorry for Maddy. But what could I do? Girls got crushes. Her crush was on the wrong person. It wasn't my problem. I was only supposed to look after her through the jazz festival.

Something was going to happen. I got this gut feeling. Don't ask me what it was. I was glad when Tom came back and I could move away from the claustrophobic ticket sales booth. I didn't care where I sat. If something was going to happen to Maddy, I had to be there on the spot, close enough to whisk her away to safety.

Something did happen but it wasn't what I expected. A man in the fifth row was starting to talk rather loudly, beating his fists as if he was holding drumsticks.

'Call that playing?' he shouted. 'Just cos you got fancy hair and a posh name. You don't know nothing about the drums. Get off the stage, kiddo.'

'Hell's bells. He's drunk,' said Tom, wearily. 'He's been in the same seat since this morning. I bet he's got a couple of vodka bottles in that bag. Both empty ones.'

'Shall I ask him to keep quiet?'

'Get off the stage! You're a disgrace, young upstart! You know zero-minus about playing the drums. Go back to your playpen.'

The man was waving wildly and people were turning round and shushing him. This made him even more belligerent. He was ready to start a war.

'I can play better than you. Just watch me!' He began banging on the backs of chairs. People scattered, getting out of his way.

I had dealt with a lot of drunks during my time in the force, most of them amiable and prone to singing bawdy songs, but it was still not my favourite occupation. Tom Lucas was bigger than me and a couple of young stagehands were easing forward.

The drunk was scruffy-looking, brown tweed cap crammed on

his head, in a shabby grey anorak still damp from this morning's rain. I hadn't seen him before. He must have had a wristband or a day ticket to have got in, or had he picked a moment when the door steward's attention was diverted and slipped in?

Tom Lucas was speaking to him quietly. Several more people moved away, looking alarmed. They were standing against the canvas sides of the marquee.

'No, I won't be quiet! No, I won't come outside!' he shouted. 'Leave me alone. You ain't got no right. Take your hands off me.'

'A little fresh air?' Tom suggested.

Maddy was peering around, distracted. She looked worried and then she looked at Ross. He had noticed the rumpus but was playing through it. A bit louder if anything, as if he was bashing the man's brains out.

'Call this jazz? It's a disgrace. I want my money back.'

The man was stumbling over chair legs, grabbing at anything in sight. I whipped outside, ran down to the convenient flap and ducked under. I went straight over to Maddy.

The two stagehands moved in and were physically hustling the drunk out of the marquee. He was protesting fiercely but they were two big lads and he didn't stand much chance. He could hardly stand anyway.

His protests got fainter as they led him off the field and launched him back onto the seafront. He could go practise his drumming skills on a deckchair. The seagulls wouldn't mind.

The audience settled back, relieved that peace had been restored. Not exactly peace. Ross played even more loudly and everyone applauded with enthusiasm. He played several encores. No one wanted him to go.

'He's marvellous. He's the tops. I love him, I love him.' Maddy was beside herself with emotion, hardly able to sit still. 'Ross, Ross, I love you,' she wailed.

Ross wasn't even looking at her. He was joking with his mates, gathering up sheet music and beginning to pack his gear. A crowd of admirers gathered round the stage, wanting to chat with him. Maddy was talking to his back.

'Ross, Ross!' she cried out. She skirted round the stage so that he would see her more clearly. 'You were wonderful. It was marvellous.'

'Hi, Maddy.' He waved.

'Fab show.'

I kept out of the way, collecting up empty cans and bottles.

'Thanks, babe.' He turned his back on her. I felt for Maddy. It was such an obvious put-down. She did not seem to be perturbed. She looked flushed and happy, dancing about, clapping her hands. She had resilience in her bones.

'Do you want to go back to the hotel?' I asked. 'Change of clothes, something to eat, before the rest of tonight's gigs and the party bash?'

'Yeah, yeah, yeah,' she sang.

'Let's start walking. Ross has plenty of helpers.'

'But he might need me.'

'He doesn't need you, you can see that. Save your strength. Come on. I'm sure your hair needs washing.'

She nodded in agreement, combing her fingers through today's corkscrew style. 'My hair. It's a mess. I could do with some streaks.'

'No time for streaks.'

I steered Maddy away from the marquee, along the front and then up the hill to the hotel. It was a brisk walk and we needed the exercise. We'd been sitting most of the day, in one place or another. I was getting a square bottom.

DCI James phoned. He didn't have to come and see me anymore. Just phone. I was probably on redial.

'Elsie Dunlop has come round, a bit groggy after the surgery, but able to speak. Not too clear about what she remembers.'

'That's good news. Did she give you a description of her attacker?'

'A bit vague, but it's a description of some sort. It all happened so quickly she said.'

'Male or female?' I was thinking of the umbrella parade ladies and the rivalry between them.

'Male, medium height, slim. She's not sure about an age. He was not young, not old. She hardly noticed his clothes but remembers the cap. It was a flat cap made of brown tweed, pulled down low over his eyes.'

He heard my gasp.

'Jordan? Jordan? What's the matter?'

'A flat brown tweed cap?' I repeated. 'A man was here this morning and most of the afternoon, in the marquee. He was drunk, tried to stop the show. We've just got rid of him, dumped him on the beach.'

'What about him?'

'He was wearing a flat brown tweed cap. He was medium height, slim, middle-aged. It could be the same person. Quite aggressive.'

'I'm on my way.'

He was coming. James. He would make everything right.

TWELVE

It was creepy to think that the man who attacked Elsie Dunlop might have been in the marquee all morning, not thirty yards away from Maddy in the afternoon. If it was the same person. Elsie's description, although not perfect, had a few similarities. We needed a lot more.

'What was he doing in the marquee?'

'He was drunk. He was shouting at Ross, the drummer. He was very angry. Tom and a couple of young lads hauled him out.'

'It was a very angry person who attacked Elsie Dunlop. I'll send Ruth round to get a couple of statements from them. They may be able to add some details to the description. Hair, eyes, tattoos. It all helps to build up a picture.'

For a second, I could not remember who Ruth was. Then it came to me. The Gorgon with thrashing serpent arms. I wondered how she would get on with the genial Tom Lucas. He might charm a smile out of her.

'It's Chuck Peters' final gig tonight and then we're having a farewell party afterwards. Would you like to come? It's open to anyone.'

I couldn't believe my own ears at what I was saying. All and sundry. The hoi polloi. He did not seem to notice or perhaps he didn't mind.

'Where is the party being held?' I could hardly hear him.

'I don't know. I'll have to find out.'

'Give me a call.'

'You can bring a friend,' I said desperately. I needed my head testing. If he brought the concrete, iron-laced Ruth, I would want to die on the spot.

He rung off.

I went to see if the dining room was serving anything but it was that oasis time in the kitchen between afternoon tea and dinner when the staff got a break. The dining-room manager suggested I order a sandwich at the bar.

'Thank you, but no. I never want to see another sandwich.'

'Room service?'

'Maybe.' I didn't want to eat alone in my room. I needed people, company, noise pulsing around like a safety net. I picked up a house phone and keyed in Maddy's room number.

'Hi.' She sounded eager, as if expecting a call from Ross.

'It's Jordan. Do you want to eat out? Everyone says the fish and chip restaurant on the front, opposite the museum, is the best in town. Ross might be there. He likes it, I'm told.' Complete fabrication. The white lies tripped off my tongue.

'Cool.'

'We'll walk down. I don't want to drive. The party, you know.'

'I'll probably get a lift back.' In a flash, she had planned her entire evening. It didn't include me.

'I'll come up for you in twenty minutes.'

'Make it thirty minutes.'

I'd forgotten the layers of make-up, the frosty lashes, six changes of clothes that preceded any public appearance. I went back to my room, showered, put on my best indigo jeans, the new silky black top with straps and covered it with a fleece. I could start stripping off if the party got hot. The slinky top looked cool, as Maddy would say.

Maddy was almost ready when I called for her. It was another ten minutes while she repainted her nails and let them dry. I watched the sun go down from her window, its rays painting the sea with liquid gold. Boats bobbed on the golden water like nuggets of precious metal. Halliards tinkled. Sunsets reflecting on the sea have their own special glory.

'Look at this marvellous sunset,' I said. Maddy came over, waving her nails in the air. 'Don't you wish you were a painter?'

'I can paint,' she said. 'I go to art classes.'

'A painter and a singer, Maddy? You're full of surprises.'

She looked pleased. I'd said something right. She had her new gold lamé top on, loads of flashy jewellery, long earrings. She was ready to go.

'You'll need a jersey.'

'I'm young,' she said. 'I don't feel the cold.'

I would have replied if I could think of a retort, but I couldn't think of one. It would come to me in the middle of the night.

We walked down to the restaurant on the front. Families were packing up on the beach, going back to their guest house accommodation or their caravan, taking a few ounces of sand with them. The council had to import fresh sand onto the beach every year to replace the lost kilos.

The restaurant was busy and we had to wait for a table. People eat fish and chips at any time of day these days. It was an instant feast, loved by eighty per cent of the population. Maddy was touring the restaurant with her eyes, looking for the dark floppy hair she most wanted to see.

'He's not here.'

'Probably gone for a pint first.'

She agreed for once. 'Oh, yeah. A pint first.'

'It's a man thing.'

She nodded. She was only fourteen.

I caught sight of movement. A couple were gathering their belongings; empty plates on the table, screwed up napkins. A window table. It was perfect. I would be able to see the sea. 'Over there,' I whispered. 'Let's grab it.'

Maddy was there in a flash. She put on her prettiest smile. 'May we have your table?' They were enchanted. A young girl with good manners.

'Of course, my dear. We were just going.'

We were in the seats before they had a chance to get cold. I handed Maddy a menu. It was printed and laminated, so the food never changed.

'Scampi and chips. A Pepsi,' she said without even looking at it.

A tired-looking waitress came over, pad in hand. 'And I'll have haddock and chips and a glass of your house red.' Nothing posh here.

'Large or small?' she drawled.

'Medium,' I said.

'We don't do medium.'

'Large then, please.' I wasn't sure if she meant the fish or wine. We could always give the fish to the birds. I'd have to drink the wine. I would force myself. 'You've had a busy day?'

'It hasn't stopped. Like a swarm of starving locusts since eleven o'clock this morning. You'd think there was a famine on.' She thawed a fraction. 'I'll see if they can do a medium.'

'Thanks.' Wine or fish? I wondered.

She disappeared into the steamy kitchen.

When the fish came, it was fresh and succulent, golden batter glistening, the chips a good fat size and cooked to perfection. Even Maddy tucked in for once, though she took bits of batter off and pushed it to the side of her plate.

It was fish to dream about, freshly caught in the bay. DCI James would be in seventh heaven, again. He loved fish and chips, his favourite at Maeve's cafe in Latching, where we often met and ate together. I felt quite homesick for the steamy cafe and Mavis's raunchy banter. I would be home soon and back into my routine. I would have a lot to tell my friends, Mavis and Doris.

'Do you remember a girl at your school called Sarah Patel?' I asked between mouthfuls. Maddy nodded, her mouth full.

'Sarah? The girl who disappeared? Yeah, we all remember her. Such a fuss. We had to hang flowers on the gate in remembrance, and teddy bears and letters. Everybody was being questioned when we all knew she had gone off with one of the teachers. She was fifteen, I ask you, old enough to know her own mind.'

I was surprised. No mention of murder. Nothing about a body

buried in the grounds of Corfe Castle. It was merely the usual kind of mad, under-age elopement.

'So who was the teacher?'

'Not sure. Art, I think. It's usually art, isn't it? Long untidy dark hair and cords, quite a dish. Our new art teacher is a frumpy old geezer, dyes his hair blond to look younger. Sticks it up with gel. He can't even paint.'

'Do you know anything about this younger art teacher that Sarah was keen on? Can you remember anything about him?'

Maddy screwed up her face. 'Nope, nothing. He played jazz CDs during his classes. Some of the girls complained. That's all.'

'He played jazz? He liked jazz? Is that unusual for a teacher, to play jazz during his classes?'

She looked surprised. 'It's not a contagious disease, is it? Lots of different kinds of people like jazz. You like jazz.'

'No, but it does mean that they might have come to the jazz festival here, Sarah and this teacher, three years ago. Was your dad playing?'

'Yes, of course he was. He's a regular.'

'Did you come?'

'Probably, I don't remember. I don't remember anything three years ago.'

'Did you see them here together? The art teacher and Sarah Patel?'

'I have no idea. I was eleven. Give us a break. I'm not wonder woman with a photogenic brain. I might have seen them, I might not.'

I let Maddy enjoy the rest of her chips but she had given me food for thought. If the art teacher thought that Maddy had recognized him and Sarah together, here at the jazz festival, that might be the motive for the malicious and threatening notes.

DCI James needed this new information. I wasn't great on texting but I had another go. I texted him, in words of one syllable, that Sarah Patel might have eloped with her art teacher, that he liked jazz, that Maddy had been at the same jazz festival.

But that she could not remember seeing them.

'What was the art teacher's name, the one that Sarah liked and maybe eloped with?'

Maddy screwed up her face. 'Dunno. Hal? Sam? Joe? I can't remember. Roger something, that's it. Like in old Spitfire flying movies. Roger!'

I nodded. 'That'll do for now. But if anything does come back to you, will you tell me?'

'Roger! If it's that important.'

She was beginning to fidget. She could only sit still for so long.

'No, not that important,' I said hurriedly. I didn't want to alarm the girl.

I wondered when I would get back to the charity shops. I'd seen a round copper tray that would look good displayed properly and a couple of late eighteenth-century porcelain figures that would sell in Latching. There were some Disney Wade animals that were made for my shop window. Money was jingling in my pocket. The wasp could go home laden with loot. She wouldn't complain.

And the museum shop sold semi-gem stones. I'd seen bowls of rose quartz and white quartz. I wouldn't mind another piece of rose quartz to hold when the going's rough. I had only spent a few minutes in the museum but was enchanted by Swanage's history. There was so much from the Jurassic days to the quarry industry, to all the London stone brought back as ballast and installed around the town, even some old black bollards with dates on them that were once used to stop carriages driving on London pavements.

Perhaps I would stay on a day after the festival, browsing and shopping. Chuck Peters had only employed me for the duration of the festival, hadn't he? I guess I ought to check.

There wasn't a chip left for the greedy seagulls but some batter that had not been eaten. I scooped it into a paper napkin.

'It's for the seagulls,' I explained. 'Better slightly cold batter than fresh fish.'

I left the waitress a decent tip. I was getting generous in my old age.

We walked back along the empty seafront. Maddy was easy-going for once. Shops and cafes were closed. We climbed the steep road to the field with the marquees, one still cordoned off with scene-of-crime tape.

The working marquee was filling quickly. Tom Lucas was relieved to see me. 'We need help, Jordan,' he said, indicating the jostling crowd at the entrance. 'Get them in line, can you?'

Police crowd control voice needed. I remembered mine. 'Stay in line, please. No crowding. Room for everyone.' Maddy had disappeared inside, straight for the stage, Ross and her father. She might have wanted to be close to her father after all the Sarah Patel talk.

I recognized lots of regulars after three days. The wristband routine was merely a lift of the wrist now. The last show was so popular, it was going to be standing room only. I'd be lucky to hear the music from outside. But I didn't mind. I was here to work, not listen to jazz, however brilliant it might be.

At some point we closed the entrance. There was no room anywhere. Every seat was taken. People were sitting on the ground in the aisles, others standing at the back, in front of the bar. Punters had to fight their way through to the bar. You could die of dehydration before you reached it.

I found Tom. He looked weary, drawn. Perhaps he had been up at dawn, walking Ant and Dec. 'We can't let any more in. It would be dangerous,' he said. 'Health and safety, you know.'

'They are already sitting in the aisles which is against fire regulations,' I said. I didn't have the energy to move the people sitting on the floor. 'But I won't let any more in.'

'Well done, Jordan. Keep the entrance closed. Only let people out, but no one will go while Chuck Peters is playing. The box office is closed now so no more tickets for sale. I'm going to get myself a beer, if I can get to the bar. Can I get you something?'

He looked so hopeful that I could not refuse. 'A white wine would be lovely, thank you.' I knew it would be ridiculously low in alcohol, probably 4.5 per cent, from a box, more like lemonade with a dash. A clear liquid with a slight fizz.

Tom Lucas was one of those forlorn men, locked in a suffocating marriage. But at least he had these three days of freedom to look forward to every year.

'Stay here, Jordan. You can sit on my desk. Not a good view but at least you can hear the music.'

That was kind. I was tired. I had had so many injuries to my back in the past, my spine hardly knew how to stand up. I could see Maddy's gold lamé top. She was sitting on the edge of the stage, flashing her nails. She looked ecstatically happy. Ross must have smiled at her.

Don't ask me what Chuck Peters played. It was like being shot to the stars in a rocket. One standard after another, taken to extremes, rendered new and inspirational. I could not believe what I was hearing. The audience were cheering themselves hoarse.

I wanted to tell Maddy, 'Your dad is a genius!'

I knew Chuck was a genius. No one else could extract such emotive sound from a tube of brass and some finger levers. This job had been an unexpected bonus. I was being paid to listen to jazz. I was being paid for a few days away from vertigo.

It materialized out of the air, the idea. It was a daft idea but the younger musicians were all for it. They were keyed up, hot and sweaty from playing their hearts out. They wanted to cool off. A swim seemed an ideal way and the sea looked inviting.

'I'm going swimming,' Maddy called out as I helped with the clearing up. The bigger lads were stacking chairs ready for the removal van tomorrow morning. Others were dismantling the electrics and the stage. The marquee was hired by the day, so every day saved was extra money for the kitty.

'I have to go,' I told Tom. 'I have to keep an eye on Maddy. Thanks for the wine.'

'Thanks for all your help, Jordan,' he said. 'See you at the party?'

He looked eager and hopeful. I nodded cheerfully. My response could be taken any way.

Maddy was hurrying down the steep path with the crowd. They crossed the road in a jostling swarm, halting the traffic. Some of the younger members of the audience had joined in, hoping to gatecrash the party later. They knew there would be impromptu jazz till the small hours. They didn't need sleep.

Maddy was already peeling off her gold lamé top and stepping out of her skinny jeans. She was going to swim in her bra and pants. I had no wish to join her. I scooped her clothes off the sand, shaking them free of sand. She'd be the first to complain if they itched.

The moonlight lit the waves with silver streaks as the baby waves brushed the shore. It was idyllic. Further out anchored boats bobbed on the water. I could not tell if the tide was coming in or going out. At Latching I always carried a tide timetable.

The beach was crowded with laughter, cans popping open. I was drained. I sat on a pile of folded deckchairs and watched the boisterous youngsters like a tired old lady. I was killing time. Time was killing me.

Someone had spotted something on the beach. Not many people took any notice. They were too eager to get into the cooling water. I wandered over, wondering what he was pointing at.

The rest of the beach was empty apart from this noisy crowd from the marquee. But a few feet from the lapping sea was a small, dark, square-shaped mound. It was a pile of clothes, neatly folded so all the edges lined up like towels in a linen cupboard. On the top of the pile was a brown tweed cap, the peak facing towards the horizon.

The drunk's clothes. I recognized them instantly. He had been turfed out of the marquee and deposited on the seafront. He had fancied a bit of a swim too, to swim off the cider. But that had been some hours ago.

Ross was sauntering over the sand, pulling off his black cotton shirt. He'd had to stow away his precious percussion set first. 'Maddy OK?'

'Sure. She's dancing about on the edge of the sea where the

sharp pebbles are. She probably wants you to carry her over to the deeper water.'

'She'll get dumped if she does.'

'Look,' I said, drawing him aside. 'These are the drunk's clothes, aren't they? The man who disrupted your gig this morning. You saw him, didn't you?'

'Sure. They look the same.' He looked at the neat pile with disgust. 'You don't suppose he's walking around stark naked, do you?'

'Hope not. I can't stand any more shocks.'

I shouldn't have said that. The shock goddess was having a laugh with another one up her Grecian sleeve.

There was a scream, all the more terrifying because it was carried over the water. It was a woman. Some swimmers were thrashing round an anchored rowing boat. No one could see anything in the dark water.

'It's a body!' she was screaming. 'A b-body.'

'He's topped himself,' said Ross knowingly. 'That's what drunks do.'

THIRTEEN

It wasn't the naked, dead body of a drunk floating face down on the water, bloated and glassy-eyed, that had alarmed her.

The distraught woman was brought ashore. I think she was one of the umbrella parade but without her umbrella it was difficult to tell. She had got caught up in a fishing net, left over the side of the boat for a morning catch, tangled herself in it till she thought she was going to drown. Perhaps she had touched a fish also caught in the net.

So it was not a dead drunk. If he had topped himself, then his body would have been washed out to sea. Perhaps he had swum far out, as far as his strength could take him, before letting go. They might find him in Poole harbour or Portsmouth, depending on the tide.

'Can someone look after this lady? She needs dry clothes and a cup of tea,' I said. There were several willing helpers. They'd had enough of swimming, their enthusiasm evaporating. The night air was cooling rapidly. They wanted a beer and sandwiches and crisps. Maddy was only wet up to her knees.

'What a fuss,' she said, climbing back into her clothes which I'd left safely on the deckchairs.

I made sure that the other pile of clothes was not touched. I texted James again. I was getting the hang of this stuff now. Drunk's clothes found on beach, I texted. He may have topped himself? Identity vital? (The spelling was improvised text-speak. It suited me.)

I hoped that would entice James to the party. It was being held in a pub, of course, as the marquee was now a cold, desolate wilderness. The dismantling had to be done fast. The helpers wanted to get to the party too.

James replied almost immediately. He wrote: Cordon clothes for forensic.

With what? I don't carry round a roll of scene-of-crime tape in my bag. I dragged a tarpaulin cover off one of the saucy beach paddle boats and put it over the neatly folded clothes, anchoring it down with the largest pebbles I could find. It would have to do till the uniformed arrived.

I hurried to catch Maddy. She was flagging, trying to keep up with the lively musicians who had adrenaline coursing through their veins. She was tired from lack of sleep, too much jazz, her emotions running high. Jazz is exhausting music for both players and audience.

'Hold on, Maddy,' I said. 'I'm not wearing skates.'

'My feet hurt,' she said. 'Those pebbles were nasty and sharp.'

'Yes, beaches do have pebbles, very nasty and sharp sometimes.'

'Not in the Caribbean.'

'It's different here. This is the Dorset coast, UK.'

'You could have warned me.'

I gave up. I was not going to argue with her. I didn't have the breath. My sympathy was in short supply at this time of night. The crowd were converging into the same pub as we went to a couple of nights back, the Bull and Horn. Was it only two nights ago? It felt like years.

It was already three deep at the bar, a melee of people shouting orders to the overworked staff. Chuck wasn't drinking. He had a couple of bottles of spring water on his table with a plate of corned beef sandwiches. He grinned up at me.

'Hard work, isn't it? Keeping that young minx in order.'

'We get on quite well, most of the time,' I said.

'Ross is giving her the cold shoulder. He doesn't want a fourteen-year-old following him around. He's showing a bit of sense for once. She could cause trouble.'

'Sad,' I said. 'We can all remember what it's like being fourteen and having a crush on someone.'

'I can't,' he said. 'I don't think I was ever fourteen.'

Nor could I, to tell the truth. My parents had been killed in a car crash just before my twenty-first birthday, but before that tragedy, it had been a normal childhood. So normal it was a happy blur of school and holidays. It was as if their deaths wiped out all previous memories. All I could remember was that I had thick plaits and it hurt when my mother brushed my hair. And now I wished that I had not protested so much.

'Does my employment finish when the jazz festival is over? You'll be going home tomorrow,' I asked, before I forgot. 'Sorry, but I have to know.'

'I want to ask a favour, Jordan. I need some decent shut-eye before travelling to my next gig. It's in Wigan, I think. That's a long way up north. We thought we might stay on an extra day to relax and unwind, leave on Tuesday morning. Is it asking too much, to ask you to do an extra day?'

I tried to look as if I had a dozen urgent appointments that would have to be cancelled. Terribly inconvenient, etc.

'That's OK,' I said. 'I'll take Maddy around all the historic parts of Swanage. It's got so much history. It'll be a culture tour.' Including a culture tour of the best charity shops. Maddy could buy herself some more skimpy tops.

He breathed a sigh of relief. 'You're a darling,' he said, biting into a sandwich. 'Corned beef, my favourite. I'm starving.'

Tom Lucas appeared with a bottle of Merlot and two glasses. 'Come and join me, Jordan. Let the maestro relax and talk to his fans.'

I would far rather have stayed with Chuck Peters but I could see a gaggle of women wanting him to sign their CDs. It was money, after all. Selling CDs was a business.

'Lovely,' I said brightly. Chuck winked. I had a feeling that he could sense my reluctance to join Tom. No one could play jazz the way he could without knowing how people felt.

It was an assault course getting to Tom's table. Maddy was draped over Ross's table, drinking more Pepsi, eating salted peanuts. He looked bored. There were dozens of pretty girls, almost wearing mini-skirts, cruising the room. He was eyeing them all, mesmerized by the long hair and long legs.

I could not be rude to Tom. He was essentially a very pleasant man, probably lonely, on the lookout for female company. But he was twenty years older than me, overweight, did not share my taste in food, lived over a hundred miles from Latching. At least, I think it was a hundred miles. Still, no mileage in this as a long-range romance.

Fate has a lovely way of serving up the goodies. I looked up from Tom's table and there was my saturnine James in the doorway. He was in a casual black polo-necked sweater and dark jacket. He was scanning the room for a disordered mass of tawny red hair. Then he saw me and shouldered his way over. People parted for him, like the biblical Seven Seas.

'Jordan,' he said. 'I need to talk to you. Urgently. Outside.'

'Business or pleasure?' I was going to make him pay for all those months we'd been apart. When I had suffered. I'd bought my vertiginous flat on my own, my wasp car on my own. Where was he when all this was going on?

'Would you like to sit down?' I was still in polite mode.

'No, thank you,' he said coldly. 'Come outside, please.'

DI Ruth Macclesfield slipped into my chair like a skinny eel. She must have been standing right behind James. 'I'd love a glass of wine,' she said to Tom, eyeing the bottle and the untouched glass. 'I'm off duty now.'

'Of course,' he said. 'My pleasure.'

Although I knew I shouldn't, I followed DCI James outside onto the pub balcony. It had a balcony but it only looked onto darkened back streets and alleyways, the haunts of smugglers and villains of the past. No view of the sea. Balconies should always have a view of the sea.

He pulled me into his arms and before I knew what was happening, he was kissing me. Now, this was such a shock, it was some moments before I could respond. He was taller than me and my arms crept slowly round his neck and felt the softness of his skin and his hair. I did not question what I had done to deserve this. It was enough that we were together, wherever that was, on whatever balcony. It could have been in Timbuktu or New Orleans.

'Are you all right?' he asked, relaxing his grip.

'A little shaky,' I said. 'But I could get used to this.'

'I've been worried to death about you. There's a lethal killer out there who kills anyone in his way. I thought he might target you and not Maddy.'

'I think he has drowned himself, this art teacher who ran away with Sarah Patel. She was one of his students. He thinks Maddy spotted him at the jazz festival and that's why he's been threatening her. Of course, Maddy never saw him or Sarah. She was only eleven, a mere baby, under her father's wing. Not into jazz drummers at that age.'

'The clothes and the cap are secure?'

'Under a boat tarpaulin on the beach, pinned with pebbles.'

'We need them for forensics. See if Elsie recognizes the cap.'

'You'll get them.'

We heard the sweetest sound coming from the pub. It was a strong, resonant voice but with undertones of innocence. I knew who it was and steered James back into the pub so that he could listen. I took his hand so that I would not lose him. This moment was mine.

Maddy was singing with the Ross Ensemble. She was in her gold lamé top, hair tousled, make-up smudged, barefooted. She was singing her father's old standards but with a totally different interpretation, as if they had been written for a different decade.

Chuck was mesmerized. He had never heard his daughter sing before outside of the shower. Ruth was sitting close up to Tom Lucas. She had taken off her severe jacket and loosened the top buttons of her shirt. She was becoming almost feminine.

Maddy could sing. She had a future ahead of her and no doubt would be a truculent and turbulent star. I only hoped that she would not be spoilt by fame too early. Maybe Chuck could restrain her from wasting this talent until she was ready.

'That's your Maddy?' James breathed into my ear.

I nodded. He moved some of my hair out of his face with gentle fingers.

'She's a handful,' he said into the same ear, his breath like a whisper of air. 'Nice top,' he added. I didn't know if he meant mine or Maddy's.

'I need you,' I said. 'Please don't leave me.'

'I'll be back soon,' he said, easing away from me as the crowd broke into clapping. Maddy, on the small stage, looked flushed and excited. Ross nodded and they began another standard, a swinging up-tempo number, from the thirties, something from a Fred Astaire and Ginger Rogers film, long before Maddy's time. But she sang it as if she had been there as the legendary couple danced across the ballroom, Ginger's pale swansdown gown flying in the wind machine.

'James?' But he had gone. It was more than I could stand. Here one minute, standing close to me, and the next, he'd gone. Had I imagined that kiss? No, my lips were still tingling.

My middle name was now wallflower. I was propping up a wall, not even holding a drink, which was even worse. Ruth was merrily getting through my glass of wine. Still, I had all of tomorrow. Shopping list: copper tray, Wade figures, piece of rose quartz. And I'd spotted a couple of Jacob sheep which might be Royal Crown Derby.

Ross suddenly broke Maddy's vocal spell by launching into 'Bass Drum Boogie'. He had offloaded all his percussion extras: xylophone, tubular bells, Chinese gongs and tam tams. It was a wonder he didn't have a set of military side drums as well. He leaped around like someone possessed, bashing anything that moved.

Maddy went back to her father's table, still smiling. Chuck was speaking to her, probably telling her to rest her voice, not to overdo it. He knew voices were vulnerable, especially one as young as hers.

Tom was talking to Ruth. They were swapping life stories. She looked enthralled. Perhaps I had missed out on a self-made multi-millionaire. Dorset has a few that don't need digging up.

This wallflower was wilting in the heat. I dashed out onto the pub balcony to get some fresh air, not to relive recent memories, but it was fully occupied by other smooching couples who had discovered its relative privacy.

'Sorry,' I said but no one was listening.

My head was ringing with Ross's onslaught so I escaped downstairs and out onto the open street. The pavements were glistening. It had rained while we were upstairs. I could not see James's Saab or any police cars. Had he brought Ruth along or had she brought him?

James was returning. I could recognize his footsteps any-where. He had a peculiarly different stride. Rain was spattered on his shoulders.

'I had to get uniformed to move the pile of clothes before the tide came in,' he explained. 'High tide is at twenty past midnight.'

'I don't know the tide times along this coast.'

'How could you? It isn't Latching.'

'Are we getting somewhere with this investigation?'

'Yes, it's moving. Thanks to you. I hadn't made the connection before. That's been a great help.'

I was being thanked. Was this the first time ever? Should I get a banner made? *CID thanks Private Investigator.* Vistaprint do them very reasonably. It would look great hung outside my shop in Latching.

'Do you want to go back inside? Chuck Peters is playing now. You should hear him play at least once in your lifetime. Everyone in the world should hear him play. It would transform their lives.'

'OK,' he said, taking my arm. 'He must be good.'

'He is more than good. There isn't a word in existence for him.'

Chuck Peters was on the small stage now and the room had grown quiet; not even the clink of glasses. He was playing the soul out of songs. The man had music in his veins. Angels were gathered there, dripping notes down from heaven.

James was standing behind me. I could feel his height and his warmth. His arms were somewhere, not quite sure where. But we were as one, together, a grafted fusion of bodies, listening as one.

As the clapping swelled, James bent and whispered again: 'I agree. More than good.'

Then he was gone. The man was ephemeral. He could transform himself into sea mist. I sat down at Tom's table, traitor that I was.

'So how are you, Ruth?' was my opening gambit. 'Did you enjoy that?'

'Tom owns a farm,' said Ruth, her face flushed with triumph. 'He's going to teach me to ride.'

'Wow,' I said. 'A farm? That's brilliant. What do you farm?'

'Pigs,' he said modestly. 'I've a thousand pigs.'

Perhaps he was eating his own produce in all those burgers. I was glad he had a horse. Ruth would look good on a horse. That upright, legs-astride look. I would be all over the place, probably fall off into a cow pat.

'Do you know them all?' I asked. It was a very silly question. 'Your pigs?'

'Some of them have names,' said Tom with a reluctant grin. 'I can't bear to have them slaughtered. Granpops is my favourite. He's black. He knows me. Comes over when I call him.'

I was glad to hear that. He had a heart for a black pig.

'I never eat meat,' I said.

'I know,' he said with a trace of sadness, as if I had let him down. Perhaps he had imagined something more growing between us, something illicit. But I couldn't change. I enjoyed his company but I could not change my life.

The evening was coming to an end. Everyone was exhausted, players as well. Many had long journeys ahead. Playing jazz was work. They had other bookings lined up. It paid the bills, or some of them.

The pub staff were tired too. I could see it etched on their faces. Maybe the bar takings had soared but their feet hurt.

Tom was giving Ruth a lift home. Chuck was driving Maddy

back to the hotel. Everyone had forgotten about me. Ross had picked up one of the blondes. I was the only stranded female. I guess I would have to walk. The night air would freshen my brain. I slipped into my fleece before I left the hot room.

The rain had cleared again and as I walked downhill to the seafront, my spirits rose. Nothing awful could happen on such a starlit night. More people should be walking and not driving about in stuffy cars, polluting the air.

There was hardly anyone else about. The narrow promenade alongside the sea was deserted. Even the seagulls had gone to bed, to wherever they hang out on the crowded cliffs, heads tucked under a wing. It seemed a pretty uncomfortable way to sleep.

Then I heard footsteps. They had suddenly come from nowhere. The footsteps were quickening. I felt a quiver of alarm and tightened my fingers on my torch. It was a useful weapon.

'Jordan, don't be scared. I couldn't let you walk home alone.'

It was James calling, yet I hadn't recognized his footsteps this time.

'I didn't hear you coming,' I faltered, relieved to see his dark figure.

'Sorry, I took a shortcut over the grass. I had to catch you up.'

He swung into step beside me, not touching me or taking my hand or anything. But it was enough to know that he was there, that he had been concerned, that he had not forgotten me. He looked tall and dark, strong and comforting.

'Nobody offered me a lift,' I said as if I had to explain my lonely state.

'They probably all thought someone else was giving you a lift.'

'I guess so.'

The dark tide was high, washing against the steps of the beach huts. The pile of clothes would have floated away if James had not had them bagged and moved. White horses glistened on the waves further out in the bay, rowing boats bobbed, the halliards on the tall masts of the yachts in the harbour tinkled like small voices.

'Beautiful, isn't it?' said James, for once having time to look.

'The sea is always beautiful. And now, in my new flat, I have a view of it, day and night, whenever I want to stop and look. You must come and see it sometime.'

'Sounds perfect. Lucky you. I'm currently living in a rented flat in a farmhouse with a view of sheds and tractors.'

'I hope it isn't a pig farm.'

'No pigs. Arable.'

We were climbing the hill now towards the Whyte Cliffside Hotel. It stood solid and white in the distance. This steeper part of the hill always took my breath away. Damned asthma. And I didn't have my inhaler as usual.

I put my hand on James's arm. 'Could we s-slow down a bit?'

'I forgot. Sorry. Are you all right?'

I nodded, taking a few deep breaths to regulate the intake. For a moment I leaned on him. I could hear my heart thudding. Another moment to treasure even if I couldn't breathe.

We began walking again and James took my arm as if to propel me upwards. The wind was freshening and I could taste rain again. James was going to get wet, returning for his car parked somewhere near the party pub.

'Where's your car?'

'I don't exactly remember.' He grinned.

We went into the driveway that led to the brightly lit hotel entrance. Chuck had left his car at the side, as if too tired to put it in the car park. He had parked askew and they had got out, leaving it there. They had not looked at the boot.

Scrawled across the boot in luminous paint were two words: YOU'RE NEXT!

It was like a scream in the dark.

FOURTEEN

'He's here. He's somewhere near,' said James. 'That paint's not even dry. A drowned man didn't do this.'

I could see that. I hoped neither Chuck nor Maddy had spotted it when they got out of the car. They'd gone straight into the hotel and up in the lift to their suite.

James was already on his phone. 'I need uniformed over here, forensics and a photographer.' He gave the address. 'I know it's late. I don't care if it's late. Wake them up. No sirens.'

He would get a lift back in a police car now.

'You'll get a lift?' I asked, knowing the answer. 'And I had thought of offering you half of my very comfortable double. You could have the best side.'

'What a kind thought, Jordan,' he said, peering closely at the letters as if there might be some fingerprints. 'I'll take a raincheck on that one.'

'I don't do rainchecks.'

'Very wise. You don't know who might take them up.'

He pushed me towards the automatic doors of the hotel and they yawned open for me. I knew he wouldn't change his mind. He wasn't that kind of man. I walked into the abyss out of the rain. I wondered when it would ever stop raining.

The car had gone in the morning. They had towed it away for a thorough forensic search. There would be some clue. The man would have left some hair, some fibre or soil from his shoe. It was amazing what they could find.

I went up to Chuck's suite at breakfast time to tell him what had happened. He was still in his dressing gown, a room-service tray on a table with a continental breakfast. He poured out coffee.

'Join me, Jordan. I can drink from a tooth mug.'

'I've had my breakfast, thank you.' Another omelette. Smoked salmon and cream cheese, recommended by my friendly waiter. Out of this world on the gourmet taste scale. It would become a favourite. I wondered if Mavis could make one.

Chuck was shocked by the news from police but had agreed that he could do without his car for a day. He needed it back early the following morning. 'So more threats?'

I hadn't told him the exact wording. 'Sort of.'

'Thank goodness Maddy didn't see it. She would have freaked out.'

'We don't want to alarm her.'

'I've got to get to Wigan.'

'Could you hire a car?'

He nodded. 'I could. But I need my instruments. They are all locked in the boot. I hope they're not damaged. Worth thousands. Insured, of course. But their sentimental value is off the chart. My first ever trumpet.'

'I'll phone DCI James and make sure they are safe.'

'I'd be obliged. I can't work without them.'

'How's Maddy?'

'Still asleep. Worn out by the party. She can sing good, that girl of mine.'

'She can sing good. She has a future.'

'Her mother was a jazz singer.'

'That's where she gets it from. Great genes.'

I left Chuck. I think he was going back to bed and I didn't blame him. The man was a genius and a genius needs pampering.

I'd slept well when I'd finally got to bed. I'd waited in reception with James till uniformed arrived in unmarked cars. Then he was busy. He spoke to the night duty receptionist but he had seen nothing unusual. Forensics searched around and they found a footprint, half spotted with paint.

'A bit of a drip here, guv,' they called out.

'Good work. Take a cast or dig up the drive.'

James bent and gave me the briefest kiss on the cheek. 'Go to bed, sleepy-head. I'll need your brain in the morning.'

I wanted him to need my body, not my brain, dumb-cluck.

There was no word from James so Maddy and I got ready to do the town tour. She was not keen on the history and culture, preferring to comb the charity shops.

'They have great old-fashioned jewellery, you know,' she said. 'Vintage stuff. All the rage. The stuff people throw out.'

I saw Chuck stuff a wad of notes into Maddy's hand. She would probably spend it all. I wanted to show her what I had learned about Swanage's past history from the tourist office walkabout leaflets. And I wanted to go into the library to look at microfilm. They were a well-equipped library, small, oddly octagonal in shape, but up to date in services. We went there first.

Maddy was happy to go on the internet and email all her friends. I asked for microfilm of the local paper, three years back. It was eye-aching work scrolling through all the tiny print. I was looking for pictures, photos taken of the jazz festival three years back.

The photographers had been there again this year, snapping anything that moved. And every year back, I reckoned. Local papers needed news and a jazz festival was news.

The umbrella parade, three years back, looked identical to this year's. I spotted Elsie Dunlop, same outfit, different umbrella. It was a Star Wars theme. She had gone to town. Probably won first prize.

There was another photograph, taken down on the harbour front. I recognized several more umbrella ladies. In the background were two peering faces. One was a young girl, Asian-looking, long black hair, and the man was tousle-haired, good-looking in a careless sort of way. It was only head and shoulders of them both but something rang a bell.

I called Maddy over. It was hard to prise her off Facebook or Twitter or whatever she was on.

'Look, Maddy,' I said. 'Please look carefully. Do you recognize these two faces?' I zoomed in. They came up fuzzy, but larger.

'Sure, that's Sarah and that's the arty art teacher, Roger whatshisname. Is that the jazz festival?'

'Three years ago.'

'So, I don't remember it.'

Maddy went back to her infinitely more interesting social twittering.

I got a print of the photograph on the microfilm. They both looked happy but Sarah had a wistful look as if she knew her parents would be worried about her. I texted the news to James. There was no answer. I didn't expect an immediate response.

'Cup of coffee?' I suggested after logging off. I needed a caffeine boost. Then it was history and marathon charity shops. Maddy had all that money to spend. She would not be able to resist a spree. Her fingers were twitching.

I thanked the library staff. They had been so helpful, especially when I was hopeless at working the microfilm machine. At least I didn't break it.

One of the library staff recognized Maddy. 'You're the girl who sang at the youth big band concert? You were so good.'

Maddy was pleased and went out, beaming. That compliment had made her day. The next hour also made her day.

You'd have thought she had nothing else to wear, that her wardrobe was as empty as Mother Hubbard's cupboard. She raked through the racks, tossing garment after garment over her arm, whether they were her size or not, taking what she fancied. She would make them her size.

I concentrated on the rick-rack shelves. I bought the Wade figurines, the copper tray, a square vase which might be early Troica, fingers crossed, and the spotted sheep. If the vase was Troica, I could sell it on. A watercolour painting of Swanage bay caught my eye but I could not read the painter's signature. It was quite faded and old. But there was something about it that I liked.

My new flat at Latching, the fourth-floor flat with amazing views, was twice the size of my former two bedsits. It would need more furniture. My furniture consisted of a bed, a coffee table, a big sofa, a desk and a microwave. And it had walls that need pictures.

So when I saw this pink velvet footstool, I was hooked. Velvet is my downfall. It would fit into the wasp.

'I'll pick it up tomorrow morning,' I said, handing over a fiver.

'We'll put it out the back for you. What name?'

'Lacey. Jordan Lacey.'

'She's Wonder Woman Lacey,' said Maddy, grinning and following me to the counter with a pile of clothes. 'You're my bestest friend.' Then she did an unexpected thing. She draped a necklace of azure blue beads over my neck. It still had its price tag hanging from a string. It was chunky and modern.

'For you,' she said. 'Pressie. Cos you're nice.'

'I love it, thank you.'

One up for me, it seemed.

Maddy obediently followed me on the history tour, mildly interested in the story of the stone artefacts which were brought back from London and installed round and about in Swanage. She particularly liked the old jail house or 'cooler', re-sited behind the town hall. She peered through the grilled door into the dark interior.

'Creepy,' she said with a pretend shiver. 'I wouldn't like to be stuck in there, especially at night.'

'No chance of that. It's kept locked.'

There were ancient faceless statues of the once-famous politicians of London in the garden of Purbeck House, now a three-star hotel in town, but Maddy showed little interest in them, not even in the old arch from Hyde Park Corner. Some of the statues had lost their heads so it was not surprising. The gothic London Bridge clock tower was more to her liking as the unusual downstairs space looked as if it had plenty of room for a party.

'It was originally called the Wellington Tower built on the south side of London Bridge but it got in the way of the traffic so they moved it. There's no actual clock,' I said.

'This would be great for a party,' Maddy enthused, not listening to the historical facts. 'We could have a Ye Olde London theme party. I could come as a lavender seller. I need to look for a long skirt and a frilly blouse. Can you buy lavender? How about tonight?'

More shopping. 'But surely all your friends will have gone home?'

'I'll make some new ones.'

I got an unexpected text from Mavis, the owner of my favourite cafe in Latching. She was latching into this technology. (Joke – I must remember to tell her.) 'A geezer came into the cafe, asking if we'd got a detective in town. I told him about you. Do I get commission if it's a new case?'

I texted back. 'Yes. Back sometime tomorrow.'

A new case. That was what I needed: something to take my mind off vertigo and buried girls.

'About this party,' Maddy went on. 'I need to buy Pepsis, beer and Breezers, crisps and nuts. It's going to be great. We can bring some taped music, go dancing under the stars.'

'You may need permission,' I said dubiously, seeing another late night steering Maddy back to her bed.

'Why? It's public property, isn't it? Who's to know anyway?'

'Are you asking your dad to the party?'

'Heavens, no. No old people. But you can come,' she said graciously. 'I'll make an exception for you.'

'How kind,' I said, equally gracious.

But James would not be included. Practically ancient.

I could see another hectically busy afternoon, the wasp ferrying party food and crates of drink from the big supermarket near the station. Maddy was not able to buy the beer and the Bacardi Breezers. She was underage. I had to do it. So I was useful. I existed solely as her dogsbody. Did Shakespeare invent that phrase? It sounded Shakespearean. He invented most of today's phrases.

I got a second text from Mavis. This man wants his wife

found, she wrote. Ye gods, another domestic. I texted back: 'Have got brilliant new car, can find anyone, anywhere.'

The afternoon passed in a haze of shopping. I never wanted to see another shop, only mine. I went into a trance. I could drive on automatic pilot. Hotel to shop. Shop to hotel. Dump supplies at clock tower. I was in taxi mode. 'You've got to dress up,' said Maddy, still on a high.

'I'll come as a street vagabond. I'll find a shawl.'

'Cool.'

Ross wasn't there but some of the jazz lovers had hung over, not wanting to go home yet. I recognized a couple of musicians from the youth jazz band. Maddy had texted them. The news had gone round. I was glad to see her transfer interest to a younger generation. Ross would hurt her eventually.

Breezers or a Pepsi? Not exactly my drink but then I was driving. A slight drawback emerged when it was found that the clock tower was locked at night, but the party transferred itself to the rock and shingle garden walk below. No one seemed to mind. Most of the fancy dress was unidentifiable. Anything flowing or weird was Ye Olde London. I was shawl and tramp.

I had to be there. The paint maniac might strike again. He might be any of the gyrating youngsters in costume. How could I recognize a drowned man in a cowl and monk's robe? I don't know why that thought came into my head but it was the perfect disguise. We had several monks. They were popular in London, begging, living off hand-outs. Much like today's homeless but not selling the *Big Issue*.

At some point while I was drinking my Bacardi Breezer diluted with Pepsi, which was revolting, I noticed that Maddy was not there. She was not dancing on the walk below nor snuggling up in one of the clock tower recesses.

My wasp was empty although she could not have got into my car without breaking a lock. She would not have gone swimming on this particular stretch of water: no beach, just a shelf of pebbles. It would need a lot of lavender to improve on the fishy smell.

I started to spread the word. 'Has anyone seen Maddy? When did you last see her? Do you know where she has gone? She is only fourteen.'

'No idea. We thought she was dancing.'

A few of the more responsible youngsters fanned out, looking for her along the walk and the gardens. She might have gone anywhere.

Someone found her basket of lavender. It was strewn on the pavement leading back to town. I was getting a really bad feeling. There was a stampede into town, hunting along twittens and alleyways. The booze had run out anyway so the party was over. I followed, my head buzzing with possibilities. I was sick with worry.

It wasn't me who found her or heard her. It was the top trumpeter from the youth jazz band. She was in the jail house, the 'cooler', locked in, a creepy dark place, screaming her head off. There was nothing I could do, except talk to her through the grille. I sat on an uncomfortable stone ledge nearby. The uneven edge bit into my bottom. But I had to stay there.

'Calm down, Maddy,' I said. 'You are safe now. What can you tell me? How did you get in here?'

'It was a m-monk,' she sobbed, from within the depths. I couldn't even see Maddy in the dark. She was huddled somewhere. 'He said he was a friend of Ross. He said he had a gift for me. Something s-special from Ross. Ross has n-never ever given me a present before.'

Ross? No, he was not the present-giving type.

'We'll get you out,' I promised.

'Save me, Jordan!' she howled.

'I am saving you,' I said.

FIFTEEN

Maddy was not a happy bunny when she was released in the early hours of the morning. She was wet and cold and terrified out of her mind. Her teeth were chattering, her skirt and blouse torn, and she was barely coherent. It took time to wake up someone who could unlock the old jail house and the custodian then took further time trying to find the key.

I wrapped my everpresent fleece round her shivering body when she stumbled out and tried to rub some life into her arms. She needed a warm bath and hot tea and fast.

'I'll take Maddy back to her hotel,' some young man volunteered from the crowd.

'No!' she screamed, clinging to me. 'I'm not going with anyone except Jordan. I won't leave her.'

My car was parked down along the front, near the clock tower so that we could have made a handy escape from the party. Not so handy now. It was a ten-minute walk away. I doubted if Maddy could walk that far. Nor could I, with Maddy clinging to me.

'Can you phone for a taxi?' I asked the same helpful young man. 'I'll pick my car up later.'

'OK,' he said, taking out his mobile. 'If I can find one at this hour. It's pretty late.'

'Please try.' I didn't want to phone James. The man needed his sleep.

There was one taxi driver still awake and driving. He'd taken a couple back to Wareham after a show at the Mowlem Theatre. He was relieved that we only wanted to go to the Whyte Cliffside Hotel.

'Get in,' he said. 'I couldn't stay awake for another long drive.'

It was only a short journey through the town and up the hill and the back of his car was still warm. I paid him twice what he asked for. He was worth it.

The night receptionist looked curiously at the bedraggled Maddy.

'A little mishap,' I said.

We went up in the lift to the top floor. 'Don't wake your father,' I warned her. 'We don't want to worry him.'

She was still shaking from shock and it was easy to propel her into the bathroom and run a warm bath. There were several bottles of complimentary bath foam and I poured them all in. The mixed fragrances might be soothing.

Her fancy dress outfit was torn and dirty. I peeled it off and tossed it into the waste bin. The hospitality tray was well stocked. I made two cups of tea and took them into the bathroom.

Maddy was up to her neck in foam. She was beginning to look better and took the tea. A few sips were reviving.

'You must never, ever leave me,' she said, her foam-covered hand clutching my arm. Suds dripped onto the floor, making a puddle on the bath mat.

'I have to go home. I have my own life to lead, a business to run. Your father only employed me for the jazz festival.'

'I'm not safe any more. Someone wants to kill me. I know it. But why? I haven't done anyone any harm.'

I didn't know how much she knew and I wasn't going to tell her. That was up to Chuck Peters and I felt sure he did not want his daughter alarmed.

'So what on earth makes you think that?' I said lightly. 'It was just a silly joke to lock you in the jail house. Some stupid drunk. Nothing sinister.'

She was calming down a bit, leaning against the back of the bath, drinking the tea. I had to admire her recovery.

'The same drunk that shouted at Ross?'

'I doubt it.'

'It was more than a silly joke,' she said. 'The monk had a knife to my throat. He said he would kill me. He said I knew too much for my own good. But I know nothing! Nothing at all. I am ignorant and thoughtless, only clothes mad.'

'You are being very harsh on yourself,' I said. 'You are intelligent and observant. You may have seen something, perhaps unconsciously, that he doesn't want you to have seen.'

'Tell me, tell me,' she said urgently. 'What could I have seen?'

'Did you see Sarah and Roger, the art teacher, here at the jazz festival three years ago?'

'I can hardly remember last week,' she howled. 'Only saw that photograph that you showed me at the library. How can I remember three years ago? Have a heart.'

She had a point.

'Before you forget, Maddy,' I said, hating that I had to do it, 'can you give me a description of the man, the monk? Any detail might be helpful.'

'I don't want to think about it any more,' she protested.

'I know. That's why you have got to tell me now. Tomorrow might be too late. A fresh memory is always more reliable. Try and be sensible about this. We want to catch this awful man, don't we, even if it was a joke?'

She swallowed the mini lecture. 'He was medium height, not tall like Ross. He was thin, I think, although it was difficult to tell. He was wearing a monk's dark clothes and a hood thing pulled down and a mask over the lower half of his face. I only saw bits of his eyes. They were horrible, glinting with evil.'

Too many vampire films. 'Age? Voice?' I prompted.

'Not actually old. Sort of twenty to thirty, I suppose. I don't know ages really. His voice? Just an ordinary male voice. No foreign accent. Full of menace and threatening, as if he was full of hate. He hated me. Why should he hate me?'

'Did he say anything special?'

'Just that I knew too much and he was going to kill me.'

Her voice was trembling. She lay back in the suds. She had had enough of the cross-examination.

'Did you see his hands?'

'No, he had gloves on. But I think he was wearing one of those string bracelet things on his wrist, like for a religion or a charity.'

'What did he call you?'

'Nothing. Perhaps he had the wrong person.'

'So he didn't kill you, did he? It was only words, a threat. He bundled you into the jail house and left you there. Somehow he had a duplicate key.'

'I could have died if no one had found me.'

'You would have been found the next morning. There's a cafe in the same yard, behind the town hall.'

I made more tea, wrapped her in warm towels, put her to bed like a baby. I had never had a baby. I might be a good mother. There was still time. But a baby needed a father and James had too much personal luggage. He might not want another family.

'Don't leave me,' said Maddy, snuggling down against the pillows.

'My room is only a floor below.'

'No, no, Jordan. Sleep here, please.'

I was longing for the comfort of that bed, bones aching. I took the spare pillows and blankets from the wardrobe and laid them on the floor. The floor was hard but would be good for my back. I eased off my boots and wriggled out of my jeans.

'I won't leave you,' I said. It was my job.

Chuck Peters woke me some time before dawn. An eerie grey light was filtering through a crack in the curtains. I blinked hard, wondering where on earth I was.

The floor had got harder during the night, as floors do. I doubted I could unbend myself and stand up straight.

'Jordan,' he whispered. 'Jordan? Wake up. Come into the sitting room where we can talk.'

The sitting area was the adjoining factor of the two bedrooms of the suite. I followed him in a bent, decrepit state as if my spine had fused unnaturally during the night. I grabbed a towelling robe for decency.

Chuck had made coffee from the hospitality tray and two cups stood on the small table. I was immediately uplifted. Wonderful man, and he could play the trumpet.

He closed the door carefully as I sank into an armchair and reached for a coffee.

'Your DCI James phoned this morning. Apparently he had a plain clothes constable at Maddy's party who reported back what happened. I am eternally grateful that you found her and took care of her back here. She could have died of fright in that creepy jail house.'

'Your daughter is made of sterner stuff,' I said. I felt a mild glow, the way Chuck had said 'your' DCI. If only he was.

'Tell me all that you know.'

I went through it all again. Perhaps I should have had Maddy tied to me with reins like they use with toddlers. Too late now. Chuck nodded now and again, poured me some more coffee.

'Maddy is a wilful girl, a handful. But perhaps now she will be a little more amenable. She's had a fright.'

'Quite a fright.'

'I understand you've left your Mazda MX5 somewhere along the front. You ought to go and collect it before it gets vandalized by some mindless thugs.'

'But I can't. I promised Maddy I'd stay with her.'

'I'll be here with Maddy. I'll sit in an armchair in her room and compose a line or two. It will be good for me. I don't write enough new stuff these days.'

'Dancing Ledge?'

I was back in my 410 bedroom, and out again in five minutes. A quick face wash and hair brush and I was jogging down to town. Everywhere was empty. Only me and a few early-rising seagulls. Daylight was edging behind the Jurassic cliffs, throwing them into strange formations and colours, embedded with the fragmented bones of dinosaurs. The sea was brushing the sand soundlessly, as if forbidden to make a noise too early.

My footsteps on the promenade were muted. I ran along the front, along the harbour wall cobbles and the quarry rail lines towards the old Wellington clock tower. All signs of the party had gone apart from a mound of bottles and cans by a council refuse bin.

The wasp was all right, glistening with dew. It looked forlorn as if it did not like being left out all night in a strange place. I unlocked the car and slipped into the driving seat.

'Sorry,' I said as I turned the ignition. 'Hadn't forgotten you.'

It responded easily without a single early-morning cough. I drove slowly back to the hotel, relishing the empty roads. Daylight was on its way now. I wanted to stay up and watch the dawn but I knew it would be foolish. I needed a few more hours' sleep before that long drive home to Latching.

I didn't go into breakfast for a very good reason. I overslept and the dining room had stopped serving. There was only tea and biscuits from the hospitality tray. Chuck and Maddy had ordered room service.

They invited me to join them to finish up their croissants, which were good even when cold, although butter wouldn't melt on the flaky bread.

Maddy was not quite her old self. She looked subdued but she was wearing a new fringed cotton top and new straw sandals, both loot from yesterday's shopping spree, so that was a good sign.

'So everyone is going home today?' I said brightly.

'We are not quite sure of our plans,' said Chuck. 'DCI James is coming to see us this morning and has asked us to wait till he gets here.'

'I'm not going anywhere,' said Maddy stubbornly. 'I'm never going to leave this room again. I'm going to stay here until I am very old, at least eighteen.'

'You'll soon get bored, stuck in this room with only books to read and repeats on television. I could get you some jigsaws. Perhaps your school will send classwork for you. You could do it on your laptop.'

'I need police protection,' said Maddy. 'I shall get that detective to arrange it. A woman constable, sitting here with me, day and night. Or I could go home with you, Jordan. That's a great idea. My father would pay you to look after me all the time.'

My heart sank. Run my shop, investigate cases, put my new flat straight and take care of Maddy, day and night? I'd get more than vertigo. I'd get chronic bi-polar.

'It's a one-bedroom flat and extremely small,' I said weakly.

'I won't take up much room, promise. We could buy a camp bed and a sleeping bag,' she said with growing enthusiasm. 'I can sleep somewhere. I've always wanted to go camping. I won't be any trouble. It'll be such fun.'

My mobile rang. It was DCI James. 'I'm here but don't open the door until you've checked who it is,' he said. 'They had room service in room 520 this morning. Who delivered it?'

'I've no idea.'

'I'm coming up now.'

He rang off. No enquiry about my health. Nothing had changed.

'That was DCI James,' I said. 'He's on his way.'

'Good,' said Chuck. 'Now we'll get something done.'

I didn't quite know what that meant but I felt sure he didn't mean to sound so blunt or lacking in confidence in my ability.

'Hopefully they will have already caught him,' he added hastily, reading my expression.

There was a knock on the door and Maddy got up to open it but I stopped her.

I went to the door and spoke through it.

'Who is it? Identify yourself, please.'

'Detective Chief Inspector James. I phoned you from downstairs.'

'Password, please.'

'We didn't arrange a password.'

'You could have a gun jammed into your back.'

'No gun.'

'Or at your head.'

'Open the door, you idiot. I've got work to do.'

I turned the key and opened the door a fraction. He was alone and he looked only slightly amused. 'Come in,' I said. 'You're in time for a cold croissant.'

'My favourite.'

Maddy retold her story and gave her description of the man. DCI James made notes and asked a few questions. The young man who had offered to drive Maddy to the hotel was his undercover police constable.

'How did you know the party was on?' I asked.

'Maddy put it on Facebook,' he said. 'Not a sensible thing to do these days, young lady. You were lucky that hundreds didn't turn up.'

'I might have been safer with hundreds of people there,' she said morosely.

DCI James ignored the interruption. 'We found a brown monk's robe rolled up and stuffed into a refuse bin. We need you to identify it and then it will be taken to forensics.'

'I won't even look at it,' she said stubbornly. 'I'm not going out.'

'You'll do as you are told,' said Chuck.

'You won't have to, Maddy. I've brought it with me.'

James had left a green M&S carrier bag by the door. He opened it up and laid a dusty brown robe on the floor. It was creased and muddy. Maddy took one look at it and went white. Then she began to cry, quivering sobs, hiding her face in her hands. Chuck put his arms round her.

'I think you've got your answer, James,' I said.

'I guess so. We'll get it checked out. Might be a trace on it.'

A trace of what? I didn't like to ask.

'May I have a look at your hairbrush, please, Maddy?' he went on. He'd already got out a plastic sample bag. He was going to take a few of her hairs and see if they matched any on the monk's robe.

She went next door to her bedroom, glad to have a chance to repair her face. While she was gone, there was a discreet knock on the door and a voice called: 'Room service.'

'Come in,' said Chuck.

It was the same smart waiter who had been serving me such lovely breakfasts. He gathered up the used cups, plates and cutlery and put them on his trolley. He smiled at me.

'No omelette this morning, Miss Lacey? I had very special one for you, for your last morning at Whyte Cliffside Hotel.'

'Unfortunately, no. I overslept. I shall miss those omelettes. But thank you just the same.'

He reached over for the empty croissant dish. I froze. His hand was a few feet away from me. It was only for a second. But one glimpse was enough. Partly visible from under his white shirt cuff were a few inches of plaited string, the meditation kind, the charity kind, the save the world in friendship kind.

SIXTEEN

'The young lady? She does not want any breakfast?' the waiter enquired casually.

I thought quickly, on my feet, though I was sitting down. 'She's gone out,' I said. 'To the library. She had some books to return.'

'Ah, that is good that the young lady likes to read books,' he said as he wheeled out the trolley. He opened the door and took the trolley out onto the corridor.

Chuck Peters and DCI James looked at me in surprise.

'Jordan? What was all that about?' His voice was low.

'I didn't know that Maddy had borrowed any books,' said Chuck, bewildered. 'She only reads magazines.'

I waited until I heard the footsteps receding and shook my head, miming 'no questions, please'.

'They make a lovely breakfast here, don't they?' I said brightly. 'I've had several delicious omelettes.'

James caught on immediately. 'The hotel has an excellent reputation, that's why it's always full.'

'I've been coming for years,' said Chuck, wondering what on earth was going on. 'It's the best.'

'So, Jordan?'

I thought I heard the service lift doors closing.

'The waiter's wrist,' I said, lowering my voice. 'He was wearing one of those string things. Maddy said that her assailant wore a string wrist band.'

'Lots of youngsters wear them,' said James. 'They are very

popular. A charity thing. A friendship thing. They never take them off.'

'But not always people at the same hotel as me and Maddy,' said Chuck. 'And not one who asks where Maddy is. Who knew all our movements.'

James flicked on his phone. 'I've a constable waiting outside in an unmarked car. Pete? Watch the staff entrance, see if a young man comes out, about thirty, slicked-down dark hair, slim build. See if he goes towards the town. Get another plain clothes to get to the library immediately. Let me know if this guy goes any-where near the library.'

There was a long pause.

'What will you do? Take him in for questioning?' asked Chuck.

'Ask where he was last night?' I said.

The constable was back on the phone.

'Coming out now, guv, yeah, in a bit of a hurry. Jeans, blue T-shirt, dark hair, making for the town. Walking quite fast. Lighting a cigarette.'

'Get someone to the library immediately. I'll come down now. We'll follow him at a distance, then take a different route once we get to the front.'

James switched off his phone. 'Well done, Jordan. You'll make a detective yet.'

The charm of the man. He could really lay it on. No wonder I was insanely mad about him.

Maddy came back into the room. She was wearing different sandals. 'The others hurt,' she said. 'And the straw itched.'

'I think they are probably made for the beach,' I said.

'You stay here, Jordan,' said James, getting up to leave.

'I'm coming with you.'

'No, you're not. You're staying with Maddy. We might do an identity line-up if we pull him in. You'll need to bring Maddy to the station.'

'I actually want to go home to Latching,' I said desperately. 'I've things to do. My life to live. A new case to solve.'

'They can wait.'

'The jazz festival is over.'

'So?' James looked at me coldly, no warmth in those granite eyes. 'Are you a clock-watcher now? That's not like you, Jordan. You usually stick to a case until it is resolved, one way or another.'

'This is not my case. It's your case.'

'Are you two having a row?' Maddy asked with interest. 'That's cool. Do you know each other that well? Have you got a thing going on?'

I could see James struggling. It was a moment I quite enjoyed. 'No,' he said, at last, straightening his face. 'We don't have a thing going on. And we are not having a row. Jordan will follow her conscience.'

Maddy came over and flung her arms round me. She smelt of some strident new perfume. 'Jordan is my bestest friend. She'll look after me. For always and always and forever.'

I wondered if she had been drinking. Had she got some left-over Bacardi Breezer stashed away in her room? But I gave her a hug back. I think the girl needed a few hugs.

'Off you go then,' I said to James. 'Do your Sherlock Holmes sleuthing. Don't trip over your pipe.'

Maddy thought this was funny and started laughing. It was good to see her laugh.

'I'll borrow some jigsaws from the lounge. I am serious about the jigsaws. I'll get a really difficult one, loads of sky.'

'Do your worst,' said Maddy, jumping about. 'I'm brilliant at sky.'

'I still have to drive to Wigan,' said Chuck, even more bewildered by what was going on. He seemed to have lost the plot.

I turned to him. 'Off you go, Chuck Peters, jazz maestro, go do your Wigan sell-out concert. I'm sure the police will have finished with your car by now. We will look after Maddy. She is the most important person here, you'll agree. But please keep in touch: email, mobile, text, landline. Whatever suits you, but Maddy will be safe with me.'

I knew I sounded optimistic. But his Wigan concert was

important. I'd looked it up on the internet. Thousands of tickets had been sold.

James had gone. I hoped he would keep in touch. Swanage was a delightful place. I loved it as a watering hole from the past. But the view from the hotel was limited. Even if it was the same sea that I loved.

While we waited for the call from DCI James, I took the opportunity of packing Maddy's things. No easy job, since she had bought a ton more. It was easier to pack my belongings. There was only the black silk top to add to my wheelie bag. It went in without protest.

Maddy was playing games on her laptop when I got back from my room. She did not seem at all perturbed at my brief absence. She had recovered.

Chuck was ready to leave for his long drive to Wigan and I assured him that Maddy was in good hands. He was reluctant to leave her. The police had returned his car, precious instruments safe.

'It's best for this malicious person to think that his plans have gone awry and that you are not at all worried and work is back on schedule.'

'Are you sure?'

'That's how he would think.'

We were booked out of the hotel before anyone could know. No trail. No forwarding addresses. Chuck met all the bills. I drove Maddy down to the police station, only stopping to fill up with petrol and collect the pink velvet stool. The wasp only did about twenty-eight miles to the gallon. She was a thirsty girl. I parked her discreetly out of sight, in a side road.

'Where are we going?' asked Maddy, not looking up from her laptop. She was playing a game. She was some wonder woman shooting down monsters with rapid fire.

'You are going to do an identity parade,' I said. 'It'll take about ten minutes.'

But it took considerably longer because Maddy was reluctant. She'd put on a baggy pink fleece with the hood pulled forward as if she didn't want anyone to see her face; she was also wearing big sunglasses. They told her to stand behind a double glass wall, reassuring her that no one could see in.

'Are you sure? I can see them.'

There were six young men, five of them off the streets, all dressed identically in something dark with a hood over their heads, lined up against a wall. The station sergeant couldn't get six monk's cowls. The five men off the streets got paid. I'd seen the advertisements. Not a lot, but it was beer money.

Maddy was breathing fast. She didn't like this. At first she wouldn't look at them.

'Take your time, Maddy,' said DCI James, who had recovered the more kindly aspect of his nature. 'They can't see you. Just say which man looks like your attacker.'

It was impossible. The poor girl had no idea. They all looked the same. She did try but I could see that the whole procedure was gruelling. She couldn't identify the wrong man. She had not been told that the waiter from the hotel was among the six. I knew which was the waiter immediately from his height and the shape of his head. But then I had seen him many more times than Maddy.

'I don't know,' she faltered. 'It could be any of them. Number three or number six, but I'm not sure.' Number three was the waiter. Something about the taut body language. 'Five is a bit too tall.'

After the identity parade, when the six were all dismissed, Maddy was asked to help with a police identikit drawing. But again, this was useless. Loads of grey shadow, more hood than head. I was itching to depart, especially if the suspect waiter was returning to the hotel. He might be on lunch duty and discover that we had booked out. As far as the hotel was concerned, Maddy had left with her father, on her way to Wigan.

I didn't ask DCI James what happened when they detained the waiter or on what grounds he was included in the identity parade. The less I knew the better.

We went outside, instantly energized by the sea air after the stuffy offices. Maddy looked ready to take a dive to the shops again but I was having none of that. She was totally my responsibility now.

'Ready for our drive to Latching?' I said. 'It's quite a way. We'll take the scenic route.'

'Hit the road, Jack,' she sang.

It was an exhilarating drive. The wasp seemed to know she was homeward bound. She was not exactly on automatic pilot, but near. Perhaps she had a homing instinct, like a sea bird, and the Latching seashore had a different smell to the fishy Swanage Bay.

'Am I really going to stay in your new flat?' Maddy asked.

'Yes, for the time being. I'm not quite sure how we'll manage. It's very small.'

She was watching me at the controls of the wasp. 'Will you teach me to drive, Jordan? Dad will never let me.'

'Quite right too. You are too young to drive.'

'But I ought to know what to do in case you have a heart attack or a stroke.'

She really knew how to cheer me up.

There was some logic in her argument. I talked her through the basic controls, told her what I was doing and when. She took a genuine interest.

'I'm going to have a car exactly like this, when I'm sixteen.'

'You'll be lucky. The Mazda MX5 is unique. They don't make them like this any more.'

We stopped at a small nondescript wayside cafe for coffee and the ladies room. The single-storey building needed a lot of paint-work. I was paranoid about Maddy being recognized.

'Pull your hood up,' I said. 'I'm going to call you something different in the cafe. Not Maddy. What name would you like?'

'What fun, like in a film? In case we are being followed? I'd like to be called Summer. I love the name. Summer. Can I switch off for you?'

I nodded. She leaned over and switched off the ignition and took out the key.

I pocketed the keys, in case she decided to take off somewhere. She probably thought she could drive now.

We went into the cafe, sat in a corner where I could see the door, and ordered coffee, Coke and toasted teacakes. Maddy had decided to call me 'sis'. She had either upped her age or reduced mine. Either would work.

'This is a crummy joint, sis,' she said.

Not the moment for a lecture in politeness. 'It'll have to do, Summer,' I said. 'As long as the loos are clean.'

'Shall we go to the cinema tonight, sis? I'd like to see the new Bond film. That is, if there is a cinema. Where are we going?'

'Eastbourne,' I improvised quickly. 'I've booked us in at the Grand. Right on the front.'

Maddy gobbled down the toasted teacakes. Her appetite had recovered too. We found the toilets. They were clean. Paper towels. We were back in the wasp in fifteen minutes.

'Can I switch on for you?' she asked expectantly. I let her. I didn't see any harm. It was all part of her education. Her father would buy her a car as soon as she was old enough. Driving lessons were expensive.

It took several hours but the wasp ate up the miles. I would have put the hood down except I didn't know how to do it.

Maddy liked the look of Latching as we cruised into the town, especially the amusement arcades. I drove along the front so that she could get some idea of how wide and spacious and safe it looked, so different from the claustrophobic Swanage Bay. Then I turned in towards the long and tortuous climb to the car parking area of the flats. She was still impressed.

'But this is lovely,' she said. 'It feels so safe. No one can get in without your parking pass. The security arm won't rise. Let me do the pass, please. I can reach the screen. Look.'

Maddy leaned over and activated the parking pass without any trouble. She was flushed with achievement.

We heaved our cases and carrier bags out of the car and took the lift up to the top floor. I was beginning to get the dreaded vertigo feeling. No James to talk me along the walkway. Would

Maddy notice my hesitancy?

But she was talking non-stop and we were dragging along so much luggage, the walkway seemed crowded. I got a few waves of unsteadiness but nothing like the dizzy sickness of before. I left the velvet stool in the car for the next day.

We were at my front door. It looked like home. I almost apologized to it for going away. The moment I switched on the lights and the bathroom night storage heater, it became warmer and more welcoming. Maddy danced through the two rooms and was soon out on the balcony, leaning over the rail, watching the crowds walking below along the promenade. The sea was washed out, far to the horizon. The pier stood on black spidery legs across the sand.

'I love it,' she said. 'It's like a doll's house. So tiny. I could sleep out here, Jordan, on the balcony.'

'No way. The pigeons will wake you at dawn, fly down and nibble your ears.'

'I won't be a nuisance, I promise. Can we go on the pier?'

'We'll see. One shred of nuisance and I'm packing you off back to your father.'

'Wanna bet, sis? Then that nice detective won't like you any more.'

Maddy had certainly recovered her spirits.

'I'm going down to the leisure and camping shop to buy an inflatable mattress for you. I've got a sleeping bag. Do you want to help me choose? I might get the wrong colour.'

'Sure, sis,' she said, casually, coming back into the sitting room. She had already unpacked her belongings. My sofa was strewn with clothes. Her cosmetics were stood all along the windowsill.

'Always close the balcony door. We don't want an inquisitive pigeon hopping about, looking for scraps.'

The shopping didn't take long. It was pink, of course. Dark pink one side and bright pink the other, with a hand pump. Maddy produced a credit card. 'Dad slipped it to me,' she whispered. 'Battle of Hastings.'

Chuck ought to change his pin number. It was too easy. We

also bought some milk and a few essentials. I wasn't into cooking. My repertoire was still soup, salads and sandwiches. Maddy would have to get used to it.

'Veggie's OK with me,' she said. 'Healthy, isn't it? I don't like meat anyway.'

'You eat burgers.'

'They're not meat, are they?'

'Sort of meat, bits and pieces.' I was not going to elaborate.

Maddy was actually enjoying herself. I left her pumping up the air mattress. This was a novelty. She might even go to bed early. After our supper snack, on the balcony, watched by a row of beady-eyed pigeons, we went for the promised walk along the pier.

She loved it. The freedom, the space, the strolling holidaymakers enjoying the late evening sunshine. The tide had turned and the sea was washing round the sturdy timber struts. We walked the circuit then went into the amusement arcade. Now she was in her element. She got a pound's worth of change from a machine and was trying them all.

Jack, the owner, sidled up to me. As always, unshaven, T-shirt stained with coffee. My long-time admirer. 'Who's this with you?' he asked.

'A visitor. Not staying too long, I hope, or I'll be exhausted.'

'At least she's spending money, not like some I could mention.' He grinned.

'Looks like we'll be coming in every day,' I sighed.

'I'll give you a discount.'

There was a whoop of joy from Maddy. She had managed to grab a large pink elephant out of the soft toy machine but it was too large to go down the chute to freedom.

'I'll get it for you, missy,' said Jack, shaking out a fearsome bunch of keys. 'No one has managed to snatch the elephant before.'

'He's cool. He can sleep on my bed.'

'What's your name, missy?'

'Summer,' said Maddy, all smiles. She was doing her

enchantment role. Jack was amused. He usually got a bad mouth from the youngsters who came into the arcade.

'See you tomorrow, then?'

'You bet.'

Since Maddy now had a prize, I managed to get her to leave. The sky was beginning to darken and I wanted to be back in the safety of the flat. I had work to do for the morrow. There was this new case to contact and my shop to open.

'Where's your television?' she asked as we went in. No trouble with vertigo. The timed lights were illuminating the walkway but I couldn't see the height.

'I don't have a television.'

'You don't have a television? You're living in the Middle Ages, lady. First thing tomorrow then,' she said mysteriously. 'Dad's card, remember? Twenty-one-inch flat screen. It could go in that corner.'

'Now I have some work to do. I have a new case tomorrow and a shop to open up.'

Her eyes opened wide with surprise. 'You've got a shop? Wow! What does it sell? I can help, you know. I'll be your assistant. Please? Please?' She was looking through my old jazz tapes. 'I see you've got some of my dad's.'

'I'm a big fan. Remember?'

'Can I phone him?' She was suddenly homesick. 'On his mobile. I want to talk to him.'

'Ask him to pull over if he's still driving.'

'He knows that.'

'Of course, Maddy. But don't say exactly where you are, in case your phone is being hacked.'

I left her talking to Chuck on the phone. I thought we had covered our tracks rather well. I thought we were pretty safe. But I was wrong.

SEVENTEEN

Maddy slept on top of the sleeping bag inside a folded sheet with a pillow in a clean pillow case. She kept the pink elephant beside her. It had a reflective sort of face. It was her comfort mascot.

I slept in my own bed with the door open. It was a joy. My bed was so comfortable. It was always my one luxury. The mattress was the right degree of firmness for my back. I slept the sleep of the good and deserving, though what I had done to deserve Maddy indefinitely I was not sure.

In the morning I made mugs of tea, marvelling at the view of God's country from the kitchen window, the South Downs, now National Trust. My two previous bedsits had one view only, the street below: refuse bins, stragglers on the pavement, cruising cars, gutters with debris.

'Wake up, sleepyhead,' I said, putting the tea down beside her. 'The day has dawned.'

'This is far too early for it to have dawned,' she mumbled.

'Don't forget, I'm a working woman. I have a shop to open and a client to interview.'

She brightened a fraction. 'I'd love to work in your shop and sell things. Can I? How shall I know all the prices?'

'Everything has the same price. Six pounds. It makes life easier. The books are priced individually, inside the cover, unless they are on a fifty-pence shelf or in the sad and abandoned twenty-pence box.'

I'd arranged for the new client to come and see me at half ten. He'd sounded really agitated on the phone.

'Can't I come now? It's really urgent.'

'I'm sorry, I'm busy, winding up another case.' The lie came out as smooth as treacle. 'Tomorrow is the earliest. Don't worry, Mr Taylor. I shall then be able to devote my entire time to your case. Half past ten tomorrow.'

'I suppose I shall have to make do with that, then. Or I could find another detective.'

'It's entirely your choice,' I said politely. I was beginning to dislike him already.

We had a quick breakfast of muesli and sliced banana, sitting on the balcony in the early-morning sunshine. The novelty was enough to keep Maddy absorbed in the panorama below, cruising the promenade, cyclists, joggers, dogs being walked, prams being pushed.

'Look at all those dogs. I'd love a dog, a little fluffy one. We can't have a dog because pets are not allowed at our flats. We live in a modern block in Hampstead. No decent view at all. Can't even see the Heath.'

I had sorted the new wares for my shop and they were bagged ready to carry. I didn't want to take the car. It would be quicker to walk.

First Class Junk had a deserted look. The corner shop needed a dust and fresh air. Even the two small window displays had a tired feeling. People had stopped looking at them. They looked boring.

'I can do a window,' said Maddy. 'Let me do a window. I've always wanted to be a window dresser.' Her ambitions had no limits.

'All right. You do the side window. I'll do the front. Keep it simple. No clutter.'

'Simple and classy,' she sang out, beginning to remove the unsold items. 'I need a theme. We learned that at school.'

She had learned something at that expensive school. Not all of

Chuck's money had been wasted.

I checked that she was handling everything carefully and left her to it. I was no expert. My talent was entirely amateur. I went purely on instinct and what was available.

She put a row of the Disney Wade figures at the front. At the back she stood a *Girl's Own Annual*, circa 1950. Then at one side she put an Elizabeth II Coronation mug and four un-matching silver teaspoons.

'That's pretty good,' I said. 'For a first-timer. I like the un-matching spoons, a nice touch.'

'I don't know why. It seemed right to put something that didn't match.'

'So what is your theme?'

Maddy thought about it, screwing up her face. 'Childhood. The un-matching spoons are parents breaking up.'

I said nothing. Maddy was talking from experience.

I had two choices when Mr Taylor arrived. Leave Maddy in charge of the shop or close it for the duration of his interview.

'I can do it,' said Maddy. 'It'll be a doddle.'

'Any problems, please come back and ask me.'

'Sure,' she said. She was busy dusting everything in sight with my special magnetic feather duster. It was supposed to collect the dust, not merely distribute it.

'I can cope. And I'll do the right change.'

'Brilliant.'

I knew it was Mr Taylor, the moment the man arrived. His appearance matched his voice, disgruntled and annoyed. His sandy hair hadn't seen a comb. His raincoat was not fastened properly and he didn't own a pot of shoe polish.

'Come in, Mr Taylor. Come into my office,' I said, putting on a welcoming smile which was entirely false. It hurt my face.

'I'm on time.'

'Excellent. I like a punctual person.'

He sat down on my Victorian button-back chair without being invited. The coffee percolator was already giving out its wonderful aroma. I didn't use my best bone china mugs in case

156

they got broken. Two sturdy pottery ones were filled instead.

'How can I help you?'

'My wife has left me. I want her back.'

I was not surprised. Any sane woman would leave him if he was always like this. Still, there were always two sides to every story.

I drew up a lined pad. 'Please give me the details. Everything that you can remember.'

'Her name is Doreen Taylor. She's forty-three, that's ten years younger than myself. We've been married fifteen years and have a semi-detached house in Farm Road, north of the station. I've done everything for her: never short of money, nice house and furniture, nice car. Holidays, everything. She wants for nothing. But she's walked out on me. No reason, no letter, nothing.'

'What did she take with her? And when was this?'

He looked stunned for a moment, as if he had not properly checked around. 'Nothing, as far as I can see. No clothes, no savings book, no jewellery. It was a week ago. I remember the day exactly because I had to go out in the evening and there was no supper ready.'

'So she might not have walked out on you. There might be another reason for her disappearance. Have you checked the hospitals? People can fall, get concussion and lose their memories.'

'Of course I checked the hospitals. Do you think I'm stupid? There's no trace of her.'

'Did she take her handbag?'

'Her handbag has gone. And a photograph of her parents. Don't know why she took that. They died years ago.'

'What was she wearing?'

'I don't know. She normally wore jeans and a T-shirt of some sort. A fleece or a windcheater. She always looked a mess. I kept telling her to smarten up. It wasn't as if I didn't buy her clothes. Always the best.'

'You chose her clothes?'

'She had no taste.'

No taste in men either, by the look of it. 'And what did Doreen look like?'

Again, he was stunned for a moment, as if he didn't remember. 'She's thin even though we have the best of food. Brown hair tied back in a ponytail. I don't know why she didn't go to a hairdressers and have it properly cut and set. Eye colour? I don't know. I never looked.'

But how many husbands do know their wife's eye colour? This was not unusual. He had watery eyes, no colour at all.

'Have you brought a photograph of Doreen?' I kept mentioning her name before she disappeared into the mists of the unknown, the unremembered.

'Of course I've brought a photograph. It's a holiday snap, last year at Margate. On the beach. It was one of those annoying photographers. We had to buy a copy to get rid of him.'

They were sitting in deckchairs so I couldn't see Doreen's height or build. But I could see her face. She had a certain frail prettiness which had long been dampened by sadness. Reg Taylor, on the other hand, was a picture of annoyance, stiff with disapproval.

'I'll keep this, if I may. I'll get it copied and circulated. Someone may have seen your wife.'

'I want her back.' He hadn't touched his coffee. Perhaps he preferred instant. 'I can't manage on my own. She's got to come back.'

I took out a contract form. I was nothing if not businesslike. 'My rates are ten pounds an hour or fifty pounds a day. The day rate is a bargain. A whole day and often half a night.' I tried to lighten my voice, turn it into a joke.

Reg Taylor was also a miser. I was not surprised. 'Ten pounds an hour? That's outrageous,' he said.

'Cleaners get paid more than that these days.'

'Fifty pounds a day? Do you think I'm made of money? How many days will this take?'

'It depends on where she is and what has happened to her. I'm not a medium. I can't see into the past.'

Maddy put her head round the door. 'Sis? A moment, please.'

'This is the contract, Mr Taylor. Please sign it if you want me to find your wife.'

I went out into the shop and leaned on the counter, taking deep breaths.

'I thought you needed a break,' said Maddy. 'I've sold two Wade figures already. The money is in the drawer. Do I get commission?'

I had to laugh. Maddy was looking really pleased with herself. 'I'll think about it. You may put me out of business.'

'A nice lady called Doris came into the shop. She brought some fruit for you. She's going to bring me some Pepsi. Her shop sells food and drink and lots of things.'

'That's great. I'll thank her. Doris has a shop a few doors down. I must go back to Mr Taylor. He may have changed his mind about employing me, in which case we are back on the breadline.'

'Not exactly,' said Maddy. 'You're forgetting my dad's card.'

She seemed to think that her dad's card was the answer to everything and I suppose it was.

Reg Taylor had filled in the details, signed the contract and thrown ten crumpled notes onto my desk. 'There you are, two days' full money. That's all I'm going to pay. And I expect results in that time.'

'Is that all Doreen is worth to you?' I could not stop myself asking.

'I'm not made of money. And you can't count this as a whole day.'

I had forgotten to ask Reg Taylor what he did for a living, what bought the nice furniture, the nice car, the nice holidays. But it was too late now. He had stalked out of the shop, slamming the door.

'Are all your clients as nasty as that one?' asked Maddy. She was sorting through books and had put one aside that had glossy photos of current pop stars in it.

'No, some are really nice. I found a lady's lost tortoise. We are still friends. Sometimes she brings me a cake.'

'Probably a tortoise cake?' Maddy fell about, laughing at her own dreadful joke. It was the first time I had seen her almost normal. She'd had a childhood without a mother, surrounded by jazz musicians, packed off to boarding school. Nothing normal. Except that her father loved her. That was obvious. 'Can I have this book? It's got some great photos.'

'Yes. It can count as your commission.'

She looked at the price inside the cover. 'That's fair. Thanks.'

'I think we both need some lunch,' I said later. The copper tray had gone. I knew it wouldn't stay long in the window. 'I know a good Mexican restaurant just along the road.'

My dear Mexican friend, the owner, was not there, but his staff remembered me and we got the best of service. Maddy was careful. She had not had Mexican food before and some of it was very hot. The staff brought her a glass of iced water.

'You know some nice people,' she said, tucking into a chicken enchilada. 'As well as some nasty people.'

I spent the afternoon rechecking the West Sussex hospitals and A&E departments. I did not trust Reg Taylor's account. Doreen Taylor could be anywhere, concussed, blissfully tucked away from the dominating Reg.

But they had no record. I got the holiday snap photocopied and pinned them up around the town, followed by Maddy.

'This is awful,' she said. 'It's like those lost cat photos you see on lamp posts.'

'We have to do it. Someone may have seen her. They need only get in touch with me. I'm a sort of middleman.'

'Middlewoman.'

Maddy was flagging. She had never had such a busy day. It was normal for me. I was used to long hours on my feet. We headed back to the flat. It was still daylight. I felt the usual apprehension as we got out of the lift and began the trek along the open walkway. I did not look down. I still had to fetch the pink velvet stool.

'Look, there's your car,' said Maddy, peering over the rail. It was no surprise. It was where I had parked it. 'Can we go for a drive? What do you call it? The bumble bee?'

'The wasp.'

'But wasps have stripes. Your car hasn't any stripes.'

'The luggage rack has black metal stripes. And the engine buzzes.'

Maddy went into inventing new names for my car. It was a new game. She suggested banana, milkshake, yellow pepper, lemon and by the time she got to scrambled egg, we had reached my front door. As I put my key in the door, a tall figure emerged from the far end, where the walkway rounded a viewing corner. It gave me a shock to see him. He paused and then came striding towards me.

'Hi there, Jordan. Maddy. Had a busy day?'

'Jordan! It's your nice dishy detective. He's come to see you. That's good, we can all sit on the balcony and drink wine. Have you got any wine?'

I was glad to see him but knew instantly this was not a social call. James wouldn't have driven all the way from Dorset to find out how I was and drink wine on the balcony.

'Hi there,' I said. 'How did you get in past the door code?'

'One of your neighbours buzzed me in. She thought I looked a reliable sort of visitor.' He caught my stricken look. 'Sorry, Jordan, that's not exactly true. She recognized me from when they had vagrants sleeping in the foyer and she called 999. I answered the call.'

'Come in. I'll make some tea,' I said, bustling straight into the minuscule kitchen. I loved the light wood fitted cupboard doors and granite-style worktops. The microwave was installed at one end, my toaster at the other. I remembered my bedsit kitchen corner with its draining board and a tap.

'Wonderful view,' said James, looking out at the South Downs. 'A bit different from your other place.'

'I've gone up in the world.'

Maddy was already dragging the bathroom stool out onto the

balcony. The beach was drenched in late sunshine, still warm. The tide was coming in, thrashing against the shingle, the unicorns dancing on the waves. I had certainly gone up in the world. Quite a long way up. Vertigo up.

'I need to talk to you alone,' he said.

'What do you suggest I do with Maddy? Send her out to play on the beach?'

'We'll think of something,' he said, taking the tray from me. Doris had given me a packet of assorted biscuits as a welcome back gift. I opened them and arranged them on a plate. It was all immensely civilized.

'So do you like it at Latching with Jordan?' James asked as he set the tray down on the balcony table. Some previous tenants had left behind a table and two basket chairs. They were bleached and worn from sun and rain. The tiles on the table were uneven from the rain seeping underneath.

'I love it! I love it!' Maddy enthused. 'I'm going to stay here for ever and ever. I shan't go back to school. I've got a job in Jordan's shop now. I do window dressing and sell things.'

'It all sounds very professional,' James agreed.

'But Jordan hasn't got a television. I have to look at things on my laptop. It's not the same.'

'Jordan is a little behind the times or it may be that she is short of money,' said James, stirring his tea.

'We're not short of money,' said Maddy, mysteriously patting her pocket like a gangster.

'So is this a flying visit?' I could not resist asking.

'No, my enquiries have moved to this area. I shall be based here for a few days. I'm staying at the Travelodge nearby. This is my room number if you need me.' He'd written the number on a scrap of paper. 'I have a sea view too, although no balcony to sit on.'

'I bet the Travelodge isn't as nice as Jordan's flat, even though she hasn't got much furniture.'

'The pictures are nicer here,' he said, looking in at my collection of Jack Vettriano waiting to be hung on the wall. I'd got 'The

Singing Butler', of course, and three others. There was also my early eighteenth-century map of West Sussex, when Brighton was only a fishing village and Latching wasn't even named on it. I don't think James had seen that acquisition.

It had been a lucky buy at a charity fair along the front. No one else had spotted it in the box of framed prints. I could not believe that it had been thrown out, or that no one wanted the print. *Flog It!* would love it. Doris had told me about *Flog It!*

I could not stop my heart from soaring at the news. James was here for a few days. I might see him again though Maddy would be my constant chaperone. I could hardly dope her Pepsi with Valium so that she went to bed early. She was a late bird like her dad.

'More tea?' I asked like a society hostess.

James followed me through to the kitchen, leaving Maddy hanging over the balcony wall, eating her way through the biscuits.

'You were followed,' he said. 'He must have seen you getting into your yellow car. We were tracking you by satellite when we noticed a motorbike following you. He stopped at the same cafe. Left a few moments after you, followed you all the way to Latching.'

I could not stop a shiver. I nearly spilt the milk. 'How do you know it's not a coincidence?'

'The waiter did not return to the Whyte Cliffside Hotel. He was calling himself Carlos at the hotel. He's left everything behind. We've gone through his things in his room, his hairbrush, etc. We are ninety-nine per cent sure he is Roger Cody, the art teacher who was last seen with Sarah before she was murdered. The DNA on cigarette ends we found in his room nearly matched cigarette ends found near Sarah's makeshift grave. The torrential rain hasn't helped. We've a feeling he's been back to Corfe Castle.'

I shivered again. It was macabre. Going back to the grave.

'And now he's in Latching?'

'Somewhere in Latching. We've lost track of him. But he's here. Probably got a job or is laying low.'

'At the Travelodge?'

'I hope not. Maybe. It's reasonably priced.'

'How am I going to cope if I can't take Maddy out with me? I have a shop to open and a runaway wife to find.'

'Maddy could come with me to the station tomorrow, play on our computers, watch our television, re-organize the holding cells.'

I gave him a quick hug. It was very quick. Enough to feel the hardness of his body and the freshness of his skin. A long time no hug.

'Caught you,' said Maddy, from the doorway. She was grinning with satisfaction. 'I knew you two were up to something.'

EIGHTEEN

Maddy spent the evening on the phone to her dad. Every minute of the day was recounted to him in detail. He seemed reassured to know that DCI James was in the area.

'But he's only come to see Jordan,' Maddy said knowingly. 'They are cool about it but I could tell.'

'Don't play gooseberry then,' he said.

'As if I would. Jordan is my bestest friend.'

'I'm glad to hear it.'

'She hasn't got a television. Isn't that cool? I thought everybody had a television. So we are going to play cards instead. And we are going to play for money! Dig that, Dad!'

I didn't point out that 20p would be our highest stake. Supper was on a tray, cheese and nibbles, radishes, celery and nuts. By ten o'clock, Maddy was flagging. She had won 50p off me. She played a few of her dad's tapes and flaked out on the air mattress on the floor.

I was glad to retreat to my bedroom with my notes to go over. If I found Doreen Taylor, it was odds to even she would not want to go back to Reg. Or she might already be in London; hitched a lift, walked, cycled. I hadn't asked if she had got a bike. Probably not. A bike would have given Doreen a certain amount of freedom and the sanctimonious Reg would not have allowed that.

Tomorrow I would go to the library, comb the local papers, see if anything sparked an idea. Latching had a summer of public events. I might spot Doreen in a crowd picture. I would show her photo around the station staff, the bus crews, the National Express office. Maddy would be safe at the police station in DCI James's care. He would probably ask one of his young officers to keep an eye on her.

I struck lucky at the railway station. One of the women staff customer personnel (they used to be called porters) remembered seeing someone like Doreen Taylor behaving oddly.

'Yeah, I think that's her,' she said, squinting at the photograph. 'I noticed her because she was so nervous. Kept dropping everything. Yet she only had a couple of stuffed carrier bags. Nearly fell down the subway steps in her hurry to get to platform two opposite. Then she shut herself in the ladies loo and I thought she must be doing drugs or something. I nearly knocked on the door. Can't have that, you know, not on the station. Against the law.'

'But you didn't and she wasn't?' 'Nah, she came out in another mad rush and flung herself on a train at the last moment before the doors closed. It was a wonder she didn't get squashed.'

'Where was she going?'

'I dunno. It was the slow train to Brighton. The fifty-six. Stops all along the line.'

'Thank you very much indeed,' I said, giving her my business card. 'You've been very helpful. Please give me a ring if you think of anything else.'

'What she done? Robbed a bank?' The woman was curious.

I shook my head. 'Gone missing. Her family are worried.'

The woman nodded wisely. Perhaps she knew the feeling. 'That fits,' she said. 'She looked like she was running away from something, poor soul.'

Brighton was a good place to get lost in. It was crowded with holidaymakers in any season, cafes and restaurants, hotels and boarding hotels thriving. Doreen could hole up there for weeks and never be found. And I would never find her either.

But she would have to have money to live on or get a job.

The miserly Reg would probably have kept her short, made her account for every penny of housekeeping spent. No chance of saving much, if anything, out of the purse.

She needed money. She needed a job. And to get a job she would need an address. Employers always wanted an address. They didn't employ the homeless.

Brighton was my next stop. I called DCI James and told him of my schedule for the rest of the day.

'Can you keep Maddy for me?' I asked. 'I'll be back before it gets dark.'

'She's teaching my officers how to do funky dancing.' He sounded amused for once.

'Very useful in police enquiries.'

'Don't take your yellow car. He might follow you and you won't be safe.'

'I was going to go on the train. Ask passengers if they saw my missing person on the day she went missing.'

'So you have a lead?'

'A good one. She was seen at Latching Station in a state.'

'A state?'

'Nervous, not wanting to be seen, hiding in the ladies.'

'Roger Cody seems to have been swallowed up in Latching. We're checking all the hotels. He may be staying at one or working at one. He must have had false references to have worked at the Whyte Cliffside.'

'No problem these days with photocopiers. You can falsify any document. Nothing is valid if you know how to do it.'

'Be careful, Jordan. This man is a killer. Elsie Dunlop is surviving but she was lucky. She's still in intensive care.'

The fast train to Brighton only took half an hour. None of the passengers had seen my nervous Doreen, dropping carrier bags. Brighton railway station was teeming with passengers, a grey, smoky building with a dirty glass roof that did nothing to enhance its appearance. The fearless pigeons were everywhere, searching for dropped crumbs from the numerous take-away cafes.

I combed the cafes, the restaurants, the hotels, walked a dozen streets, showing everyone Doreen's photograph. They might have seen her, employed her, given her a free mug of tea. But no one recognized the fragile Doreen.

The pier and the amusement arcades were next, then the succession of tiny cave-like shops underneath the promenade, that led directly onto the beach. The beach was crowded, not an inch to spare between glistening bare brown bodies. Yet only a short distance up the coast there was Latching with four miles of sand and shingle and plenty of room for everyone.

Doreen would hardly be sunbathing, with her carrier bags as head rests.

She could be anywhere among this seething throng.

'Yeah, I've seen her,' said a swarthy stallholder who ran a whelk stall. 'She's bought a couple of punnets off me yesterday. Looked half starved. I gave her some crisps and a cup of tea.'

'How kind,' I said, noting his name. 'Have you seen her lately?'

'Nope. She paid me in pence, like money out of a child's money box.'

'I'm looking for her. I need to find her.'

He shook his head. 'Homeless, I should think. Have a look under the pier or on Rathbone Street. That's where the homeless go to get free stuff. Free soup dished out at night from a van or something.'

The sun was going down, taking the warmth. I was glad I had my fleece. Somewhere I read that fleeces are made from recycled plastic bags. I wondered if I was wearing Tesco or Waitrose?

I found Doreen Taylor, wrapped in nothing but her coat, trying to sleep in a narrow doorway in The Lanes. She looked dreadful, gaunt and unwashed, a scarf wrapped round her head. I had nothing on me except a packet of Rolos and some mints. Talk about prepared to save the starving.

'Doreen Taylor? Don't be alarmed. My name's Jordan Lacey and I have come to help you. Will you come with me?'

'I don't know who you are.' She sat up, blinking and wild-eyed, against the shop doorway. 'What do you want? Leave me alone.'

'I know. You will have to trust me.'

'You could be anybody. You could be the police. I'm not going anywhere with you. I don't know you.'

'I'm not the police. I'm a friend.'

She took a lot of persuading but hopefully my harmless face and friendly disposition calmed her fears. Also the doorway was draughty and hard. She was cold and hungry.

I took her to a dimly lit all-night cafe that would not mind her bedraggled appearance. I ordered two coffees, cheeseburgers and chips. I ate a few chips to be sociable and drank the coffee. Doreen demolished the rest. She still had a faint air of prettiness about her. Reg had not been able to wipe away all her confidence. She had found the courage to run away.

I had to tell her. 'I'm a private investigator, i.e. that's a detective, employed by your husband, Reg Taylor, to find you.'

She shot up frantically, ready to escape, but I managed to calm her and get her to sit down again. I kept my hand on her arm. She was trembling.

'You said you were my friend.'

'So I am, don't worry, Doreen. Please sit down. I'm not going to split on you. Reg Taylor is a vile man and I don't know how you stood him for so long. You deserve a better life, but not by sleeping in doorways in Brighton. That's not a better life.'

'I don't know what else to do,' said Doreen, forlornly. She had a sweet, clear voice. It was her best asset.

'What can you do?'

'I was a telephonist for a big pharmaceutical firm.'

'Go back to the same firm, try to get a job with them. Tell them any story you like. Say you are divorced, single, whatever. But you must find yourself a room, an address, however cheap, get a few good nights' rest, keep yourself clean and decently fed and warm.'

'But I've no money. There's only a few pence left.'

'Yes, you have,' I said. 'Your husband reluctantly gave me a hundred pounds to find you. You can have it. Here it is, take it.

I've only spent a train fare and I can afford that.'

Doreen looked at the folded crumpled notes in bewilderment. 'He gave you a hundred pounds? So you could find me?'

'My fee for two days' work. I charge fifty pounds a day. But I want you to have it. I know it's not a lot but it will pay for a dry roof over your head till you sort yourself out. There are a lot of bed and breakfast places, back of the town, vacancy signs in the windows. Find somewhere that looks clean and homely.'

She fingered the money as if it was contaminated. 'How do I know this isn't a trap?'

'I promise, Doreen. It's all above board. We'll leave separately. You can go first, if you want to. Please take my card and if you need any help, phone me.'

Doreen stood up uncertainly, pushing the notes into her bag. 'And you won't tell Reg that you found me? You promise me that? I can't go back to him.'

'I'll tell him that my enquiries have gone dry. I won't mention Brighton at all. But please tell me something. I'm curious about this man. What does Reg do for a living?'

'He's an income tax inspector. At least, that's what he said.'

It was dark by the time I reached Latching police station to collect Maddy. She was glazed with boredom. She rushed at me.

'Thank goodness you are here at last, Jordan! Can we go on the pier? The amusement arcade stays open quite late. They are all working here, you know. Dreadful things happen. I saw two blokes covered in blood. Everyone is so busy.'

'I should hope so. Have you got your pink fleece with the hood? OK, we'll walk home, via the pier. I'll say goodbye to DCI James.'

'He's out. An urgent call. I heard the sirens.'

I thanked the station sergeant instead and steered Maddy out of the building. She was only too pleased to get out, as if she had been set bail. I tucked her arm into mine. A breath of sea air on the pier was a good idea after a day in Brighton, a place so crowded there was barely room to breathe.

'I know some short cuts down twittens, as they're called. Used by pirates and smugglers in olden days. Probably full of ghosts. We'll go on the pier but for ten minutes only. Then it's back to the flat and no arguing.'

'I never argue,' said Maddy. I didn't comment.

Walking the pier in the dark is magic. It is strung with fairy lights which swing in the night breeze, phosphoresence glistens far out on the sea, fishing boats sail past, distant pin pricks of light denote a cruise liner sailing into Portsmouth.

The amusement arcade was packed with youngsters on a night out. The air resonated with the sound of coins cascading out of the machines. Maddy won 40p and lost a pound's worth of coins.

'Nearly fifty per cent profit,' she said happily, disregarding the true maths of her winnings.

The flat was a haven of peace and quiet. I was glad to sink into an armchair and put my feet up. I had walked miles that day, the only respite being on the train twice. But I had achieved what I set out to do. I had found Doreen and helped to set her completely free. I hoped she would find a new life.

'You looked whacked,' said Maddy. 'Shall I make some tea? Station tea is so strong. It's out of a machine. It's like brown gravy. Yuck.'

'That would be lovely. I only need a few minutes to relax and then I'll revive.'

But I fell asleep and when I woke, Maddy was out on the balcony, people-watching in the dark, and my tea had grown cold. My mobile phone was ringing. I dug it out and answered.

'Hello?'

It was James. My James. His voice was full of concern. 'Are you all right?'

'We are both fine. Weary but OK. Thank you for having Maddy.'

'Can I come round?'

'Where are you?'

'Downstairs. Outside on the street.'

'I'll buzz you in.'

He came along the walkway to my flat carrying two large paper-wrapped parcels. The smell was delicious, wafting my taste buds. 'Got any plates?' he said as if I didn't know the meaning of the word. 'I've brought supper.'

We ate fish and chips out on the balcony, the night stars twinkling in a velvet black sky. James mourned the lack of tomato sauce but I'd hardly had time to go shopping. Maddy ate with her fingers, ignoring the fork I gave her. Fish tasted better finger fed.

'So you found your missing person?' James asked.

'Yes.' I nodded. 'Mission accomplished.'

'Where was she?' Maddy asked curiously.

'Client confidentiality,' I said. 'One day I might tell you. But she is going to find a job, get a new life.'

'Are you going to tell that nasty man who came to your shop?'

'I don't think so. I don't think he needs to know anything.'

'Jordan works in wondrous ways. She rights wrongs, wrongs rights,' said James. 'Let her resolve the case in her own way. She has her own methods.' He followed me out to the kitchen with the plates. 'I must speak to you alone. Maybe I should have simply phoned you from the foyer.'

'Supper was a lovely idea, thank you. We'll go outside, on the walkway.'

'No vertigo?'

'Not at night, because I can't see down. You could stop me from seeing down by standing in the way.'

We went out onto the walkway. It was cool and dark, lights in the darkness from other blocks of flats, from far distant roads, a few winking planes flying across to the channel and Europe.

I made sure I had not locked myself out, put the safety bar across the opening of the door. It was an ingenious device.

'What do you want to tell me?'

'There has been another development. I have some bad news for you. Your admirer, Tom Lucas, he's been found dead, in one of his own pig sties.'

I steadied myself on a rail. I was devastated. That dear man. It was very dark below. I could make out the shape of my wasp.

Her light colour made her different to all the other parked cars. I could see the black lines of the luggage rack which had prompted her name. The news was hard to take in.

'How awful. He was such a nice man. Tom was kind to me,' I said slowly. 'No one special though. I think he was lonely. The last time I saw him was at the farewell party. He was getting on very well with your Ruth. Did he have a heart attack? He was a bit overweight. What happened?'

'Not a heart attack. Something far more brutal. He'd been dead at least twenty-four hours when we got the call so that puts the time of death at not long after Maddy's impromptu party.'

I felt a cold shudder. 'Far more brutal? Not another murder, surely?'

James nodded. 'It's not in any way pleasant. He was killed with a pitchfork and died among his pigs.'

NINETEEN

James didn't go into details. I didn't want to know. It was too grotesque. Poor Tom. Was it the same killer? Was the killer into pointed things? An umbrella tip, a pitchfork? How had Sarah Patel been killed?

'Yes,' said James, reading my thoughts. 'We think it is the same killer. Sarah was killed with a knife, the sort used by painters. A palette knife. Similar hallmarks. Pointed weapon. Unprovoked attack. And somehow all connected to the jazz festival. Don't tell Maddy.'

'I may appear stupid at times but it's purely a professional screen,' I said, using the ice in my voice to cover my dismay at this new murder. 'Of course I shan't tell Maddy. But you should phone Chuck. After all, he contacted you in the first place about these threatening messages.'

'I've already done that. He thinks that he should take Maddy out of school and go abroad somewhere after the Wigan gig, maybe to the States. They might be safer in another country. He says he can pick up work anywhere.'

'And that's the flaw. It'll go on the internet that Chuck Peters is playing in wherever, Baltimore, Chicago, and the killer will follow them.'

'I'll warn him of that. The internet broadcasts information in seconds. Nothing is secret any more. The world knows everything, instantly, whether it's true or not.'

James moved closer on the dark walkway and for a few

moments put his arms round me. I breathed in his closeness, the firm hardness of his body, the warm closure of his arms. I had a feeling that something at last was going to happen.

'I know you are upset, Jordan. No one likes death, especially sudden and violent death. But I see so much of it, I suppose I have grown a shell. You can do the grieving for both of us.'

Then he was gone, leaving me outside on the walkway, the warmth from his body gradually evaporating into the night air.

I was glad I had found Doreen and given her a chance of freedom. If she decided to go back to the dominating Reg, that was her choice, but I had a feeling she would find a new life on her own. I could not get Tom Lucas out of my mind; I felt guilty.

But I needed some new cases. Reg had only employed me for two days. My fame travels fast but not fast enough to pay the bills.

The next morning we opened the shop and arranged new window displays. Maddy liked doing windows so I left her to it. I had to admit she had a flair. She ravaged the storage boxes outside and brought out items that had not seen the light of day for months.

'Look at this!' she crowed. 'I love it. A golden mask, probably from one of those wicked festivals in Venice. It's fabulous.'

'I hate it.'

'Bet I can sell it.'

'Go ahead.'

'Usual commission?'

'Don't push me.'

But it sold, within minutes, to a guy going to a fancy dress party. I was glad to see it go. I'm not into grotesque, especially after the previous night's news. Chuck Peters had been on the phone to me. He asked not to speak to Maddy, not to alarm her.

'Don't tell Maddy anything. I know she's safe with you. I'll make it short,' he said.

I was in the middle of typing up my report for Reginald Taylor. I told the truth, detailing the steps I had taken. I wrote that I had found his wife but did not say where or how. I also said that for the time being she was not ready to return to him. The report left it all rather vague. He had not instructed me to bring his wife back. He had instructed me to find her and I had. As I said, mission accomplished. I would post it to him at the end of the day.

'I'll be down tonight as soon as the second gig is over. Is that all right? Expect me extremely late, if that is OK? I want to see my Maddy,' said Chuck. 'I think it's time we made a fast disappearance.'

'Any time,' I said. 'Just buzz the flat number and I'll let you in.'

It looked like being a disturbed night. How long would it take Chuck to drive down from Wigan to Latching after his last show? Several hours at least. I could see hours of dark waiting before his arrival.

Maddy had a profitable morning. Customers liked her Shirley Temple charm and bright smile. She sold a few odds and ends that had not moved before. She totted up her commission.

'I could have a holiday job with you,' she said as we munched our late lunch-time sandwiches. 'Dad would let me stay with you in your flat and I like it here. I love the pier. I could go swimming. Lots of girls have holiday jobs. I'd have to be paid, of course.'

'Of course,' I murmured. 'Only fair.'

'And you could get on with solving crime in Latching.'

'My ambition in life.'

'While I look after your shop.'

'The perfect solution.'

'I know that my commission so far today is not a lot, but I do like that scarf. The filmy one, all blues and purples, mingled.'

I knew the one. And there hung a problem.

I also liked the scarf. It was hand painted on silk and quite beautiful. It had come in a box of vintage clothes from a house clearance. I put a date of about 1920 on it. It had not yet been on sale in the shop, only used to dress a window.

It was not a plaything for a teenager. A sudden whim. Something to be cast aside or to be left behind at a disco when the novelty wore off. My possessive buttons went on hold.

The door to the shop opened, saving me from a reply. It was my friend, Doris. She was carrying a tray of goodies, fresh and canned. Vegetables, fruit, juice, rolls and cheese.

'I heard that a siege was imminent,' said Doris. 'Can't have you and your young visitor starving. Though you could lose a bit of weight, Jordan. Putting it on a bit round the waist, aren't you?'

Jazz drinking. And too much snack food. Doris was right.

'What do you mean, a siege?' I asked.

'Your knight in shining armour phoned me. He said you might not be seeing daylight for a couple of days. I'll keep an eye on your shop.'

'I have no idea what he means.'

Doris had a worried look. She put the tray down on my counter with a hand-written bill.

'He means that someone is after you, ducky. And I think you ought to get off home and put up the barricades. Like in *Les Mis*. Great film. Mavis and I have seen it twice.'

'Did James actually say that? When?'

'He phoned about ten minutes ago. He couldn't get through to you. He tried several times. Maddy? Is that her name? He said you ought to make tracks for your flat now.'

'And you waited ten minutes to tell me?' I knew why he couldn't get through to me. My phone needed recharging. Mentally I was already locking up the shop. We'd go out the back way. There was a yard at the back and a locked gate.

'I had a customer.'

'Thank you for the food. It was a kind thought.' I pressed a brown ten pound note into her hand. 'You'd better go, Doris. Don't say a word to anyone. You've got my mobile number. Please phone.'

Doris went quickly. She had left her shop unattended. Business was not that great this end of town.

'Are we closing?' said Maddy, still on her tuna sandwich.

'No more customers this time of the afternoon. No one shops this late. We might as well pack up. Doris has done some shopping for us. We'll go out the back way.'

'Why?'

'I've already locked and bolted the front. Get your things. I'd like to go now.'

'What's the hurry?'

'Don't ask, Maddy.'

Maddy caught the degree of urgency in my voice but was not dismayed. She followed me out the back way; watched me locking the back door and then the back gate.

'This is all very cloak and dagger,' she said. 'Has something happened that I don't know about?'

'I don't know. DCI James phoned. He said we ought to get back to the flat.'

'Perhaps he'd like a game of Scrabble.'

'That's probably it.'

We walked fast. I was glad I had not brought the wasp. I took short cuts through the narrow twittens. I knew every one like a smuggler of old. Their ghosts clapped their hands at my ingenuity. If we were being followed, we'd have lost them by now.

I didn't even go in the front entrance of the flat but made Maddy walk up the twisting car ramps of the multi-storey to the car park and then unlock the door to the stairway to the flats. We could have been one of many shoppers, walking up to collect any car, parked on any level.

'I love your flat even more and more,' she said. 'Two different ways of getting in and out. That's cool.'

The flat was still flooded with the afternoon sunshine. The double-glazed windows acted as solar heating. I wondered what it would be like in the winter. I wondered if I would be around to find out.

Maddy went straight to the bathroom and I heard the shower on full blast.

I hoped the water was still hot. I only used economy heating at night for the immersion heater.

I locked every door, front and back onto the balcony.

As Margaret Thatcher once said: 'Pennies don't drop from

heaven, they have to be earned on earth.' It seemed appropriate.

I made a big salad for supper, enough veggies for our daily five. We ate on the balcony, bathed in the late warmth, me with a glass of white wine and Maddy with her customary bottle of fizz. I would have rationed her to one a day, but it was an addiction and no way was I her mother. This was Chuck's problem.

She hung over the balcony rail, people watching. I knew what it was like.

The ever-rolling panorama of people walking the seafront, young and old, cycling helmets for the young and motorized chariots for the elderly. Kids were on scooters, dog walkers, runners, strollers, lovers. A moving slice of Latching life.

And there below on the beach, dogs enjoying the freedom of space and, when the tide was far out, horses galloping for miles, their manes and tails streaming. Worm diggers in Wellington boots, finding the bait for their hooks. Seagulls tossing through the flotsam of dead fish from the fishing boats. It was all in the food chain. Everybody had to live.

Maddy turned round from the rail and fixed her eyes on me. 'You don't have many clothes, do you? You keep wearing the same old thing. You need to jazz up your wardrobe.'

It was true. My wardrobe was limited and always had been. Clothes were not my first priority. They never had been. In the force, it was a uniform. Then when I left, it was another uniform. Jeans and a shirt.

'We'll go shopping together tomorrow morning,' Maddy decided. 'I'll find you a few decent things to wear. Nothing showy since you are a detective, but so that when DCI James takes you out, you'll look like decent arm candy.'

I couldn't wait to look like arm candy.

We listened to jazz tapes, played cards, talked till the light faded. I went to bed early, hoping to get a couple of hours' sleep before Chuck arrived. It might be three or four in the morning. The motorway would be fairly empty in the small hours. He might put his foot down.

'Your dad's coming here straight from Wigan,' I told Maddy.

'He'll be here by the morning, I should think.'

'Great,' said Maddy. 'I can show him your shop.' She paused, some manners returning. 'Would that be all right, Jordan?'

'Of course,' I said, hoping that the morning would bring a normal day. I had no idea what was going to happen next. 'He might want to buy some of those old LPs.'

'I spotted a signed Stan Kenton,' said Maddy. She knew more than she let on. 'They are pretty rare.'

'And I've two copies of that particular LP,' I said. 'I will never sell mine. It even has his voice on it, introducing the numbers. An absolute gem.'

Maddy was impressed. 'Perhaps I ought to buy it for my dad.'

'Why don't you take it as today's commission?' I suggested. 'Then you could give it to him as a present. He'd love it.'

I didn't want to let the LP go but I knew Chuck would treasure it. Nor did I want to let Maddy have the painted silk scarf. I was a real meanie some days.

It was nearly 5 a.m. when my entrance bell rang. I switched on the visual and it was Chuck standing there in the foyer. I buzzed him in and told him to take the lift to the top floor.

I wrapped a robe round myself and stood on the walkway outside my door. The night walkway lights were still on. Their time switch didn't think it was morning yet.

Chuck looked knackered. It was a long drive from Wigan. He came in and leaned on the kitchen counter while I made him a hot drink.

'I need a couple of hours' kip,' he said.

'We're a bit short on bedrooms here,' I said. 'But I do have a very comfy sofa, a big three-seater. Plenty of blankets. Maddy is still asleep on the floor, on an air mattress.'

'I'll take the sofa,' said Chuck. 'I've slept on a lot of sofas. All part of the life of a wandering jazz musician.'

Chuck was also on the short side so he might fit. I didn't fit. I would have to lay on my side with my knees bent. I found him a clean pillow and a blanket. My stock of linen was good.

'We'll be off and out of your hair by the morning,' said Chuck.

'I've got Maddy's passport. We are going to put a few thousand miles between us and the UK. Not a nice place to be till they have caught this rotter.'

'Maddy will be sorry. She likes it here.'

'So I've gathered.' He grinned. 'Regards your flat as her second home apparently Could live here forever, she said.'

'Not when we run out of space for her clothes.'

'Could be a problem.'

'So where are you going? The States, Australia, New Zealand?'

He put down his mug. The tea had revived him. 'I think it's better that you don't know. I know I could trust you, but the less you know the better.'

Did he think I was going to be taken hostage and tortured? Did he know something that I didn't?

'I agree,' I said. 'Surprise me when you come back. When DCI James has caught the killer and Maddy is safe again.'

'Thank you for understanding. Maddy is all I have. I have to keep her safe and I am grateful for everything that you have done. Maddy couldn't have had a better bodyguard or better friend.' He took a brown envelope out of an inner pocket and put it on the counter top. 'A little bonus for you,' he said. 'Open it after we have gone.'

We both got a couple more hours of sleep, Chuck flaked out on the sofa. Then Maddy was up, bouncing around, pleased to see her dad, telling him everything she had done. The sun was already up and we had a simple breakfast on the balcony.

'Sorry about the tatty bamboo chairs and the table. Left behind by the last tenant,' I said. Rolls, fruit, cereal and coffee. Simple was the word.

'So pack all your things, sweetheart,' said Chuck. 'We're off on our hols. We deserve a holiday.'

'A holiday? Wow, that's great. Is Jordan coming with us?'

'Not this time. It's just you and me.'

'Where are we going?'

'It's a surprise. I've phoned for a taxi to pick us up in half an hour so you had better get moving. I've parked my car in the multi-storey. I've left it in the long-stay bay and paid for two months. Then we'll be back for when school starts in September. Maybe a new school.'

'What about your instruments?' I asked. 'Your precious trumpets?'

Chuck waved towards an oddly shaped black leather zipped case, on its side in the hallway. 'I never move without them,' he said.

Maddy had forgotten about the shop in the excitement of a holiday with her dad. She flung her clothes back into her suitcase. It would barely shut. In no time the taxi driver rang my entrance bell and it was time for them to go. Maddy gave me a big hug. She was elated with the prospect of a flight to some holiday spot where she could get an all-over tan.

'I'll send you a postcard,' she promised. 'Don't forget that holiday job. I'm coming back.'

'Have a great time,' I said, hugging her back. 'Take care.'

Then they were both gone and the flat was empty. It was barely nine o'clock. The whole day seemed meaningless without Maddy. She had been the centre of my universe for the last week, every moment taken up with keeping her safe.

I stood in the kitchen, looking at the green expanse before me, now bathed in morning sunshine. The fields were dotted with specks of sheep.

Chuck's envelope was tucked behind the tea caddy. I opened it. There was a wedge of ten pound notes. I didn't count them. It seemed too mercenary to count them. Certainly enough to jazz up my wardrobe. And maybe buy new furniture for the balcony.

If I lived long enough.

DCI James seemed to think time was limited.

TWENTY

Now that Maddy had gone, I saw no point in staying in the flat or staying under cover. Maddy had been the target, not me. At least, I thought so. I needed to open my shop and be available for any new clients.

I let the air out of the airbed and put it away in a cupboard. It might come in useful if I ever had another visitor. In no time, all trace of Maddy and Chuck had gone. It took a bit longer to remove Maddy's presence from the bathroom. She had left half of her cosmetics behind. I put them in a bag and stowed them on an empty shelf in the kitchen. Maybe she would come back one day.

I went out of my flat and locked up. For once I felt no waves of vertigo as I walked along the open walkway. It was like a new freedom. I even looked over the rail to check on the wasp. It was still in her parking place. All was well.

There was a lot of activity happening on the beach. Big screens were being erected on the two beach areas either side of the lido, lengths of cabling laid along the pebbles, being secured and covered. Had I missed something?

Then I spotted the scaffolding going up at the end of the pier and another big television screen, facing the shore. Maddy was going to miss the birdman event. She would have loved it. Two days of professional and unprofessional birdmen (and women) launching themselves off the pier in various winged contraptions for the £25,000 prize for the longest flight.

It would be such fun. Hundreds of people were already packed on the beach below. Not an inch of sand to spare. Coastguards were preparing their orange rubberized boat to go out to rescue birdmen who ditched in the water, dragging their flight machines back to the shore. They would be busy.

But I still had to work. I walked to First Class Junk and let myself in. Perhaps I ought to do birdman windows but Maddy's windows were better. There were a few customers, mostly browsing. Another Wade figure went to a good home but that was all. Everyone was on the beach, mopping up the sunshine, waiting for the first contestant.

I decided I might as well shut up shop and join them. I hadn't had a day off or a whole night off for over a week. It would do my mind good to clear it of all the grim clutter and take in some harmless amusement. There would be a police presence, on the lookout for pickpockets and other rogues who thought careless crowds meant good pickings.

There was barely an inch of sand or pebbles to spare on the beach and I only needed a few inches. A scattering of self-sown sea thrift clung to life. Thank goodness for the big screens. At least one got a close-up view of the terror on the contestant's face as he launched himself off the scaffolding and into the air. This moderate easterly wind might carry contestants into range of the prize money.

'Jordan? What are you doing down here?' It was James, in plain clothes, a black T-shirt and washed-out jeans. But his heavy belt gave him away. It was strung with various technological gadgets. I wondered if he had a laser gun.

'I've come to watch the birdmen,' I said. 'But I can hardly see a thing. There are so many people in the way.'

James put his hands on my shoulders and gently turned me round, away from the beach. 'What's that up there, perched in the air, facing the sea? Nineteen feet of what can you see?'

It was the block of flats where I lived and on the top floor, the fourth, my flat with its nineteen-foot balcony. My balcony. A pigeon was sitting on the rail, gazing down at massed humanity.

'You've got your own view, free apart from the rent, hot and cold running food and drink, a chair with a cushion. I'll even lend you my binoculars.'

I had forgotten all about my new flat. I thought I was still living in those two backstreet bedsits where the shingle was an imaginary front garden, the sea my pond, the sky my heaven.

'I'm an idiot,' I agreed.

'And maybe Roger Cody is here, among the crowds. He doesn't know that Maddy has gone. He might recognize you and that would not be in the interests of your safety. I'll see you back to your flat.'

I gave up my whole one foot square of brown pebbles and a family immediately grabbed the space and set up their territorial signs. James steered me through the crowds, the sun bleating down, hot and relentless. Unprotected skin was already beginning to redden and burn. The St John's Ambulance volunteers were going to be busy.

I punched in the code for the front entrance. James already knew it. I did not want to let him go. 'Would you like to join me for supper this evening? Something simple on the forgotten balcony? I could rustle up spaghetti or a salad.'

He nodded. 'I'll bring the wine. Don't open your door to anyone.'

'Except you.'

'Except me.'

'You need a hat.'

James unfolded a black peaked cap from a back pocket and put it on. He looked like someone from a Mafia gangster film. 'Thanks for reminding me.'

The view from my balcony was amazing. I was up above everyone and I could still read the television screens. James's binoculars were terrific. If I wanted to make loads of money, I could have sold seats for a tenner a day, fifteen with refreshments. The balcony would take at least ten people before it collapsed under the weight. Note: money-making idea for next year. This could be the start of a big business venture.

A sun hat was essential. I had to root through several bags before I found mine. I had not unpacked even half of my stuff. No wonder Maddy thought my wardrobe needed jazzing up. She had only seen the current regulars.

It was so civilized on the balcony. I took out a tray with celery, radishes, nuts and some fresh water and settled to watch the display of nerves and ingenuity. There were standard winged gliders of different sizes and designs as well as crazy flying beds, tea trolleys, prams and a bicycle with wings. The contestants fell into the sea with regular monotony. I clapped each contestant as they were helped ashore and laughed along with the crowd though no one could see me.

It was a great afternoon, relaxing and healing, plus the bonus of James coming to supper. I would need to do a quick shop downstairs at the supermarket. Shopping list: three different kinds of cheese, garlic, lettuce and tomatoes, cook-in red pepper sauce, herbs, paper napkins and a pot of fresh flowers. I was pulling out all the stops for this man.

I took the safety catch off the door and started to unlock it but the key wouldn't turn. I tried several times, different angles, different twists, different hands, both hands. The key was jammed in the lock. I couldn't get out.

There was no point in shouting.

The number of the local Dial-A-Hubby was on my essential list no girl should move without. But the hubby had switched off his mobile. He was probably sitting on the beach, his bald patch going red. This did not merit a 999 call. A jammed lock would be classed as frivolous. I would have to wait till James arrived. Supper would be on the plain side. Would radish and cheese spaghetti pass as gourmet?

I made a fruit salad, laid the balcony table, washed my face and put on a clean T-shirt and waited. And waited. The crowds were drifting off the beach. I could smell the aroma from portable barbecues. Youngsters were staying on to party into the night. They'd brought sausages, loud music, swimsuits and a lot of cans.

By eight o'clock I'd finished the nuts and decided to phone

James. I didn't know where he was. He could be out on some emergency.

'Hi, James,' I said. 'Supper on the balcony? Remember?'

There was a pause. 'You cancelled. I got a message.'

I shook my head. 'No, I didn't cancel. I didn't send any message. I've been waiting here, except that I can't get out.'

'What do you mean?'

'My lock is jammed. I can't turn the key. I needed to do some shopping but it's probably too late now. Maybe there's still some supermarket open—'

James interrupted me urgently. 'Don't touch the key, Jordan. Don't try to open your door. It could be booby-trapped.'

'What do you mean?'

'There may be a device fixed to your door. With some explosive. If you open the door, it will blow up in your face.'

It was a very long evening. I hoped James was wrong. If he was right, then the killer knew where I lived, knew which was my car. We were both sitting targets and I was more concerned for the wasp than myself. I had already lost my ladybird. I couldn't bear to lose another car.

I played some jazz but I wasn't in the mood for music. I wasn't in the mood for anything.

Even most of the beach barbeques had gone home before James arrived. He brought with him a squad of men wearing flak jackets. I watched from my kitchen window, ignoring James who waved me away.

A bomb expert, geared up in protective clothing, helmet and goggles, was peering at the door lock. He looked up, grinned, pushed up the visor of his helmet.

'Blu-Tack,' he said.

Someone had stuffed Blu-Tack into my door lock. Not exactly a high explosive but weird, to say the least. The expert cleaned out the door lock with a probe and nodded to me. The key turned and the door opened.

No explosion. Shreds of blue sticking to the key. That

threatening note had been fixed to the hotel door with Blu-Tack. Not exactly a vital clue.

The whole squad came in, searched the miniscule flat, planted themselves around on the balcony, ate the fruit salad, radishes, celery and nuts. I opened my last packet of biscuits. James followed with the bottle of wine but he kept it discreetly hidden.

'Okay,' he said. 'False alarm but it could have been worse. Home now, boys. Debrief tomorrow.'

I was shattered. Blu-Tack was not exactly high explosive nor was it friendly.

'It was a warning,' said James. 'He's not sure about you.'

'I'm not sure about anything,' I said.

'I'm staying here tonight. Is that all right with you?'

Not exactly the invitation of a lover but I had to agree to second best. James opened the bottle of wine and we sat on the balcony eating whatever was left of Doris's shopping. I didn't care what I ate. I unpacked a box of glass and china and washed my two nineteenth-century twisted-stem wine glasses. They were too beautiful to sell in my shop. The cut glass shone in the moonlight. The glasses made any supermarket wine into a special drink.

The night air was balmy. The nightclub at the end of the pier was flashing neon lights to announce that they were open. Mini-skirted girls were streaming along the pier, hoping to meet the love of their life at a disco.

'Don't you wish you were young again?' I said.

'I don't remember ever being young.'

'I love dancing.'

'I never learned to dance.'

I tried not to remember hearing about the tragedy of his wife and children. DCI James had suffered more than any human should suffer, yet had carried on working, determined to solve crimes.

'I am only going to say this once,' I said, 'but I admire the way you have carried on. It can't have been easy. It shows how much courage you have.'

'It wasn't courage,' said James. 'It was necessity or I would have gone mad. I think I did go mad, for a while. Work was my only distraction.' He stood up, yawning. 'Where shall I sleep?'

It was a tempting question. 'There are four options,' I said, keeping my voice practical and steady. 'You could sleep on the floor but it would be extremely hard. You could sleep on the sofa but you are rather too long for it. You could blow up the air mattress which takes a lot of puffing. Or you could sleep with me. A bit of a tight fit but possibly the most comfortable option.'

I didn't dare look at him. It was the most brazen thing I had ever said to James over the years. He might be shocked or he might be laughing at me.

'The fourth option is easily the most inviting,' said James, not letting me see his eyes. 'But a tight fit needs a special occasion so I'll pass on that one and start blowing up your airbed. Where do you keep it?'

I hid my disappointment but I understood about it having to be a special occasion. Any closeness with James would have to be special.

I got out the airbed, put another clean pillowcase on a spare pillow, found a sheet and the sleeping bag. I was almost asleep in the fourth option before James had finished blowing up the airbed. I listened to his breathing and the blowing slowing down. He might have given up and made do with semi-inflation. At least I felt safe with James in the next room, my door left slightly ajar.

My dreams should have been all about James but instead I found myself jumping off the scaffolding at the end of the pier. My wasp had sprouted wings and took me far out to sea before ditching in the water. I gasped as the water rushed over my head and into my mouth.

The coastguard dingy was racing out to rescue me, bouncing on the waves. 'Save my wasp, save my wasp!' I shouted but they couldn't hear me.

I woke up with a start, the words still on my lips. Dawn was filtering through the drawn curtains. I could hear quiet activity in the kitchen, water being drawn from the tap, cupboard doors opening and shutting. Someone finding their way about a strange room.

James knocked on my door and came in with two mugs of hot tea. He put one on the bedside table and sat on the end of my bed, holding the other. He looked at home, relaxed even, with stubble on his chin and wearing a creased T-shirt and boxer shorts.

'I learned something interesting last night,' he said.

I struggled to sit up and still look decent. 'Oh, what was that?'

'You talk in your sleep.'

'What was I saying?'

'Save my wasp. I think the word was wasp.'

I relaxed. No intimate secret revealed. 'So now you know. My car is special.'

He sighed elaborately. 'And I hoped I was special.'

'Second best to a car,' I said. I wasn't going to tell him first thing in the morning when my teeth needed cleaning.

TWENTY-ONE

Breakfast together on a balcony in clear morning sunshine is almost perfection even when you haven't slept with the man you love. The beach had been washed clean by the tide. The council refuse collectors were emptying the bins and sweeping the promenade. Gulls were swooping down to finish up picnic crumbs.

I found a carton of overlooked eggs from Doris and scrambled them. There were some stale cream crackers which I crisped up in the microwave. James made coffee.

'An unusual but acceptable breakfast,' said James, carrying the tray out onto the balcony. 'Have you got any tomato sauce?'

'No, sorry. No time for shopping yet. You'll have to force yourself to do without.'

'I could almost move in with you,' he said casually, buttering a cracker. But he was looking far out to sea.

'I could almost take that as a compliment,' I said. 'But I know that you are tempted by the view from the balcony, not my delectable charms.'

'Your charms are considerable, I'll grant you that. But the balcony wins, every time. Hands down.'

His phone rang. He answered it. He nodded, quickly scrapping up the last of his scrambled egg. 'OK, thanks. I'll be there in ten minutes. SOC on their way? Good.'

He ended the call and swallowed the last of his coffee. 'Sorry, Jordan. I've got to go. They've found an abandoned motorbike with blood on it. It might belong to the man we want. Don't answer the door to anyone, Jordan. Don't go out. I'll be back for you. Pack a bag.'

This is what it would be like, what it would always be like. Policemen's wives, partners, girlfriends, they all had to get used to sudden departures, long absences. It came with the job.

I didn't watch him go or do that female waving thing. He had to feel unencumbered. I was not a ball and chain. Breakfast on the balcony was some compensation. I could imagine that he was still sitting opposite me.

Why had James told me to pack a bag? Were we off on a jolly holiday? No, he was probably taking me to a safe house. I hoped it wasn't that one in Brighton, where I had escaped by jumping out of the bedroom window.

My rucksack didn't take much but I managed to squeeze in a torch, wire, string, a candle, matches, screwdriver and scissors. They might come in handy. All wrapped up in a couple of T-shirts, some clean underwear, socks and the perennial, now boring, fleece.

I was washing up, dreamily gazing at God's green-hilled country, when a delivery man walked past to another flat. He was carrying a large pizza box. Pizza for breakfast? I had not met my next-door neighbours yet. I had not met any of my neighbours.

There was an urgent knock on my door. 'Breakfast delivery!' someone shouted. I opened the door.

'Sorry, I didn't order any breakfast,' I said.

'Oh yes you did, sister,' said the delivery man. He pushed the door open, the plates balanced on the flat of his hand. A touch of work experience. I should have known immediately and slammed the door shut but I was too slow. It was the waiter from the Whyte Cliffside Hotel. Carlos, the one with a string bracelet on his wrist. The one we thought might be Roger Cody.

'No, I didn't,' I said, leaning hard on the door. But he was stronger.

He threw the breakfast on the kitchen counter and grabbed me by the hair. He had a penknife – no, it was a palette knife – in his hand, the flat cold blade hard against the side of my neck.

I decided not to struggle. I needed my neck.

'You're coming with me,' he said. 'Don't make any trouble. Walk normally.'

'I need my inhaler,' I whispered. 'I've got asthma. I could die.'

'Get it. Be quick,' he said, following me, hand still grasping my hair, knife on my neck.

I bent sideways and picked up my rucksack. He didn't check its contents, wanting to make a fast exit. He pushed me along the walkway. None of my neighbours were visible. They were probably out shopping or already on their balconies, waiting for the second day of the birdman competition to start. I wondered where he was taking me and if he was indeed Roger Cody, the art teacher from Sarah's school. It would be better if I pretended not to know.

'This is very silly,' I said as we got into the lift. 'Why are you doing this? I don't know you. Who are you? You don't know me.'

'Shut up. You know too much.'

Could I make a dash for it when we reached the pavement outside the supermarket? The crowds would already be massing for the stampede onto the beach. No one had won the £25,000 prize yesterday so competition would be strong.

But the lift stopped with a rattle, doors opening. We were not at the ground floor, we were only at the second floor. I saw the flashing light on the second button. He pushed me back along the familiar walkway, which was only a few feet higher than the car parking area. My wasp was parked on the other side. I barely glanced at her. She was safe.

He put a key into a front door and kicked it open, then pushed me inside. The flat was empty. It was completely empty. Not a stick of furniture. Nothing at all. Only a rather unpleasant orange patterned carpet on the floor and a sense of stale air everywhere.

'I hope you will feel at home here,' he said. 'It's a replica of your flat two floors up but none of the home comforts. I have heard of your reputation for escaping so I am going to make sure that this time you don't. You are going to stay here until I have no need of you. Meanwhile, Jordan Lacey, you will be a very useful bargaining factor.'

He was tying me up with window cord. No point in struggling with that palette knife on my neck. Hands behind my back. Ankles tied together and laced behind to my wrists. I lay on the floor in a strung-up, bowed position. It was extremely uncomfortable.

I was able to take a good look at him. He was in his mid thirties. Dark tousled hair, no longer gelled down, waiter-style. Slim build. Long, slim fingers. String bracelet. He fitted the description of Roger Cody and the drunk at the gig. And there was no doubt of his identity at the hotel.

'What about my mushroom omelette? It was always so good.'

'Not today, lady. You're back on a strict diet.'

'This is a waste of time,' I said in a reasonable voice. 'Let me go and I'll pretend that this has never happened. Be sensible.'

'I'm very sensible,' he said. 'Don't you know that yet? Elsie Dunlop recognized me and so did the wife of that steward, the overweight pig farmer. And look what happened to them. I suggest you keep quiet.'

'I need some water,' I gasped.

'Plenty in the tap,' he said, putting a strip of duct tape across my mouth.

I heard the door slam shut and a key turning. I was two floors below my own flat. I supposed this one was for sale or between rentals. No one would come house-hunting today while the birdman was on. And an estate agent would have difficulty explaining my presence.

The carpet was not dirty but the awful colour was an eyesore. I rolled over so that the view changed. It was exactly the same size as my sitting room but the loud patterned wallpaper was as bad as the carpet. The blinds had been pulled down so the room was in semi-gloom. I couldn't even see the birdman.

Roger Cody had forgotten about my rucksack. I'd hung onto it but dropped it behind a door as he opened it and pushed me into the sitting room. My shoulders felt as if they were being pulled out of their sockets as the cord tightened between my ankles and my wrists.

Moving my legs made the traction worse but salvation lay in that rucksack and I had to get to it. I could hear the crowds below cheering and clapping as another contestant ditched into the sea. How could they all be down there enjoying themselves, when I was only a few hundred yards away, trussed up like a turkey and dying for a drink?

I dragged out the rucksack from behind the door and unfastened the two straps with my fingers which could move. It was not easy but it worked. I felt around for the shape of the scissors and pulled them out. Somehow I had to saw through the window cord with an open blade. Window cord is tough stuff and they were only ordinary nail scissors.

I sawed for ten thrusts then took ten deep breaths. It was a way of conserving energy. Window cord is made up of separate strands. I teased them out separately, a single slender strand being easier to saw through.

Suddenly the cord strung between my ankles and my wrists tore and snapped. The relief was exquisite as I could stretch out my legs at last. They were hurting like mad. I lay on the floor, breathing heavily. I shuffled over to a wall and somehow sat myself upright, legs outstretched. Sitting up was a relief but there was no way I could get my bonded wrists that were tied behind me to the front of me. My legs were too long to buckle up and contort like a gymnast.

I still had the scissors so went back into the saw and breathing rhythm again. It was a fraction easier with the wall behind me acting as a board. I was tiring and it seemed to take hours. But then the cord broke and my wrists were free. It was a moment of triumph. My head fell forward. My wrists were bleeding where the scissors had sawed skin instead of cord.

I tore the tape off my mouth. That hurt. It took off skin and hairs. A depilatory job without moisturiser and painkillers.

Now this was easier as I could see what I was doing. The

scissors snipped away at the ankle cords, severing strand after strand. The crowds were still cheering below on the beach, enjoying themselves. I had no idea of the time. I didn't have an inner clock like Jack Reacher.

Then the last cords gave way. I sat, leaning against the wall, trying to plan what to do next. Finding more energy would help.

Once my ankles felt liberated, I tried to stand up but I couldn't balance. All my muscles had gone to jelly. I crawled into the kitchen, opening cupboards for anything: a mug, a pot, a saucer. There was nothing. I used the cupboard doors to pull myself up onto my feet and turned on the tap. I let the water run for a few minutes, then cupped my hand and drank furiously. Water had never tasted so good. Doris would be pleased if I lost weight.

I took stock of my position. No phone. It was still charging in my flat. I needed to be prepared if Roger Cody returned. And somehow I had to get a message out for help.

I tore down all the blinds from their window fitments and jammed them against the front door. There was no tape, no nails, no way to fix them, but their size was some kind of obstacle. I cut off the window cords and tied them from bathroom door handle to kitchen cupboard door handles very tight, making a criss-cross maze. A crazy spider's web. I could duck under them but if Roger managed to get in, it would delay him. More cord went from open door of linen cupboard to sitting room door handle. Another hurdle.

There was no way of getting out onto the balcony. The door had been locked and the key removed. I doubted if I could break the double-glazed glass with my bare hands. No furniture to hurl through it. My rucksack wouldn't even dent it.

They had left behind the shower curtain. It had a grotesque pattern of frogs on it. The bathroom suite was that avocado green that went out of fashion years ago. I tore down the shower curtain and hung it from the bathroom light to the hallway light. It might fall down and envelop anyone trying to come in. Worth a try.

More water. I would certainly lose weight at this rate. I slowed down and went through the flat, inch by inch, to see if anything had been left behind. There was nothing, nothing at all, not even a roll of toilet paper.

So all I had was my rucksack and my few items for emergency. I could wave the torch at the window but who would see it? The birdmen were still launching themselves off the scaffolding. I could try to unscrew the lock plate but the screws were on the other side of the door. I could set fire to the place with the candle and matches but not exactly a sensible move. Besides it might spread and my flat was two floors higher.

I was free to curl up on the floor now, in any position that was marginally comfortable, and think. This thinking had better be one hundred per cent dynamite thoughts. Roger Cody might be back any time. I was determined not to be victim number four.

My rucksack was useful as a pillow. I thought through its contents. How could I attract attention and get help?

I switched the torch on and stood at the window, waving it, flashing SOS in Morse Code. The current birdman was one of the best. He flew quite a way, skimming low over the waves, strapped to his contraption, before nose-diving into a trough. No one was looking up at the window. A cheer went up as he came ashore, dripping, dragging his soggy flying machine.

I started knocking on the walls of the flats on either side. Someone must be in. They might be sitting on their balconies but surely they needed a drink, or ice, or the bathroom at some time. I staggered from the kitchen to the bathroom opposite and back again, knocking on the walls. But the insulation must be good. No one knocked back or shouted at me to pack it in.

This second floor was alien territory. I knew no one. They might all be empty or between rentals. The owners might be crowd haters and at this very moment walking in the peace and quiet of the South Downs, or having lunch in the garden of an inland country pub.

The thought of pub food sent waves of hunger through me. I cupped my hands and drank more water. There must be something I could do to attract attention.

I tipped out the rucksack. The packing had been rushed

and without much thought apart from some emergency items, which were currently being of little use. Two T-shirts, one black, one blue. Some clean underwear. Pair of socks. Toothbrush and toothpaste.

I laid out the T-shirts on the ghastly carpet and cut up all the side seams and across the necks. Fond farewell to T-shirts. I am committing you to a far, far better fate. So now I had four quite large pieces of material. My drawing skills are not Royal Academy standard but I can spell. Each of the four pieces was cut carefully into a capital letter, as large as possible.

I would use the sitting-room window as it was the biggest. No glue or tape, only the piece of duct tape Roger had put across my mouth. Toothpaste had a certain adhesive quality. It might last but the sun was now beating through the double glazing and the room was becoming unbearably hot.

Candle grease? It might work. I had no idea and nothing else. I lit the candle and mixed toothpaste and candle grease together on the working top with the toothbrush handle.

I cut the duct tape carefully into four pieces and fixed the top of each letter high up on the window. Then I used my home-made glue to attach various parts of the letters so that one word was spelled out across the window pane.

There was some glue left over so I glued each sock on to the bedroom window and with my mascara drew in the dot under-neath in the form of an exclamation mark.

People in plane crashes had done this. People marooned on the top of snowy mountains. They had found something . . . pebbles, sand, wood, boulders, anything, to spell out the word that was universal. SOS.

H E L P ! ! said my window message.

It had been exhausting. What else could I do? Ninety-nine per cent of the sunburnt population of Latching would think it was a joke. There was only one person in the world who would take it seriously and I had no idea where he was.

James was working. A motorbike with blood on it? It could be a ruse.

TWENTY-TWO

There was only one more thing I could do with what was left of my home-made glue. I poked some of the stuff into the keyhole of the front door with the handle of the toothbrush, as Cody had filled my keyhole with Blu-Tack. Maybe it would slow him down if or when he came back.

I took my one and only lipstick and wrote *Help* on the kitchen window in large raspberry-coloured letters. Then added *Call 999* underneath. But I had little hope of anyone seeing it. No one had walked past on the walkway all day.

There was nowhere to sit. I didn't want to stand for hours, watching the birdmen. My appetite for spectacle had gone. I propped myself against a wall and wrapped the fleece round my legs. They were still aching. I might have to wait a long time.

How long could a person survive without food or water? I didn't know. I had unlimited water so that gave me a few days. Roger might be planning to leave me here to rot. I'd heard of plane survivors eating strange things like wood and grass and berries. There was nothing here except the revolting carpet. If I was vigilant, I might catch a spider or two. You can live on insects. They contain protein.

I tried the light switches but the electricity had been cut off. No chance of flashing them on and off once it got dark. Some idiots would think it was a private disco party and walk on by.

I might eat the left-over bits of T-shirt material. Cotton must be edible. It's a plant after all. Then I could chew on my rucksack even if it ruined my teeth. I could still clean my teeth. That was an encouraging and hygienic thought.

Two discoveries cheered me up immensely. I found some paper lining the bedroom drawers. They smelt of mothballs but paper is edible. Spies swallowed secret messages in films, and lovers chewed up illicit letters. In the fitted wardrobe I found a dry cleaner's wire hanger. This could be a weapon of sorts.

It took me some time to untwist the wire and bend it into a holdable blade shape with a double hook on the end. Not exactly lethal but it might inflict some nasty damage if I aimed the hook at his face.

The cheering from the beach had died down. It was all over. People were packing up to go home. Whoever had won was going to celebrate at the nearest pub and have his photo taken for the local paper, waving the cheque.

Soon no one would be able to see my message in the window. I began walking up and down, shining the torch behind the letters. Someone might notice this erratic behaviour and report it.

I drank more water, ignoring the hunger. Chewing the paper would start at dawn tomorrow. The mothball taste might have evaporated.

It was growing dark. The streets lights had come on and the string of swinging fairy lights that were strung between each lamp post. Kids were throwing stones at them. Flags were flapping from a south-westerly direction. The nightclub was festooned with blinking on-and-off lights. My torch was poor competition and the beam was getting weaker.

The candle would not last long either and I had no way of carrying it, or protecting the flame. I contrived a candle holder with the toothpaste lid, screwdriver and rags. It was the best I could do.

I paced the HELP circuit till the flame gutted and hot wax fell on the T-shirt rags protecting my hand. No more light. The only light came up from the yellow street lamps. There was nothing I could burn. No books (sorry, all you striving authors), no junk mail, no bills.

A few hours' sleep would help restore my energy, with my rucksack as a pillow, fleece as shoulder warmth, carpet as a mattress. It was more soothing when the colour was lost in the gloom. I dozed off, ignoring the hunger.

A series of loud bangs woke me up. It sounded like some sort of manual work going on. I peered through the balcony window. Several lorries were lined up in the street, unloading fresh goods for the supermarket below, huge containers being trundled inside on wheels.

I waved frantically but who was going to look up when they had limited parking time and several tons of stuff to unload? I banged on the window but they were making more noise than I was.

It was barely dawn. I could only guess the time, somewhere between six and seven o'clock. The sky was streaked with layers of light creeping over the horizon. It was beautiful, as always. Maybe I could catch another hour of sleep. I looked forward to breakfast. A paper sandwich and cold water flavoured with rust.

Another series of loud bangs woke me. Someone was trying to get in. The front door was shaking. I crawled under my web trap of cross-hatched window cord and into the bedroom and shut myself into the fitted wardrobe, my wire clothes hanger weapon at the ready.

I was trembling; tried to freeze my limbs or the sound would give me away. But if he got in and found me, I was ready to put up a fight. The hooked ends would cause some damage. Might even take an eye out: a nasty thought but I would fight for my life.

I heard the front door give way and come crashing in. Then I heard muffled oaths as my spider's web of window cord and shower curtain slowed down whoever was coming in. Footsteps stomped into the flat. It was more than only Roger Cody. Had he brought along some of his mates to deal with me?

I held my breath, hoping they would think I had fled, got out somehow. Then the wardrobe door was flung open and I launched myself at the intruder. He was masked and helmeted, like something from Spiderman, but I clawed at him just the same, ripping the fabric.

'Hold on, miss. Calm down. Police. We're friends.'

I did not know the voice. I did not believe him for one instant. Launch number two was a panic attack. If I could get out of the flat, I could run along the walkway, jump over the wall and into the car park, get lost in the multi-storey, then hide behind some 4x4 till the owner arrived and could drive me away.

It seemed a good plan at the time. But I missed my chance.

Two men were holding me, firmly but gently, prising the coat hanger from my stiffened fingers. I then recognized the navy flak jackets, the helmets, the goggles, and the array of gadgets strung along their belts. Their battering ram lay on the floor.

'Are you the police?' I gasped. 'Have you rescued me? I was being held prisoner. A hostage. I must get out before he kills me.'

'That's right, miss. You're safe now but we want you to come along to the station and make a statement.'

I still didn't trust them. They could be anybody, dressed up.

'Who told you I was here?' Not exactly a fluent question.

There was movement at the door.

'It was me, Jordan. I was opening up the arcade and happened to glance up towards your new flat. Always like to check where my friends live. Just made out your message, knew it had to be you, that something awful had happened, so I phoned the police.'

It was Jack, unshaven and grinning, the owner of the amusement arcade on the pier. He was beaming with pride. I hugged him, coffee-stained T-shirt and all. Jack, of all people, the owner of the arcade where I had once tackled and captured two robbers. We were quits now.

'Thank you, thank you,' I almost sobbed. 'I thought no one had seen my message. The birdmen and everything.'

'Cost me a bomb, those birdmen. Hardly a soul playing the machines. Until it got dark. Then business perked up. I've brought you some coffee, girl. Thought you might need it.'

It was not a mug of his usual thick brown stewed coffee but

a capped foam beaker from the new take-away cafe that had opened halfway along the pier. Normal cafe coffee taste but it was bliss at this particular moment. Jack offered two packets of sugar and a plastic spoon.

'Thank you, Jack. I need this drink. Bless you.' There were tears in my eyes but I tried not to cry.

Jack strolled through the flat looking at everything. 'Wow, what a place,' he said. 'I might move in. Like the carpet.'

The police car took me to Latching police station. I didn't know these particular officers and they didn't know me. Jack followed in his posh blue Jaguar. He was quite a wealthy man. People lost a lot of money on the machines.

They took a statement from me not in a normal interview room but a room that had status. The status was a potted plant and a picture of Ye Olde Latching fishermen's cottages on a wall. The grey plastic chairs had cushioned seats. As they recorded my story, a chunky cheese and tomato sandwich appeared from the cafeteria. I was in heaven, well, almost. My jaws had forgotten how to work.

'So you are working on the Corfe Castle case in conjunction with DCI James?' They seemed impressed at my connections.

'Yes, it was the same man, Roger Cody. The man that they are tracking down for the original Sarah Patel murder, and maybe for two others.'

'You were very lucky, Miss Lacey. You might have been his next victim.'

'He said he was going to use me as a hostage. Not sure what he meant. But it didn't sound nice. It could have been his intention.'

The police photographer took photos of my wrists and ankles though I had to explain that some of the cuts were self-inflicted with my scissors.

Jack had gone back to his amusement arcade on the pier. He had to open up for the holidaymakers anxious to lose their money. He nodded to me from the door before he left and I tried to smile my thanks. I was not very successful. Shock was setting in.

I wanted to lie down and sleep. I was exhausted by all the energy I had spent on getting myself free and booby-trapping the flat. It had taken its toll.

The door of the interview room opened and DCI James came in. The only man I wanted to see. He looked as tired as I felt. His clothes were dishevelled. He hadn't shaved. It seemed a permanent state these days.

He sat down opposite me and took both my hands, turning them over, looking at the marks on my wrists. The police surgeon had put medicated plasters on my cuts. 'It's all my fault. I should never have left you. I should have known that Roger Cody would come after you. I'm so sorry, Jordan.'

'He said I was a hostage. He was going to bargain me for Maddy.'

'He put a message on Facebook saying just that. He would exchange you for Maddy Peters. He put a time limit and said then he was going to blow you.'

I didn't want to know the details.

'But I'm not on Facebook. I haven't got the time.'

'That's beside the point. He told the world what he wanted. I'm not on Facebook either.'

'So how did you get the message?'

'Detecting is a strange process these days. There's a whole department of experts at Scotland Yard scrolling through Facebook and Twitter and blogs and other social media sites. They have a high level of access. They pick up all sorts of useful things, using a set of coded words. Some people think it's clever to boast on the net about what they have been up to.'

'Can I go back to my flat now and have a shower and go to sleep?'

'It's not safe. I'm taking you back to my room at the Travelodge. I'm not letting you out of my sight for one minute.'

This was hardly the romantic declaration that I would have liked but it would have to do. He steered me out the back exit of Latching police station, the route usually used when taking prisoners to and from court. I was given a blanket and told to hold it over my face as prisoners often did.

There was an unmarked car, not James's Saab, but a dark green Ford Fiesta. He drove to the Travelodge on the seafront and parked outside.

'You'll get a parking ticket,' I said.

'No, I won't. The car will be picked up in a few minutes by the owner who kindly loaned it to me.'

I got out. The pavement felt good. A breath of sea air blew across my face. I wanted to walk the pier. I wanted to walk the promenade.

The reception area was not busy and James put his arm round me and shielded my head against his chest. Another hardly romantic manoeuvre. Perhaps the ratings would improve once we got to his room.

James was booked into the last room at the end of a long white-washed corridor. It was a standard Travelodge bedroom with a duvet-covered double bed and a big settee that would pull out and make another bed. A long polished wood counter housed a hospitality tray and television set and space to write cheques or thank-you letters. A door obviously led to the bathroom. Everything was spotlessly clean and white, with a touch of colour. The duvet and the settee were both cornflower blue.

James drew the long curtains at the tall windows. It was daylight but I had no idea of the time. 'Shower and sleep,' he said. 'No television. If you want a clean T-shirt, take one of mine.'

'Have you got any bras?'

'Sorry, Jordan. Quite forgot to pack any.'

I disappeared into the bathroom. It was all I wanted. Practical and plain, no comparison to the Whyte Cliffside Hotel, but the towels were clean and white, the water hot and the soap miniscule but adequate.

When I came out towel-wrapped, James had made mugs of tea. There were two packets of oatmeal biscuits. He had also put out two clean T-shirts, one white, one navy.

'Thank you,' I said. I wriggled into the white T-shirt. It was as big as a mini-dress. Quite suitable for the current circumstances.

'I'm going to lock you into this room, Jordan. So get some sleep and don't open the door to anyone except me. I will phone in advance of returning here.'

'Aren't you going to stay? You're a bit short of sleep, aren't you?'

'I've been following up Roger Cody leads all night. The bike was his. The blood was from Tom Lucas. His wife is all right but in shock. Cody is as slippery as an eel. But I can't stop now. We're very near to getting him. And you have been a marvellous help, Jordan.'

'My message on the window? Brilliant, wasn't it?'

He nodded and grinned. His face was all I ever wanted to see. 'Pity you put the E the wrong way round. Otherwise it was perfect.'

TWENTY-THREE

I think I was asleep before James was even out of the door. When I awoke some hours later, I could have discovered the time by putting on the television, but that didn't occur to me. My first thought was more tea, wash my hair, more sleep, in that order. It was very therapeutic.

Hunger also came to mind. One cheese sandwich and two oatmeal biscuits were hardly sufficient to nourish a growing girl. I doubted if Travelodge did room service. I could hardly phone out for a pizza. We'd run out of those fiddly little milk cartons so it was black tea and black coffee.

Perhaps a girl would come to 'refresh' the hospitality tray as they so quaintly put it these days. I didn't know that James had put the *Do Not Disturb* sign on the door handle. I didn't dare draw the curtains to see what the world was doing outside. A peek through the merest chink between folds told me that it was high tide and the waves were thrashing the shingle. How I wished I was down there, in my bare feet, letting the cold water trickle through my toes, dodging the unexpected crab.

I put on the television. I needed the time.

The only book to read was a shiny Travelodge brochure extolling the virtues of their chain of hotels. I was halfway through it when I heard a key in the lock and a deep voice.

'It's James. With provisions.'

'Enter James with provisions.'

I was still so scared, I ran to stand behind the door, the remote control of the television in my hand ready to conk any unfamiliar head.

James strolled in and shut the door. He looked at the remote. 'Didn't know you were hooked on the soaps.'

'It's all that pub food,' I said, putting the remote down.

'I promise you a decent pub lunch as soon as this is all over,' he said. 'And it will be over soon. But for the time being, this is the best I can do.'

I pounced on the plastic bag he was carrying in a less than ladylike manner. Food from the Garden of Eden. Some apples, oranges, a ready-made prawn salad, some cheese scones and a packet of butter.

'Unfortunately this is not all for you,' he said, unwrapping the plastic cutlery that came with the salad. 'I bought this lot at your downstairs supermarket while they were fixing the door upstairs.'

'Fixing the door? Which door? Why?'

'The battering ram made a bit of damage. And the flat doesn't belong to Roger Cody. We don't want to be sued. We are also removing all your ingenious entrapments. You certainly had some bright ideas considering the lack of useful items.'

I let the compliment swim over my head. James handed me a fork. He was using the knife to spread butter on the cheese scones.

'Why was it empty? Are all the flats on that floor empty?'

'Everyone has moved out for a month. They are doing some reconstruction work on the balconies. Some of them are showing signs of concrete stress.'

'Is my balcony showing concrete stress?' I was alarmed.

'No, your floor has been tested and is OK. It's only the floor nearest to the supermarket. So, of course, health and safety have moved in.'

'Why did you say it would soon be all over?'

'You know that Cody has been trying to barter your safety for the whereabouts of Maddy Peters? Now since we have no idea where Chuck and his daughter are now, it isn't going to work. So we are guessing that he will either leave you in the second-floor flat to die of hunger, or he will come back to finish you off.'

'Charming.'

'We arranged twice to meet him with false information but he never turned up.'

'Is this supposed to ruin my appetite?'

'Don't talk. Just eat. I haven't much time.'

'So tell me, Detective Chief Inspector James, how is this all going to end, and when?' I nearly added, love of my life, but decided it wasn't appropriate.

'We shall be waiting in the second-floor flat, a couple of officers and myself. We'll set up a trap. As soon as Roger Cody enters, we shall arrest him. And we'll have men not just in the flat. I shall have men in the car park and on the stairs, near the lift. End of story.'

The tiny pink prawn from Thailand or wherever was delicious but my brain was still working. I'd read something about the eating habits of prawns.

'Cody will know it's a booby trap. He'll smell it a mile off. That man is not stupid. There has to be some evidence that it's not a trap, and I suppose that evidence is me. I have to be still there, on the floor, strung up, as he left me. Otherwise he won't come in. Come on, James, you know that's right. You have to have bait.'

'This is not how it's planned.'

'Re-plan it. I know what I'm talking about.'

'You are not going to be involved.'

'Then he'll run. One look at an empty flat and he'll be off on his motorbike, conveniently parked on the other side of the wall.'

'No way. We've got the motorbike. We have the car park under surveillance. He can't get in or out.'

'Supposing he's already there, watching you?'

'All our men are in plain clothes. Cleaners, collecting rubbish, the postman.'

'He could be two floors up, in my flat.' The thought gave me cold shivers. I would have to move out. I could not bear to live there. He might have trashed the place.

'Don't worry, Jordan,' said James, reading my mind, as he often did. 'Your flat is safe and secured. Nothing has been touched. We found the door open and an empty pizza box. There is a constable on duty outside, making sure he doesn't return. Cody would expect us to put a watch on your flat.'

'Thank you,' I said weakly, spearing another prawn. 'But you do need me if he is to walk into your trap. He needs to see me where he left me, trussed up on the floor.'

'No way.'

'I don't need to be tied up; just a bit of window cord artistically arranged so that it looks as if I'm tied up. You know it makes sense, James.'

James finished the other cheese scone. He obviously liked them. Perhaps I should learn the recipe. It couldn't be too difficult. Besides, I had a proper kitchen now. I ought to be able to do proper cooking.

He was on his phone. 'Save a few bits of that window cord,' he was saying. 'Put them in the linen cupboard, out of sight. I'll be along as soon as it gets dark. After the last rendezvous.'

'What rendezvous?' I asked.

'No more questions. Get some sleep, sleepy-head. It might be a long night.'

It was growing dark before James came back for me. He was holding another carrier bag but he kept it out of my reach. He was turning into a domestic shopper.

'This is to stave off our midnight starvation,' he said. 'Time to go.'

'Am I to be the bait then?'

He flinched. He would not look at me. 'Don't make me change my mind.'

I grabbed my few possessions and packed them in the plastic liner of the bathroom waste bin. Somehow my rucksack had gone the way of old rucksacks with my clean underwear.

'How am I going to get out of here without being seen?'

'There's a staff back entrance. We'll use that.'

'Then?'

'We'll walk along the front like any other couple out on a date. Romantic, carefree, eyes only for each other.' It sounded too good to be true.

This was a totally new side of DCI James. 'Can you do romantic and carefree?' I asked.

'I've been practising.'

I hoped not with the Gorgon. Then I remembered Tom Lucas and was stricken with remorse. He had been such a pleasant man. He didn't deserve such an awful death. Still, maybe he had been with his beloved pigs and he had saved his wife. That might have been some measure of comfort.

'Let's go catch him,' I said, unable to keep the bitterness out of my voice.

The cool night air was bliss on my unmoisturised face. James had pushed a cap on my head that hid my giveaway tawny plaited hair. I tucked my arm into his, swinging the bathroom plastic bag on the other. Our thighs touched occasionally. I could have walked forever, say at least to Hove and back.

'Is this carefree enough?' I asked.

'You're doing fine,' he said.

'When do we get to the romantic bit?'

'How about now?'

He turned and kissed me, a sort of light but meaningful kiss. Nothing chaste about it but also not overly passionate. It was acceptable for a street-side kiss, not in broad daylight, but in growing darkness. I could see a crescent moon. It was supposed to be lucky to see the new moon but I had no money to turn over.

'We'll have to assume the eyes only for each other bit now,' he said, drawing away. He sounded a bit breathless. I remembered past days when he had rescued me. Did he know how much I cared for him? 'If we are to keep walking.'

'Not easy without genuine practice,' I said.

'Needs time.'

'Lots of time.'

We had reached the front entrance to the flats. There was

a tramp lighting a cigarette, leaning against the supermarket railing. Across the road was a courting couple waiting at the 700 bus stop. Some youngsters were playing ball on the beach. Several cars were in the nearby parking spaces.

They all looked like coppers to me.

James keyed in the door code and showed me into the lift. A cleaner in green overalls was vacuuming the foyer carpet. She had a box of cleaning materials.

'Overtime?' said James.

'Overtime,' she said, biting back the *sir*.

We went to the second floor. Now I was getting the jitters. Supposing Cody was already there, waiting to pounce? James had me firmly by the arm.

'Don't let me down now, Jordan,' he said quietly. 'We can't put the lights on. Everywhere will be dark, only the light from the street below. But you are not alone. You are in no danger. No vertigo. Be brave.'

The door had been repaired where they had battered in the lock. The police had obtained a set of keys from the leasing agents. James used one of these now to let us in. Then he locked the door behind us. I was beginning to shake. I was terrified.

'Come and meet the gang,' he said.

The small bedroom was crowded. Three men, all police officers, were sitting on the carpet, trying to play cards by street light. It was not easy. They were wearing flak jackets. Helmets and guns and a pile of other stuff were on the floor.

'Hi,' said James, keeping his voice down low. 'This is Jordan, heroine of the hour, about to re-enact her ordeal. Give her space, try not to frighten her, reassure her of our protection.' He turned to me. 'Are you feeling better now?'

They stood up, all tough young men, nodding, shaking my hand. I was very reassured. James put the food down on the floor.

'We shall be next door in the original hostage room. Half of this food is for you, half for us. Take your choice. Use the bathroom only when necessary and silently. I want no noise or movement whatsoever. Cody may come back any time.'

'Right, guv.' It was a whisper.

James found the bits of rescued window cord coiled onto a shelf of the linen cupboard. He also had the police blanket which had shrouded me when I left the station yesterday. Was it yesterday? I had no idea of the day or the time. Had life once been that easy? Had I listened to jazz half the night, walked Maddy back to the hotel from parties? Had we played shop, lost money at the amusement arcade? It was all a dream.

I showed James how Cody had tied me. Wrists together behind my back, ankles together, then the two joined by another excruciatingly painful cord laced between them. It had a name but I didn't know what it was.

'Not really tying you up,' he whispered into my ear, winding cord round wrists and ankles, separately and loosely. 'You will only need to look as if they are strung up behind your back.'

'There's no electricity,' I said.

'The street lighting is enough to illuminate the room if he comes back now. I reckon he'll wait till dawn when the supermarket deliveries make all that racket. Here's some apple juice for you and some blueberry muffins if you get hungry in the night. You're into healthy food, aren't you?'

'Got to keep healthy.'

James folded the blanket under my head, then to make things even more perfect, he lay beside me like a spoon, sharing the end of the blanket, one arm holding me, as if making sure no one was ever going to touch me again. I could have stayed that way forever.

It was not the most romantic of nights but it would have to do. I know James left me a couple of times to go into the bedroom, checking that if two of the back-up slept, one kept awake. He used his phone in the bathroom, which was the most insulated room as far as light and noise were concerned.

Everything and everyone were in place. We only had to wait.

'Not long now,' he whispered into my ear, curling up beside me. 'You are being very brave. Nothing will happen to you. We are all here.'

'I don't want to die.'

'You aren't going to die. I promised you a pub lunch. I'm looking forward to it. We'll have a great time.'

Dawn began its icy-fingered advance. No blinds hung at the windows. Would Cody notice that the blinds had gone? It wouldn't matter if he did. He was walking into a trap.

James stretched out his long legs on the floor. 'Damned hard floor,' he groaned. 'Ghastly orange carpet.' He stood up and put the carrier bag behind the door. He removed the blanket. 'Sorry, it has to go,' he said. That went behind the door, too.

Then he arranged me on the floor, like a doll, so that Cody would see me the moment he came into the sitting room, facing him, but he would not see that my wrists and ankles were not joined or tied up.

James gave me a drink of juice, taking it away afterwards and putting it on the floor, out of sight.

'Whatever happens, keep still. He must not know that you are free. I shall be here with you, standing behind the door. The other three will cut off his retreat. He can't get out onto the balcony.'

James was putting on a flak jacket. They all had flak jackets except me.

'Supposing he knifes me?' I whimpered. Jordan Lacey, private investigator, had stopped being brave. So much for heroics. So much for vertigo. I could cope with that.

'I'll shoot him.'

TWENTY-FOUR

The last minutes of waiting were an agony. I could hear the forty-foot trucks on the street delivering trolley loads of bread and fresh fruit and vegetables. Did they realize how much noise they made? When decent folk were trying to get some sleep?

Footsteps were coming along the walkway. My hearing was needle-sharp. I gasped two words.

'He's here.'

James got up, left me and went silently behind the door. There was not a single sound in the flat, only my breathing. Cody would expect breathing. Unless I had died of fright or cramp. Could cramp kill?

We heard a key go into the lock and turn. He came into the hallway, not alarmed by anything. It was as he had left it. An empty hall. Tap dripping in the kitchen. He came into the sitting room and saw me lying awkwardly on the floor, still bound and trussed up. He didn't look like the sleek waiter any more or like the tousled drunk on the beach. He looked like a cold-faced killer. Yet Sarah Patel had fallen for him, or had she? There was no proof that she had eloped with him. It was all hearsay.

'They didn't play ball, Jordan, isn't that a shame? It was a perfectly genuine gesture on my part. Tell me where Maddy is and I'll tell you where Jordan is. But apparently they are not too concerned about your welfare.'

He wandered over to the window. My HELP message had been taken down. 'It's such a lovely day, too. Your last day,

215

Jordan. I'm going to heave you into the bath and cut your wrists. Not horizontally but vertically up the artery of each arm. You'll bleed faster than way.'

We had made a mistake. I had no tape on my mouth. Would he notice? I turned my head slightly and pressed my face into the carpet, as if crying. The drama queen of my schooldays added a few convincing shudders.

'So, sadly I have no need of you any more. You like the sea, don't you? Perhaps you'd rather have an early-morning swim? The tide is on its way out. You'd soon be carried into the Channel. I'd like to get it right.'

I made a sort of gasping protest.

'And I always get it right,' said James, stepping forward. 'Roger Cody, I am arresting you for the murder of Sarah Patel, Tom Lucas, the attempted murder of Elsie Dunlop and the abduction and unlawful detention of Jordan Lacey. And I daresay I am going to find a dozen other things to charge you with. Anything you say . . . ' He rapidly repeated the Miranda warning. Reading him his rights, as they used to say before they changed the words.

The room was suddenly full of policemen. The three officers from the bedroom came charging in, guns at the ready. Roger Cody went white, looked frantically from the door to the balcony as if seeking some way of escape. But the balcony door was locked. He was trapped. One of the officers pulled Cody's hands behind his back and cuffs were clasped on, metal gleaming.

'You can't do this to me. I don't know what you are talking about. This is outrageous. I don't even know these people you mention.'

'Take him downstairs. Put him in a holding cell at the police station, give him a chance to start remembering some names,' said James. 'I'll be along straightaway. Miss Lacey may need medical attention.'

'I demand to see a lawyer!' Cody shouted.

'No problem,' said James.

I hadn't moved. I was evidence. If I suddenly jumped up, Cody would deny all knowledge of kidnapping me as a hostage. I had a mouthful of orange carpet, which was rather unpleasant.

Cody didn't go quietly. He was protesting violently. It took all three of them to get the man out of the flat and along the walkway.

'He's gone. You can sit up now, Jordan.'

'I might need medical attention,' I said in a feeble voice.

James took another carton of juice out of the carrier bag, pierced the hole and stuck a straw in it. 'This will work wonders,' he said.

'Aren't you going to check my pulse or anything?'

'I'm going to check that your flat upstairs is all right, then take you to the police station for your statement. I'll need a statement while everything is still fresh in your mind. Is there anything you want from your flat?'

'Some clean knickers.'

'Sure.'

'And mascara, please,' I said. 'In case you want to take my photograph.'

'Whatever for?'

'Heroines expect their picture to be hung on your wall of fame.'

I was seeing too much of the inside of Latching police station. It was as if I was still working there. My favourite desk sergeant, Sergeant Rawlings, had retired a few years ago. They put me in the room with the spider plant pot again. The earth in the pot was as dry as a bone and I gave it half of my bottle of water. We were instant earth buddies.

A different detective took my statement. This was a relief. I did not want to go into details about my time with James at the Travelodge or on the orange carpet. It was too personal.

'So DCI James took you to a safe house,' he said, filling in the gap. I nodded. Travelodge could add that to their glossy brochure. *We are a safe house.* 'Then the fake hostage situation was set up. Kindly tell me your part in that.'

I left out the sleeping together on the floor bit. It was hardly relevant. It happened by accident, you could say. James could have been standing behind the door all night, as far as anyone else knew. He has that kind of stamina.

'Have we nearly finished?' I asked. 'I'm very tired.'

'Of course, Miss Lacey,' he said. 'I'll get a printout of your statement and if you will sign it, then you can go.'

It's all computers these days. No handwritten statements, hardly legible, written by people who barely knew punctuation or grammar.

Any minute now I could go home. I gave the rest of the water to the spider plant.

It was the most beautiful day. I wished Maddy was there to enjoy it beside me. I walked along the front, enjoying the sun on my face and the sparkling sea washing the shore. I had no idea whether the tide was going in or out, but it was simply there.

I strolled onto the pier to thank Jack for alerting the police. He went into the brown coffee routine in his cubby-hole. I would have to drink it. My stomach was taking a beating these days.

Even the air was cleaner, fresher. It had been air-washed just for me.

'I knew the sign was you instantly,' he said. 'No one else would think of such a daft idea. Of course, I had no idea how serious it all was. Did they catch the bloke?'

'He's under arrest.'

'Lock him up for life, that's what I say. Where's your young friend, the big spender?'

'I have no idea. She's on holiday with her father.'

'Welcome here any time. Great girl. You know I fixed it so she got that pink elephant? No one else ever won it.'

I had to smile. Jack was so generous. 'I did wonder. It was too big for the chute. But she loves it.'

A woman was waiting outside my shop. She was thin, grey-haired and wearing drab eighties-style clothes that should have long gone to a charity shop. She sighed with relief when she saw me.

'Miss Lacey? I'm so glad to see you. A friend of mine recommended you. It's rather personal . . .'

'Of course. Come inside,' I said, unlocking the shop. 'We'll go into my office at the back and I'll put on some coffee.'

'My friend said you were really nice and understanding. It's a very long story. I hardly know where to begin.'

This decent and worried woman, once she had relaxed on my Victorian button-back chair, and drunk some decent coffee, told her long story and became my next case. Quite an involved one. It was a complicated tale about her missing younger sister. And a dispute over a house inheritance. And some missing letters.

Thank goodness I had a new case. I had work at last. First Class Investigations was back in business.

I waited three days for the promised pub lunch to materialize. DCI James had to go back to Swanage to take a statement from the now recovering Elsie Dunlop. James discovered that Miss Dunlop had also taught at Cowdry Private School, then in a male role. Maths was his subject. It was all rather confusing.

'It's now obvious why Cody had to get rid of her. She knew him at the school, knew what was going on and knew that he had abducted Sarah against her will. It was not an elopement at all. Cody is denying everything.'

'So it wasn't two lovers running away together?'

'No, Sarah may have had a crush on him but she had been brought up by caring parents and it didn't ring true that she would elope with him. We have been experimenting with a polygraph lie detector at Scotland Yard and even though his lawyer is protesting, we hope to carry out a test. There is no bruised or torn skin evidence still in existence, but we believe he raped Sarah, forced her to submit to him. There are traces of a street drug in her remains.'

'She must have been terrified, poor young woman.'

'He killed her because Sarah showed courage. She fought back.

There's skin tissue under her nails. He knew that she would go to the police and he would be found guilty, get a long sentence for kidnap and rape of an under-age girl. It was easier to kill her and bury her body in the grounds of Corfe Castle.'

I hated to think of what Sarah had gone through in those few days. The newspapers carried so many stories of similar crimes to girls even younger than Sarah. I hoped they would put Cody away for a long time, never let him out.

'So Elsie Dunlop had seen Cody forcing Sarah into his car outside the school. Then she spotted them together at the jazz festival soon after. She didn't know what to do. She was in the middle of a personal identity crisis and decided not to do anything that would draw attention to herself. A decision she now bitterly regrets.'

'I'm glad she is recovering.'

'And she identified the knife found buried at Corfe Castle. It's a school palette knife, the kind used in their art department. It has traces of Sarah's blood on it. The fact that Cody is refusing to take the lie detector test is in itself incriminating although, as yet, the results are not admissible in court.'

'And Tom Lucas's wife? How was she involved?'

'She's not into jazz but she came to the marquee to tell Tom that the drunk she saw being thrown out was a fake. She'd seen him, sitting on the beach, smoking, eating a burger and reading a newspaper. Then she saw him go into the public gents but he never came out again which she thought was suspicious.'

'Of course, he came out of the gents as Carlos, an off-duty waiter from the Whyte Cliffside Hotel.'

'Exactly. Tom told Ruth Macclesfield his wife's story. She passed the information on to the station and somehow it leaked and it was enough to alert Cody. He went along to the pig farm to silence them both.'

'But he killed Tom Lucas. How sad.'

'Mrs Lucas wasn't there. I presume Tom refused to say where she was and got brutally slaughtered for his attempt to protect her.'

'Is she all right?'

'Recovering. Apparently she's going to sell the pig farm but is keeping one black pig. She says it's tame.'

The Falcon was one of West Sussex's most delightful country pubs, a white and stone-fronted conversion of adjoining farm cottages. We were sitting out in the garden, well away from any eavesdroppers. There were bees and dragonflies darting about, from flower to flower, the rolling South Downs framing the distant view.

James returned from the bar with a cold lager for himself and a glass of good red wine for me. We had ordered from the chalked menu over the bar and were waiting for our food. I hoped we weren't going to talk about the case any more.

'Did you see DI Ruth Macclesfield while you were back in Swanage?' I couldn't stop that useless green-eyed monster getting a word in.

'She's asked for a transfer. Took quite a shine to Tom Lucas apparently. Sad really. It was his wife who was involved, not Tom at all. She was not another of the umbrella ladies, or one of Elsie's rivals. She spotted Cody on the beach and told Tom .'

'But poor Tom got killed.'

'Cody meant to kill the wife, or both of them. We'll never know. He won't say. He's now pleading total amnesia. Still refusing to take the lie detector test. But we have strong DNA evidence that links him to Sarah's death and to Tom's death. His fingerprints are on the handle of the palette knife but he says he used it at school. He's been refused bail.'

'These lie detector tests. How reliable are they?'

'They monitor the heart rate, brain activity, sweating, electrical skin response and blood pressure during questioning. If you have six people tested with the same questionnaire and one is a suspect, the difference is beyond question.'

'What about the threats to Chuck Peters and Maddy?'

'He's not admitting that either. Cody thought he had been seen with Sarah at the jazz festival. And as Maddy went to the same school, he thought Maddy would have recognized Sarah with him. Of course, Maddy hadn't. A delightful young girl but she can barely remember last week's soaps.'

'So where are Chuck and Maddy?'

Our meals had arrived. A large medium-rare steak and chips for the good detective. Vegetable lasagne and salad for the starving private eye. It was the first proper meal I had had for weeks. I hardly remembered how to eat.

James didn't answer straightaway. He too was savouring those first few mouthfuls. He ate mostly on the run. I wondered where his next posting would take him. When would I see him again, if ever?

'I told Chuck not to tell anyone, not even me. But I got a text this morning from someone called Summer. It said: *Ask sis about her favourite nut.* Can you shed any light on this?'

'Brazil,' I said. 'That's where they are.'

'How do you know?'

I didn't tell him. 'It's a big country.'

'Big enough. And soon Cody will be behind bars for a very long time. We'll break him down. He may change his plea.'

'But I think it will be a long time before Chuck plays again at the Swanage Jazz Festival. Too many bad memories. Still, there are many more jazz festivals. He won't be short of work. Maddy will probably change schools. It would be good for her. She doesn't need any reminders of the last few days.'

I tried to change the subject. I didn't want any reminders either of the scary part, though I had to admit there had been one or two compensations.

'Where are you going to be stationed now, James?' I had to ask although I didn't want to know. It would be Aberdeen or Arbroath or somewhere completely off the beaten track.

'I don't know,' said James, offering me the last chip. It was cold but I ate it out of politeness. 'I'm taking a few days' leave first. I'm owed a lot of time and if I don't take some of it soon, I'll lose it.'

A girl came to take our plates. James didn't even look at the dessert menu. 'Have you got any strawberries?'

'Yes, sir. Freshly picked this morning. Local fruit farm.'

'How does that sound to you, Jordan?' he asked me.

'Perfect.'

'Two strawberries and cream, then,' he told the girl. He turned his attention back to me as if he had never stopped. 'So I'm taking holiday leave. Would you like to come with me, Jordan?'

I had been waiting for years to hear James say those words. I would like them inscribed in gold ink on parchment, framed and hung on my wall. The joy rushed through me, then fell instantly to the grass beneath my feet. My toes curled in my sandals.

'I can't.' I could have wept.

'Why not?' His face did not change. I couldn't tell if he was disappointed or relieved. 'It's only a few days. I'm not planning to go off on a year's sabbatical.'

'I've got a new case. A very sweet woman who's terribly worried about her missing sister. I've already started the investigation. I can't let her down. And I'm having some professional cleaners in to give my flat a thorough spring clean and redecorate. Cover up the cracks. Fresh paint.'

'Then you'll have to move out for a few days anyway.'

'I was going to sleep overnight at my shop.'

'No way, Jordan. That air mattress is damned hard work to blow up. How about I decide to take my holiday in Latching? I've never really seen this beautiful coast or the South Downs, not the real Latching. Always too busy on a case. I've never walked the path to Chantonbury Hill or explored the Iron Age entrenchment on Cissbury Ring. And it's not far to drive to Chichester, which has an excellent theatre for shows. We could check what's on at the Pier Pavilion. We could eat out every evening: Chinese, Italian, Indian, fish and chips.'

'Do you like Thai food?'

'I'm willing to try anything. Do you fancy sharing that kind of holiday with me? You could still fit in investigations for your new case while I catch up on my sleep or sit on your balcony, admiring the view.'

The girl arrived with two bowls of luscious strawberries